Heartfelt Praise for
Joi

"Jonathan Carroll has the magic. He'll lend you his eyes, and you'll never see the world in quite the same way ever again."
—Neil Gaiman

"A surrealistic yarn told so frankly it seems wholly plausible."
—*U.S. News and World Report*

"Jonathan Carroll is as scary as Hitchcock, when he isn't being as funny as Jim Carrey. If you've never read this wonderful fantasist, buy this book. You'll stay up all night and thank me in the morning."
—Stephen King

"Jonathan Carroll is a master of sunlit surrealism—his beguiling, impossible novels are like Frank Capra films torn open to reveal the Philip K. Dick or Julio Cortázar mechanisms ticking away at their cores. *The Wooden Sea* is one of his funniest, strangest, and most melancholy offerings."
—Jonathan Lethem

"Though critics may try, there's no way to pigeonhole *The Wooden Sea*. The novel includes time travel, religious doctrine, philosophy, talking animals, reincarnation, juvenile delinquency, murder, and megalomania. But mostly it's a great love story in which the protagonist is willing to give up everything for the woman he loves."
—*Rocky Mountain News*

"*The Wooden Sea* is a treat, and I'm heading out to look for more Jonathan Carroll titles. It's gorgeously imagined And the style is impressive. Frannie, the worldly war-stung small town cop, hits classic status for me. His luminously hard-boiled American voice is smart, funny, and devastatingly decent. Kind of guy you're glad to follow anywhere—even into the strange zones of *The Wooden Sea*."
—Katherine Dunn

Books by Jonathan Carroll

The Wooden Sea

Jonathan Carroll

TOR®

A Tom Doherty Associates Book
New York

THE WOODEN SEA

This book is printed on acid-free paper.

Book design by Heidi Eriksen

A Tor Book
Published by Tom Doherty Associates, LLC
175 Fifth Avenue
New York, NY 10010

www.tor.com

Tor® is a registered trademark of Tom Doherty Associates, LLC.

Library of Congress Cataloging-in-Publication Data

Carroll, Jonathan.
    The wooden sea / Jonathan Carroll.
        p. cm.
    "A Tom Doherty Associates book."
    ISBN 0-312-87823-0 (hc)
    ISBN 0-765-30013-3 (pbk)   ISBN 978-0-7653-0013-3
    1. Police chiefs—Fiction. 2. Dogs—Fiction. I. Title.

PS3553. A7646 W6 2001
813'.54—dc21   00-047938

Printed in the United States of America

P1

To Ifah2 at Augarten heaven

The Wooden Sea

Old Vertue

Never buy yellow clothes or cheap leather. That's my credo and there are more. Know what I like to see? People killing themselves. Don't misunderstand; I'm not talking about the poor fucks who jump out windows or stick their sorry heads into plastic bags forever. No "Ultimate Fighting Championship" either, which is only a bunch of rabid crewcuts biting each other. I'm talking about the guy on the street, face the color of wet lead, lighting up a Camel and coughing up his soul the moment he inhales. Good for you, Sport! Long live nicotine, stubbornness, and self-indulgence.

"Let's have another round here, Jimmy!" croons King Cholesterol down at the end of the bar. He with the rosy nose and enough high blood pressure to launch him and his whole family tree to Pluto. Gratification, mass, texture. The heart attack that'll nuke him will last a few seconds. The cold beer in thick mugs and perfume of grilling T-bone steaks are forever until he dies. It's worth the trade-off. I'm with him.

My wife Magda says getting me to understand is like throwing peas at a wall. But I understand fine; I just don't usually *agree*. Old Vertue is a perfect example. One day a guy walks into the station house leading a dog the likes of which you have never seen. It's a mixed breed but is mainly pit bull covered by a swirl of brown and black markings so he looks like a marble cake. But that's where his normalcy stops because this dog has only three and a half legs, is missing an eye, and breathes weird. Sort of out the side of his mouth but you can't really be sure. The way air comes out, it sounds like he's whistling "Michelle" under his breath. There are two deep raised scars across the top of his head. He's such a mess that all of us stare at him like he just arrived from hell on the Concorde.

Fucked up as he looked, the dog wore a very nice red leather collar. Hanging from it was a small flat silver heart with the name "Old Vertue" engraved on it. That was how it was spelled. That's all; no owner's name, address, or telephone number. Only Old Vertue. And he's exhausted. In the middle of everyone there, he collapsed on the floor and started snoring. The guy who brought him in said he found the dog sleeping in the Grand Union parking lot. He didn't know what the hell to do with it but was sure it was going to be run over napping there, so he brought it to us.

Everyone else thought we should take the dog to the nearest animal shelter and forget about it. But for me it was love at first sight. I made a bed for him in my office, bought dog food and a couple of orange bowls. He slept almost continuously for two days. When awake he lay in his bed and stared at me with gloomy eyes. Or rather eye. When someone in the office asked why I kept it around, I said this dog has been there and *back*. Since I'm chief of police, nobody protested.

Except my wife. Magda believes animals should be eaten and can barely stand the nice cat I've had for years. When she heard I was keeping a three-legged, one-eyed marble cake in my office she came by for a look. She stared at it for too long and stuck out her lower lip. A bad sign. "The more goofy they are, the more you like them, huh, Fran?"

"This dog's a veteran, honey. He's seen *battle*."

"There are kids starving in North Korea while you're serving this mutt food."

"Send those kids over here—they can share its Alpo."

"You're the mutt, Frannie, not him."

Standing nearby, Magda's daughter, Pauline, started laughing.

We looked at her with surprise because Pauline doesn't laugh at
anything. Absolutely no sense of humor. When she does laugh
it's usually at something weird or totally inappropriate. She's a
strange girl who works hard at remaining invisible. My secret
nickname for her is Fade.

"What's so funny?"

"Frannie. He always goes left when everyone else goes right.
What's the matter with your dog? What's he's doing?"

I turned around just in time to see Old Vertue die.

It had managed to stand, but all three of its legs were trembling badly. Its head was down and it swung it back and forth
like it was saying no.

Typically, Pauline started giggling.

Vertue stopped shaking its head and looked up at us. At me.
It looked straight at me and winked. I swear to God. The old
dog winked at me as if we shared a secret. Then it fell over and
died. Its three legs twitched a few times then curled slowly in
toward his body. There was no question where it'd gone.

None of us said a thing; just stared at the poor old guy.
Finally Magda went over for a closer look. "Jeez, maybe I
shouldn't have said such mean things about him."

The dead dog farted. A long one—its last breath going out
the wrong door. Moving back fast, Magda glared at me.

Pauline crossed her arms. "That's so weird! It was alive two
seconds ago and now it's not. I've never seen anything die."

One of the few advantages of being young. When you're
seventeen, death is a star light-years away you can hardly see
through a powerful telescope. Then you grow older and discover
it's no distant star, but a big fucking asteroid coming straight at
your head.

"Now what, Doctor Doolittle?"

"Now I guess I gotta go bury him."

"Just make sure it's not in our backyard."

"I thought under your pillow would be good."

We locked eyeballs and smiled at the same time. She kissed the air between us. "Come on, Pauline. We've got things to do."

She left, but Pauline hesitated. As she moved slowly toward the door she stared at the dog as if hypnotized. Once there she stopped and stared some more. Outside my office there was a sudden big burst of laughter. Obviously Magda telling the others the sad news.

"Go ahead with your mother, Pauline. I want to wrap him up and get him out of here."

"Where *are* you going to bury him?"

"Someplace down by the river. Give him a nice view."

"Is that legal to bury him there?"

"If I catch myself doing it, I'll arrest me."

That broke her trance and she left.

Even in death the old guy looked beat. Whatever kind of life he'd had, he got to the finish line on all fours (all threes) with nothing left. He used up everything he had. That was clear after one glance at him. His head was turned into his body; the thick pink scars on top were vicious-looking things. Where the hell had he gotten them?

Bending down, I gently wrapped the ends of the cheap blanket around his body and slowly rolled him into it. The body was heavy and loose. His one good front paw stuck out. Maneuvering it back inside the blanket, I stopped and shook it. "My name is Frannie. I'm your paw bearer today."

I lifted the bundle and went to the door. Without warning it swung open and Patrolman Big Bill Pegg stood there, trying hard not to smile. "You need help, Chief?"

"No, I've got him. Just open that door wider." A bunch of people stood outside and applauded as I passed.

"Very funny."

"I wouldn't start a pet shop if I was you, Fran."

"Waddya got there, pigs in a blanket?"

"Nice guest—you invite him in and he drops dead."

"You guys are just jealous he didn't die in *your* office." I kept moving. Their laughter and jokes followed me out the door. Old Vertue was not light. Lugging him to the car wasn't the easiest thing I'd done that day. Once there, I lowered him onto the trunk lid and fished car keys out of my pocket. I slipped one into the lock and turned, but other than the click, nothing happened. The body held the lid down. Hefting him up over a shoulder, I turned the key again. The lid popped up. Before I had a chance to do anything, a loud voice a foot away from my left ear boomed "Why you putting that dog in your trunk, Frannie?"

"Because it's dead, Johnny. I'm going to go bury it."

Johnny Petangles, our town idiot, went up on his toes and leaned over my shoulder for a better look. "Can I come with you and watch?"

"No, John." I tried to push Vertue against one wall of the trunk so he wouldn't slide around when I drove, but someone was in my way. "John, *move!* Haven't you got anything to do?"

"No. Where are you going to bury him, Frannie? In the graveyard?"

"Only people get to go there. I haven't decided yet. Would you please move over so I can get him settled here?"

"Why do you want to get him settled if he's dead?"

I stopped moving and closed my eyes. "John, would you like a hamburger?"

"That would be very nice."

"Good." I took five dollars out of my pocket and handed it to him. "Eat a hamburger, and when you're done, go up to my house and give Magda a hand bringing in that firewood, okay?"

"Okay." Holding the money in his hand he didn't move. "I'll be very quiet if you let me come with you."

"Johnny, am I going to have to shoot you?"

"You always say that." He looked at the Arnold Schwarzenegger watch I had given him a few years before when he was going through a *Terminator* phase. "How long do I have before I go over to your house? I don't want to eat too fast. I get gas."

"Take your time." I patted his shoulder and moved to get in the car.

"I didn't know you had a dog for a friend, Frannie."

"Dogs know how to love, John. They wrote the book."

Driving away, I checked in the rearview mirror. He was waving at me as a child would—his hand flapped up and down.

Magda believes you can tell a person's personality by what is lying around in their car. Stopped at a light on April Avenue, I looked down at the passenger's seat and saw this: three unopened packs of Marlboros, a cheap cell phone mangled from having been dropped often, a paperback collection of John O'Hara short stories, and an unopened envelope from the town hospital containing the results of a barium enema. In the glove compartment was a tin of Altoids breath mints, a videotape of *Around the World in Eighty Days* and CDs of seventies disco music no one but me wanted to hear. The only interesting things in the whole car were the Beretta pistol under my arm and the dead dog in the trunk. The contents depressed me. What if we were living under Mount Vesuvius and at that moment it decided to blow again? Lava and ash would kill and perfectly preserve me in my two-ton Ford coffin. Thousands of years from now archaeologists would dig me up and guess who I was judging by what was around me: cigarettes, KC & the Sunshine Band, the results of an asshole exam, and a dog carcass. *What's My Line?*

Where was I going to bury Old Vertue, and with what? I had no tools in the car. I'd have to go home first and get a shovel out of the garage. I took a quick left and headed down Broadway.

On his eightieth birthday, my father swore he would never again read a set of instructions. He died a month later. I say this now because I had used the same shovel to bury him. People thought I was cracked. Cemeteries have backhoes for that purpose, but I thought there was something ancient and good about making my father's final bed. I couldn't say Kaddish, but I could scoop him a hole with my own hands. In the middle of a hot summer day I dug his grave with a smile on my face. Johnny Petangles sat on the ground nearby and kept me company. He asked where we went when we died. Bangladesh, if we're bad, I said. When he didn't understand that I asked where he thought we went. Into the ocean. We turn into rocks and God throws us into the ocean. Was that where my father was now, hiding some Greek calamari? Driving along, I wondered what Johnny would have said about where dead animals go.

The two way radio crackled. "Chief?"

"McCabe here."

"Chief, we've got a domestic disturbance up on Helen Street."

"Schiavo?"

"You got it."

"All right, I'm near there. I'll take care of it."

"Better you than me." The dispatcher chuckled and clicked off.

I shook my head. Donald and Geraldine Schiavo, née Fortuso, had been my classmates at Crane's View High School. They were married right after we graduated and had been at war ever since. Sometimes she hit him on the head with a pot. Sometimes he hit her on the head with a chair. Whatever was closest. For years people had pleaded with them to divorce, but the two lovebirds had nothing else in the world besides their hatred so why should they give that up? I would guess once a month their mutual simmer turned to boil and one or the other got dented.

A group of neighborhood teenagers were standing on the sidewalk in front of the Schiavo house, laughing.

"What's up, troops?"

"Fuckin' *Star Wars* in there, Mr. McCabe. You shoulda heard her screaming before. But it's been quiet for a while."

"They're resting between rounds." I walked up the path to the door and turned the knob. It was open. "Anyone home?" When no one answered I said it again. Silence. I walked in and closed the door. What first struck me was how clean and nice-smelling the house was. Geri Schiavo was a sloppy, lazy woman who didn't mind having a house that stunk. Ditto her husband. One of the annoyances of prying them apart month after month was going into their house, which invariably smelled of BO, rooms where windows had been closed too long, and old food you didn't ever want to taste.

Not this time. A new store had opened recently in town that sold a wide assortment of exotic teas. I don't drink tea but found as many excuses as I could to go in there just to enjoy its aroma. After my initial shock wore off at the order and shine in the Schiavo house, I realized it smelled like the tea shop. A potent, wonderful fragrance that gave your nose delicious things to think about.

The surprises didn't end there either because the house was empty. I moved from room to room searching for Donald and

Geri. Nothing had changed since the last time I visited. The same cheap couch and prehistoric BarcaLounger sat side by side in the living room like bums at rest. Family photographs on the mantle, a scrawny piss-yellow canary hopping around in its cage, all the same. But there was that orderliness and shine to everything I had never seen before in this house. It was as if the couple had prepared everything for a party or an important visit. But as soon as they had everything ready, the owners left.

I went to the basement, half worried that down there would be a rough answer to the mystery upstairs: both Schiavos hanging from matching rafters, or one standing over the other's body with a gleeful look on their face and a gun in their hand. Didn't happen. The basement was only full of tidily stacked magazines, old furniture, and junk. And even that had been neatly arranged in a corner. Down there it smelled good too. It was the damnedest thing. What the hell was going on?

Their backyard was as big as a bus stop but the lawn had been mowed. I had never seen the grass out there less than five inches high. I'd once even offered Donald the use of my lawnmower, which he grouchily rejected.

Back in the house I sat in the BarcaLounger to think things over. And almost went right on my ass when it tipped all the way back on nonexistent springs. Touch and go for a few seconds, I managed to wrestle the thing back upright. That's when I saw the feather.

There was a sealed-up fireplace on the other side of the room. As I fought gravity to get the stupid chair back on earth, I saw a flash of incredibly bright color on the floor in front of the fireplace. Wiggily kneed from the battle, I went over to the feather and picked it up. About ten inches long, it was a mixture of the most brilliant colors imaginable. Purple, green, black, orange—more. I couldn't imagine a more inappropriate object to be in the house of these slobs, but there it was. I stared at it while I called the station house and told Bill Pegg what I'd seen.

"That's a new one. Maybe they got beamed up to the mother ship."

"Captain Picard wouldn't want *them* on the *Enterprise*. You've gotten no reports, Bill? No car crashes or anything?"

"Nope. Wouldn't it be great if they died? No more having to go up there. Nothing's come in."

"Call Michael Zakrides at the hospital and check with him. I'm going home to get something and then down to the river. Call me on my pocket phone if you hear anything."

"Okay. What'd you do with the dead dog, Chief? Why don't you leave it for the Schiavos for when they get come home. Put it in their oven! *That* would shut Geri up for five minutes."

I flipped the feather back and forth in my fingers. "I'll talk to you later. Hey, Bill, one more thing—"

"Yeah?"

"Know anything about birds?"

"Birds? Jeez, I don't know. Why? What about 'em?"

"What kind of bird would have feathers about ten inches long and be incredibly colorful?"

"A peacock?"

"I thought of that, but I don't think so. I know what a peacock feather looks like. This isn't it. Peacock feathers are more symmetrical in their marking. They have that big circle on them too. This isn't one."

"*What* isn't? What are you talking about?"

I snapped out of it, realizing I was thinking out loud as I stared at the feather. "Nothing. I'll check with you later."

"Frannie?"

"Yes?"

"Put the dog in the oven."

I hung up.

How could so many colors exist on one thin feather? I couldn't stop looking at the damned thing but knew I had to get moving. Outside again, a couple of the kids from before were still standing around, probably hoping for more Schiavo fireworks. I asked if they'd seen anyone leave the house before I arrived. They said no. When I told them the place was empty they couldn't believe it.

"There's got to be someone in there, Mr. McCabe. You shoulda heard them screaming!"

I took out a pack of cigarettes and offered them around. "What'd they say?"

The kid took a light from me and blew out a line of smoke. "Nothin' special. She was calling him an asshole and a creep. But loud. Whoa, *loud!* You could have heard her downtown."

"And him? Did Donald say anything?"

The other kid lowered his voice four octaves and got a look on his face like he was about to be the life of the party. "*Bitch!* Fock you, stupid *fica!* I do what the fock I wan'!*"

"*Fic?*"

"Fica. It means, you know, pussy in Italian."

"What would I do without you guys? Listen, if you see either of them come back, call me on this number." I handed one my card.

"What's that?" He pointed to the feather.

"Beautiful, huh? I found it on their floor." I held it up. We all silently admired it.

"Maybe they were doing something in there with feathers, you know, like kinky." The boy beamed.

"You know, when I was a kid, the kinkiest thing I ever heard about was people dressing up in leather suits and whipping each other. I almost had a heart attack. But you guys know more now than Alex Comfort."

"Who's he?"

Back in the car, I slid the feather carefully under the sunshade over the driver's seat. Why was the front door of their house open? And the back door? No one leaves their doors open anymore, not even in Crane's View. Donald Schiavo worked as a mechanic at Birmfion Motors. I called there and talked to a secretary who said he'd gone out for lunch four hours ago and hadn't come back. The boss was mad because Donald had a four-by-four still up on the rack and the customer was waiting.

I shrugged it off. The Schiavos were somewhere. They would turn up. Driving home, I tried to remember where in the garage I had put the shovel.

An hour later I struck another tree root and flipped out. Flinging the shovel away, I put a filthy hand in my mouth and bit myself. I hadn't been this frustrated in ten weeks, give or take a few. My plan had been so simple: Drive down to the river, find a nice spot, dig Old Vertue a hole, drop him in, sweet dreams, go back to the office. But I'd forgotten they were laying pipe by the river and what with all the men and equipment around, it was no place for a dead dog and me.

So I drove around in those big dark woods way back behind the Tyndall house and looked till I found a prime place. Sunlight danced down through the leaves. It was quiet except for gusts of wind through the leaves and birds singing. The air smelled of summer and earth.

I was in such a good mood that I started singing "Hi-ho, Hi-ho, it's off to work we go" as I stabbed the shovel into the soft ground. Five minutes later I hit the first root, which turned out to be as thick as the underground monster in *Tremors*. Undeterred (Hi-ho, Hi-ho), I shrugged and began digging in another place. But it turned out, gee whiz, there were tree roots *all over* that old forest. And as Old Vertue stiffened in the trunk of the car, my anger stiffened into a rage hard-on thirteen inches long.

When I had finished chewing my hand and smoking three cigarettes I thought very slowly and with forced calm: I will try one more place. If *that* doesn't work . . . And this is what's interesting: Furious and frustrated as I was by the earth's unwillingness to accept my hole, not for a minute did I consider taking the dog's body to the pound and having it cremated. Old Vertue *had* to be buried. He had to be laid in the ground with gentleness and care. I didn't know why that was fixed solidly in my brain, but it was. I didn't owe him anything. No years of close companionship, a great friend whenever I was alone and down, summer days tossing him a stick in the backyard. Man's best friend? I didn't even know him. He was just an old fucked-up dog that happened to die on my office floor. Sure, part of it had to do with what Magda had said—I like losers. Most of the time I was on their side. Failures, liars, empty skulls, drunks, and felons— bring them on; I'll pay for their drinks. Old Vertue seemed to be all of the above wrapped in one. I was sure if he'd been human he would have had a voice like a coffee grinder and a brain brown from abuse. But there was something more to his having entered my life. If you asked what, I'd be lying if I said I knew. All I was sure of was I had to take care of his burial and I was determined do that. So I put my temper back in its box and picked up the shovel again. This time it worked.

Digging a deep hole takes more effort than you think. Plus it does a big bad number on the skin of your hands. But I found a spot a few feet over that let me go down as far as I wanted without putting any more obstacles in the way. When I was finished, the hole was about three feet deep and wide enough. He would be all right here.

The most interesting thing was what came up on the shovel with the last scoop. On top of the dark dirt was something much brighter, almost white. It was such a vivid contrast that no one could have missed it. I lay the shovel down and reached for whatever it was. At first I thought it was a stick that had been bleached of all color. About ten inches long, it was silvery gray and jagged at one end, as if it had been attached to something larger but had been snapped off. As I brought it up closer for a better look, the silver became a kind of creamy white; it wasn't wood but some kind of bone.

No big deal. Forests are full of animal bones. I even smiled thinking I had upset one animal's grave digging a place for another. The final outrage—a squirrel can't even rest in peace these days. Call the ASPCA! Cruelty to dead animals.

Pauline was interested in zoology. I thought she might like a look at the bone, so I slipped it into my pocket while walking back to the car to get Old Vertue.

Popping the trunk, I got a jolt looking in. The dog's eye had opened and he was staring right at me. No matter how in control you are or used to being around bodies, getting a look from the dead is never home sweet home. There's still enough life in those eyes to make you lick your lips and turn away, hoping when you look again somehow they will be closed.

"I'm just going to put you to bed, Vertue. It's nice here. It's a nice place to stop." Sliding my hands under his body I lifted him out of the trunk. He felt heavier than before, but I assumed that was because the digging had tired me. My arms shook slightly as I carried him. The sunlight through the trees went on and off my shoes. Carefully stepping into the hole, I laid him down as gently as I could. The body was twisted a little and I rearranged it. The eyes were still open and the tip of his tongue came out of the corner of his mouth. Poor old guy. I stepped out and picked up the shovel, ready to start tossing dirt in on him. But things still didn't seem right. I had an idea. Back to the car where I pulled the long feather from beneath the sunshade.

I slipped it under his collar. Like an Egyptian king going to the hereafter surrounded by his worldly possessions, Old Vertue now had a beautiful feather to carry along. It was getting late and I had other things to do. Quickly filling the grave, I tamped it down as best I could, hoping another animal wouldn't catch the scent and dig it up.

That night at dinner Magda asked where I'd put him. After I described my adventure in the forest, she surprised me by saying, "Would you like to have a dog, Frannie?"

"No, not particularly."

"But you were so nice to him. I wouldn't mind having one. Some of them are sort of cute."

"You *hate* dogs, Magda."

"That's true, but I love *you*."

Pauline rolled her eyes and dramatically stomped off to the kitchen carrying her plate. When I was sure she was out of earshot I said, "I wouldn't mind having a cat."

My wife blinked and frowned. "You already *have* a cat."

"Well, then I wouldn't mind a little pussy."

That night, after a visit from my favorite pussy on earth, I dreamt of feathers, bones, and Johnny Petangles.

Next morning the weather was so beautiful I decided to drive my motorcycle to work instead of the car. The end of summer sat on the town. It was my favorite season. Everything summery is richer and more intense then because you know it will all be gone soon. Magda's mother used to say a flower smells sweetest when it's just begun to rot. A few of the horse chestnut trees had already begun dropping their spiny yellow buckeyes. They hit the pavement with a crack or clunk on cars. When a breeze blew it was thick with the smell of ripe plants and dust. The dew hung around longer in the morning because the real heat of the day didn't start until hours later.

I have a big motorcycle—a Ducati Monster—and the evil "Fuck me—I'm a god!" sound of its 900cc engine alone is worth the price of admission. And there is nothing more pleasant than driving it slowly through Crane's View, New York, on a morning like that. The day hasn't started yet, hasn't turned the sign in its front window to read OPEN yet. Only diehards are out and about. A smiling woman sweeps her front doorstep with a red broom. A young weimaraner, its stump tail wagging madly, sniffs garbage cans placed at a curb. An old man wearing a white ball cap and sweatsuit is either jogging slowly or walking as fast as he can.

Seeing someone exercising immediately inspired me to think of French crullers and coffee with lots of cream. I'd stop and get both, but there was one thing to do first.

After a few slow lefts and rights, I pulled up in front of the Schiavo house to see if anything had changed. No car was parked either in the driveway or near the house. I knew they owned a blue Mercury, but no blue cars were in sight. I tried the front door. It was still open. We'd have to change that. Couldn't have a thief going in and stealing their painting-on-velvet of the Bay of Naples. I'd send someone over today to put temporary locks on the doors and leave a note for the elusive Donald and Geri. Not that I cared about either them or their possessions. Standing with hands in my pockets looking around, it was too beautiful a morning to have a weird little mystery like this to think about, especially when it had to do with those two jerks. But it was the job to care so I would.

My pocket phone rang. It was Magda saying our car wouldn't start. She was the queen of I-Hate-Technology and proud of it. This woman did not want to know how to work a computer, a calculator, any thingamajig that went beep-beep. She balanced her checkbook doing multiplication and division with a pencil, used a microwave oven with the greatest suspicion, and cars were her enemy if they didn't start immediately when the key was turned. The irony was her daughter was a computer whiz who was in the midst of applying to tough colleges that specialized in the field. Amused, Magda stared at Pauline's talents and shrugged.

"I drove that car all day yesterday."

"I know, Poodles, but it still doesn't start."

"You didn't flood the motor? Remember the time—"

Her voice rose. "Frannie, don't go there. Do you want me to call the mechanic or do you want to fix it?"

"Call the mechanic. Are you sure you didn't—"

"I'm sure. Know what else? Our garage smells great. Did you spray air freshener in there? What did you do?"

"Nothing. The car that was fine yesterday won't start, but the garage smells good?"

"Right."

One beat. Two beats. "Mag, I'm biting my tongue over here. There are things I want to say to you but I'm holding back—"

"Good! Keep holding. I'll call the garage. See you later." Click. If she hung up any faster I would have given her a speeding ticket. I was sure she'd done something wicked like flood the carburetor. *Again.* But you cut deals with your partner in marriage; they give you longitude and you give them latitude. That way, if you're lucky, you create a map together of a shared world both can recognize and inhabit comfortably.

Work that morning was the usual nothing much. The mayor came in to discuss erecting a traffic light at an intersection where there had been way too many accidents in the last few years. Her name is Susan Ginnety. We had been lovers in high school and Susan never forgave me for it. Thirty years ago I was the baddest fellow in our town. There are still stories floating around about what a bad seed I was back then and most of them are true. If I had a photo album from that time, all of the pictures in there of me would be either in profile or straight on, holding up a police identification number.

Unlike miscreant me, Susan was a good girl who thought she heard the call of the wild and decided to try on being bad like a jean jacket. So she started hanging around with me and the crew. That mistake ended in disaster fast. In the end she reeled away from the smoking wreck of her innocence, went to college and studied politics while I went to Vietnam (involuntarily) and studied dead people.

After college Susan lived in Boston, San Diego, and Manhattan. One weekend she returned to visit her family and decided there was no place like home. She married a high-powered entertainment lawyer who liked the idea of living in a small town by the Hudson. They bought a house on Villard Hill, and a year later Susan began running for public office.

The interesting thing was that her husband, Frederick Morgan, is black. Crane's View is a conservative town comprised mostly of middle- to lower middle-class Irish and Italian families not so many generations removed from steerage. From their ancestors they inherited an obsession with close family ties, a willingness to work hard, and a general suspicion of anything or anyone different. Before the Morgan/Ginnetys came, there had never been a mixed-race couple living in the town. If they had arrived in the early sixties when I was a kid we would have said nigger a lot and thrown rocks through their windows. But thank God some things do change. A black mayor was elected in the eighties who did a good job and graced the office. From the beginning townspeople realized the Morgans were a nice couple and we were lucky to have them.

After they moved to Crane's View and Susan heard I was chief of police, apparently her reaction was to cover her face and groan. When we met on the street for the first time in fifteen years she walked right up and said in an accusing voice, "You should be in prison! But you went to college and now you're chief of *police?*"

I said sweetly, "Hi, Susan. *You* changed. How come I can't?"

"Because you're horrible, McCabe."

After being elected mayor she said to me, "You and I are going to have to work together a lot and I want to have a peaceful heart about it. You were *the* worst boyfriend in the history of the penis. Are you a good policeman?"

"Uh-huh. You can look at my record. I'm sure you will."

"You're right. I'll look very closely. Are you corrupt?"

"I don't have to be. I have a lot of money from my first marriage."

"Did you steal it from her?"

"No. I gave her an idea for a TV show. She was a producer."

Her eyes narrowed. "What show?"

"Man Overboard."

"That's the most ridiculous show on television—"

"And the most successful for a while."

"Yes. It was your idea? I guess I should be impressed, but I'm not. Shall we get to work?"

At our traffic-light meeting that summer morning, we finished
with my giving Susan a briefing on what had been going on in
town policewise the last week. As usual she listened with head
down and a small silver tape recorder in hand in case she wanted
to note anything. There really was no interesting news. Bill Pegg
had to remind me to tell her about the disappearance of the
Schiavos.

"What are you doing about it?" She brought the recorder to
her mouth, hesitated, and lowered it again.

"Asking around, making some phone calls, putting locks on
their doors. It's a free country, Mayor, they can leave if they
want."

"The way they left sounds pretty strange."

I thought about that. "Yes, but I also know the Schiavos and
so do you. They're both emotional wackos. I could easily imagine
them having a big messy fight and storming off in opposite directions. Both probably thinking 'I'll stay out all night and scare
'em.' The only problem being neither thought to lock the doors
before they left."

"Ah, love!" Bill said, unwrapping his midmorning sandwich.

"Did you talk to their parents?"

Bill spoke around a mouthful. "I did. Neither have heard a
word."

"What's the usual time frame for filing a missing persons
report?"

"Twenty-four hours."

"Frannie, will you take care of that if it's necessary?"

I nodded. She looked at Bill and, voice faltering, asked if he
would leave us alone for a moment. Very surprised, he got up
quickly and left. Susan had never done that before. She was as

upfront and direct as anyone around. I knew she liked Bill for his wit and candor and he liked her for the same reasons. Asking him to leave meant something big and probably personal was about to land in that room. When the door closed I sat up straighter in the chair and looked at her. Suddenly she wouldn't meet my stare.

"What's up, Mayor?" I tried to sound light and friendly— the milky fuzz on top of a cappuccino you tongue through before getting to the coffee below.

She pulled in a loud deep breath. One of those breaths you take before saying something that's going to change everything. You know as soon as it's out your world will be different. "Fred and I are going to separate."

"Is that good or bad?"

She laughed, barked really, and pushed her hair back. "That's so *you*, Frannie, to say it like that. Everyone I've told so far says either 'the shit!' or 'poor you' or some such thing. Not McCabe."

I turned both hands palms up like what else am I supposed to say? "He's going off to grow chili peppers."

"What?"

"That's what my first wife said when we split up. There's this primitive tribe in Bolivia. When one of its members dies, they say he's gone off to grow chili peppers."

"Fred hates chili peppers. He hates all spicy foods." It was clear she needed something safe and inane to say to pole-vault her over the painful admission she had just made. That's why I tried to help with the chili pepper remark.

"How do you feel about it?"

She worked on a smile but it didn't work. "Like I'm falling from the top of a building and have a few more floors to go before I hit?"

"It would be unnatural if you didn't. I bought a coatimundi

when I broke up and then forgot to feed it. Do you think the separation's final, or are you just taking it out for a test-drive?"

"It's pretty final."

"Your doing or his?"

Her head rose slowly. She stared at me with flames and daggers in her eyes but didn't speak.

"It's a question, Susan, not an accusation."

"Was your breakup your fault or your wife's?"

"Mine, I guess mine. Gloria got bored with me and started fucking around."

"Then it was her fault!"

"Blame is always convenient because it's so decisive: My fault. Your fault. But marriage is never that clear-cut. He pisses you off here, you piss him off there. Sometimes you end up with a toilet bowl so full neither of you can flush it."

That conversation made me miss and realize again how grateful I was for my wife. It made me want to see her immediately so I went home for lunch. But Magda wasn't there and neither was Pauline. Different as they were, the two women liked hanging around together. Anyone would like hanging around with Magda. She was funny, tough, and very perceptive. Most of the time she knew exactly what was good for you even when you didn't. She was stubborn but not unbending. She knew what she liked. If she liked you, your world became bigger.

My first wife, the inglorious Gloria, shrunk the world like heavy rain on leather shoes and made me feel like I no longer fit in it. She was beautiful, endlessly dishonest, bulimic, and as I later found out, promiscuous as a bunny. At the end of our relationship I found a note she had written and in all likelihood left out for me to see. It said, "I hate his smell, his sperm, and his spit."

Eating lunch alone, I contentedly sat in the living room listening to my thoughts and the buzz of a lawnmower someplace far away. If her marriage really was finished, I did not envy Susan the next act of her life. In contrast, I was at a place in my own where I didn't envy anyone anything. I liked my days, my partner, job, surroundings. I was working on liking myself but that was always an ongoing, iffy process.

Over the friendly smell of my bacon, lettuce, and tomato sandwich, an increasingly pungent fragrance of something else began to butt in. I didn't pay much attention while eating, but it became so pervasive as I slipped an afterlunch cigarette between my lips that I stopped and took a long, serious sniff.

The nose can be like a blind mole brought up into the sunlight. Below ground—in your unconscious—it knows exactly what it's doing and will guide you: That stinks—stay away. That's good—have a taste. But bring it above ground, demand to know *What's that smell,* and it moves its blind head around and around in confused circles and loses all sense of direction. I asked out loud, "What *is* that fucking smell?" But my nose couldn't tell me because *that* smell was an incomprehensible combination of aromas I had loved my entire life. This is a crucial point, but I don't know how to describe it so it makes better sense.

A whore I visited in Vietnam always wore a certain kind of orchid in her hair. Her English was minimal so the only understandable translation she could come up for the flower was "bird breath." Naturally when I got back to the States and asked, no one had ever heard of a bird breath orchid. And I never smelled it again until that afternoon in my living room in Crane's View, New York, nine thousand miles from Saigon. Naturally my brain had long ago put the aroma in its dead-letter file and forgotten about it. Now here it was again. Remember me?

But it was only one in a swirling, illusive combination of cherished smells. Cut grass, wood smoke, hot asphalt, sweat on a woman you are making love with, Creed's "Orange Spice" cologne, fresh-ground coffee . . . my list of favorites and there were more. All of them were there together *at the same time* in the air. Once it had my full attention, neither my conscious nor unconscious mind could believe it.

I had to stand up, had to find where it was coming from or I'd go crazy. The trail led to the garage. I remembered that in our conversation earlier, Magda had said how good it smelled in there. What an understatement! No room freshener out of a can could have matched that deliciousness. Cloves now, the warm healthy smell of puppies. Pine, rain on pine trees.

The car was parked there looking friendly and cooperative. Hadn't the mechanic come yet? If so, why wasn't Magda using it now? The smell of new leather, a new book, lilacs, grilling meat. I kept a tool kit in the trunk. I hadn't tried to start the car yet, but since I was standing right there, why not get out the tool kit just in case?

What registered first—what I saw or smelled? I opened the trunk. The intensity of the odor multiplied by ten. And lying in there was the body of Old Vertue. Again. Under his red collar were the feather from the Schiavo house and the bone I had found in the hole I dug for him.

Ape of My Heart

George Dalemwood is the strangest person I know and one of my best friends. He is not strange in a "lives in a treehouse, wears chipmunkskin underwear and a red crash helmet" way. He's just odd. I certainly would not like to live inside his head, but I love hearing what comes out of it so long as I am at a safe distance. And for all his eccentricities, the great paradox is what George does for a living—he writes instructions for how to make things work. How do you get that complicated new camera going after it's out of the box? Read the instructions, George Dalemwood wrote. They are invariably clear, confident, and precise. Boot a computer program and get nothing but crashes? Read George and you'll be rocking in no time.

Most important, as a friend, he was unjudgmental and carried no preconceived notions about anything. Because I could not deal with what had just happened, I got into the car without another thought and drove to his house, dead dog passenger and all. Yes, the car started immediately, but I was too dazed to give that any thought. I just wanted to talk to George.

His place is a few blocks from ours. Nothing special about it—one floor, four rooms, a porch that should have been fixed twenty years ago. When I arrived his young dachshund, Chuck, was sitting on a porch step licking its balls. I stepped over it and rang the bell. No answer. Damn! Now what? Then I remembered the engine in my car was supposed to be dead. The dead dog that was supposed to be buried was in the trunk of the car that was supposed to have a dead battery. Damn!

I looked up at the sky hoping for divine guidance, or something, and saw George sitting on his roof staring at me.

"What are you doing up there? Didn't you see me ring your bell?"

"Yes."

"Well get down here, man, I need help!"

In a toneless voice he said, "I would prefer not to." Which, in spite of everything going on, made me smile. Because George had been rereading *Bartleby* over and over for the last two months and said he would continue until he understood it. Before *Bartleby* he had been reading and trying to figure out *Mount Analogue* and before that, all of the Doctor Doolittle books. Every fookin' one of them. George hoped when he died if he went to heaven, it would be Puddleby on the Marsh—Doolittle's hometown. He was serious.

"Would you like a Mars bar?"

George ate three things and only those three: boiled beef, Mars bars, and Greek mountain tea.

"No. Listen, I'm begging you as a friend, please come down and listen to me."

"I can hear fine from up here, Frannie."

"What are you doin' up there anyway?"

"Deciding the best way to describe erecting a satellite dish."

"So you have to sit up there to see?"

"Something like that."

"Jesus! All right, if you're going to be that way about it—" I went back to the car, started it, and reversed onto his perfectly kept front lawn until I was as close to the house as possible. I opened the trunk and pointed accusingly at the carcass. George slid on his ass down the roof a ways so he could see better.

He was unimpressed. "Got a dead dog in there. So?"

Hands on hips, afternoon sun directly in my eyes, I described what had happened with Old Vertue the last two days. When I was finished he asked only about the feather and the bone. He wanted to see them. I handed them up. He leaned over the edge of the roof to get them and, stumbling, almost fell off.

"Goddamn, George! Why do you make life so difficult? Why don't you just come down for ten minutes? Then you can climb back up there and be an antenna for the rest of the day."

He shook his head. After settling himself into a comfy position, he touched the bone to his tongue. If I hadn't known him I would have protested, but my friend had his own way of doing things. If you were going to hang around with him you had to accept that. After a few licks, he delicately bit it with his front teeth but not enough to break it. Standing below, I could hear the high click of his teeth against it. Sort of like castanets. I got a shiver down my spine at the thought of putting that nasty thing in my mouth.

"What does it taste like?"

"I don't know if it's really bone, Frannie. It's very *sweet*."

"It's been *lying in the ground*, George! Probably soaked up a lot of—" I stopped when I saw he wasn't listening. No matter what you were saying, if George wasn't interested he stopped listening. It was a never-ending lesson in both humility and careful word choice.

Next came the feather. That piece of evidence he smelled a long time but gave it only a glancing swipe with his tongue. That was somehow more revolting than the bone, and I looked away. I noticed Chuck had stopped licking his plumbing and joined me in staring up at his master.

"You lick your nuts and George licks feathers. No wonder you two live together." I picked him up and kissed his head while waiting for the lab report from the roof.

George pointed the feather at me. "This has a great deal to do with what I was thinking about before you arrived."

"And what was that, pray tell?"

"Conspiracy theories."

"You're on the roof being an antenna and thinking about conspiracy theories?"

He ignored me. "On the Internet there are over ten thousand sites devoted to the different secret plots people believe led to the death of Lady Diana. The essential motivation behind all conspiracy theories is egotism—I am not being told the truth. The same thing applies here, Frannie. You're a policeman; you're used to logic. But there is none here, at least not so far. You're not being told the truth. Are you more upset at the dog's reappearance or the simple fact it happened in your trunk and not someone else's?"

"I hadn't thought about that."

"There are two ways of approaching this—as mischief or metaphysics. The first is simple: Someone saw you burying the dog and decided to play a trick. When you left the forest they dug up the body and found a way to put it in your trunk when neither you nor your family were watching."

"What about the bone? I left that in my coat pocket. How'd they get it?"

He held up an index finger. "Wait. We're only theorizing now. They used the body to play a macabre clever trick on you. Which worked because look how upset you are.

"The *other* possibility is it's a sign from a greater power. It happened because you've been chosen for some reason. The dog reappears, the feather and the bone are together, and your car starts when it was supposedly broken. I'm assuming if this is the case, it wouldn't start for Magda because the dog was already back in the car, waiting for you to find it. All this is supposition;

there will be no understandable logic here because our logic doesn't apply in matters like these. Wait a minute." He moved to the far side of the roof and climbed down an old wooden ladder leaning against the house.

He came over to us and tickled the dog's nose with the feather. Chuck tried halfheartedly to bite it. "I want to show you something inside the house. But before that, I've got an idea I'd like to try. What would you say to burying Old Vertue again, in my backyard this time?"

"Why?"

"Because I'm curious to see what will happen. If he does return again, I won't have to wait to hear the news from you." He took Chuck from me, and the small dog went nuts licking his face.

"Which do you think it is?"

"Probably mischief, but I hope it's the other."

"I don't need God putting dead dogs in my trunk, George."

"Maybe it's not God. Maybe it's something else."

"That kind of shit's off my Richter scale, bud. I have trouble enough living with a teenager. Remember when I got shot? I was close for a couple hours. Magda said they were thinking of calling a priest to give me the last rites. But did I do out-of-body travel. to the big light? No. Did I see God? No." I rubbed my face. "What about the smell?"

He looked at the ground. "I don't smell anything."

"*What?* You can't smell that? Even now it's knocking me down!"

"Nothing, Frannie. I don't smell a thing."

Unlike George, his house is normal. Everything is in order; everything as uninteresting as possible. Magda and I once went over for a dinner of boiled beef and Mars bars for dessert. Afterward she said, "His house is so ordinary you keep thinking maybe it's creepy, but it isn't—it's just really dull." The only thing that stood out were all kinds of brand-new gadgets lying around, waiting for Mr. Dalemwood to explain them to confused future consumers.

"What's this?" I picked up an object that looked like a mix between a CD player and a small Frisbee.

"Don't touch that, Frannie. It's very delicate." He was searching a shelf packed full of large-format art books. "Just sit down. I'll be with you in a second."

"How come every time I come here you scold me for something?"

"Here it is." He pulled out a book as big as a door. Looking at his hand, he grimaced and wiped it on his pants. Then he opened the book and started flipping through the pages. "Wouldn't you rather be called than tricked?"

"Meaning what?" I picked up the CD Frisbee and put it down again.

"Wouldn't you like to have a metaphysical adventure rather than track down some bozo who's just trying to make you look stupid?"

"No. My family won't let me watch *The X-Files* or *The Outer Limits* with them because whenever the strange stuff starts happening, I laugh."

Judging by his expression, George had tuned me out after I said no. But when he abruptly stopped flipping pages, a smile the likes of which I had never seen rose slowly up his face like a hot air balloon lifting off. Not only that. This was the second time in two days I had seen a look on another's face that announced something big was about to arrive and I'd better put on my seat belt for whatever was coming. The first time happened right before Susan announced her separation. But George's expression was stranger because he was not given to great emotional splashes. If you didn't know the guy you could easily have mistaken him for autistic. His response to things rarely arrived with a side order of exclamation marks.

· " 'Fear only two: God, and the man who has no fear of God.' That's from the Koran, Frannie."

Whatever *that* was supposed to mean, he came over holding the book open with two hands. He put it on my lap and stepped back. I looked at him for some sign but he only pointed at the page, that bizarre smile still locked in place.

I looked down. My eyes widened to the size of planets. "No fuck-ing way!" I didn't lift my head. My eyes raced round and round the picture. I *couldn't* lift my head. "No fuck-ing way!"

"See the title?"

"*Yes, George, I see the title!* What am I supposed to do now? Huh? What am I supposed to do with this? Did I see the title? Am I stupid? I *can* read, you know——"

"Take it easy, Frannie." But he was smiling. The son of a bitch was still smiling.

On the page in the book on my lap was a reproduction of a painting by an unknown artist, circa 1750. Remember that—seventeen hundred and fifty. It is a portrait of a dog. A three-and-a-half-legged, one-eyed, marble-cake-colored pit bull sitting facing us and looking peacefully off to the right. A white bird—a dove?—with wings spread is hovering over the dog's head. Behind them in a valley is a castle. Behind that is a bucolic landscape that includes rolling hills, a meandering river, farmers at work in their vineyards. It would be easy to replace the dog with a lord or wealthy landowner standing on a hill above all he owned, all he has achieved in life, his heaven on earth, all there for us to see and envy. But it is *not* a lord nor is it a human being; it is a pit bull. And a very familiar-looking one at that.

The title of the painting was "Old Vertue."

"How did you know about this, George?"

"I remembered the painting."

I closed the book and read the title. *Great Animal Portraits.* "Does the author say anything about the picture in the introduction?"

"Nothing."

"Why didn't you tell me about this after you saw the body and I told you his name?"

"Because first I wanted to hear how you felt about it."

I was so angry I wanted to hit him on the head with the book. I was so rattled I wanted to go into the second hole I was going to dig for the dead dog and hide. I dropped the book on the floor. George started for it but when my body tensed, he froze.

"What am I supposed to *do* about this?"

He squatted down like a baseball catcher and put his hand on the arm of my chair to balance himself. Both of us remained silent. Chuck rolled over on his back and started doing that thing dogs do when they're happy or feeling goofy: Back and forth—flip flop.

"George, what would you do if you were me?"

"Bury the dog again. Then see what happens."

"Not much else I can do, is there?"

"You could have it cremated at the Amerling Animal Shelter, but I don't think that would end the problem."

"It'll come back, won't it?"

"I think so. Yes it will."

"No good deed goes unpunished. That's what I get for being

nice to a dead dog: Fucker comes back to haunt me. This is absurd. Why am I talking this way?"

"Because wonder's grabbed you by the arm, Frannie. Because it's out of your control. Something else is making the rules now."

A strange, disturbing thought arrived. I couldn't stop asking, "Is it you, George? Have you done all this? Is *that* why I came here today—because you set it up? You're weird. Maybe you're weirder than I imagined."

"Thank you, I'm flattered, but you're still looking for logical answers. Even if I *had* set you up, how do you explain that painting in the book?"

"You found a dog that looked like the picture. You put it in the parking lot knowing someone would find it. . . . This is ridiculous. There would be too many coincidences and things that could go wrong."

"Exactly. You want clear answers where there are none. What you have to do is create a real question and put it honestly in your heart. Then go looking for a clear answer. I'm *not* involved in this, but I'm very happy you came today. It's the only time I have ever seen wonder firsthand. And I believe that's what this is."

There was a big beautiful apple tree in George's backyard he planted years ago when he moved into his house. He was enormously proud of it. All year he sprayed, watered, and cared for it. A tree surgeon was called at the slightest sign of anything suspect. Although he never ate any, George spent hours in the fall carefully picking and placing the fruit in large wicker baskets he bought specifically for that purpose. He donated all of it to our town hospital. I had eaten apples from the tree and they were horrible, but don't tell him that.

Sitting under that tree, he watched as I flung dirt out of the hole. Although he had offered to help, I insisted on doing the job myself. If Old Vertue had come for me, I assumed it was my duty to dig for him.

"How old are you, Frannie?"

"Forty-seven."

"Have you noticed how the meanings of words change the older we get? When I was young I used to think old meant fifty. Now I'm almost fifty and old is eighty. When I was twenty, I thought the word love meant a sexy woman and a good marriage. Now the only love I feel is for my work, Chuck, and this tree. Yet that's sufficient."

I shoved the spade into the ground and heaved. "Aren't you just saying things are relative?"

"No, something completely different. Over a lifetime our definitions of things change radically, but because it's so gradual we're blind to them. As the years pass, our names for things no longer fit but we still keep using them."

"Because it's convenient and we're lazy." Up with another shovelful.

"Did you know the Farsi language has over fifty different terms for the word love?"

"Why are we having this conversation, George? Uh-oh! Here we go again."

"What?"

"There's something in here. In this hole too. Just like last time with the bone."

"What is it?"

I bent over and picked up the brightly colored object the shovel had just uncovered. *"Oh my God!"*

"What Frannie? What?"

"It's—it's—"

"What?" George was frantic.

"It's Mickey Mouse!" I tossed up the rubber figure I'd dug up. "It must have been in the ground ten thousand years."

Even he laughed while he jiggled the child's squeeze toy in his hand. "At least. Twenty years ago some kid was heartbroken a whole afternoon after losing this thing."

When I finished digging and hadn't unearthed any other archaeological treasures, I laid Old Vertue in his new berth and shoveled dirt over him. Chuck christened the new grave by pissing on it as soon as I was done, which was only appropriate. Ashes to ashes, dog to dog. George and I stood there a few moments looking at the spot.

"What do I do now?"

"Nothing. Wait."

"Maybe he's already in the trunk of my car."

"I doubt it, Frannie."

"But you do think he'll be back? That it wasn't just some lunkhead's prank?"

"Nope. And I think it's exciting."

"I knew this guy whose wife got pregnant when they were in their forties. I asked how he felt about it and he said, 'It's okay, but to tell you the truth, I'm too old for Little League.' It's sort of the same thing for me here—I think I'm too old for wonder."

"Pauline got tattooed." Magda's voice hit like a flamethrower the minute I walked in the door that evening. But her news was sensational. The thought of Fade making such a confident and uncharacteristic gesture made me want to clap. But if I let her mother know that she'd hit me.

I tried to sound . . . thoughtful. "Well, it *is* her body—"

She glared at me. "It is not her body when she does something as stupid as this. What'll it be next—piercing? I hear branding is very in these days. She's a teenager who suddenly wants to be trendy. I'll be your cliché tonight. Don't you dare take her side in this, Frannie, or I'll tattoo your head."

"Is it big or small?"

"Is what?"

"The tattoo."

"I don't know. She won't show me! She just announced she'd done it and left me standing there with my jaw on top of my foot. My daughter has a tattoo. I'm so ashamed."

"I thought you two were together today."

"We were! We went to the Amerling mall. After lunch we split up for a couple of hours. When we met up later, she told me what she'd done. She's such a quiet kid, Frannie. Why on earth would she do something so loony?"

"Maybe she doesn't want to be quiet anymore."

Magda crossed her arms and tapped her foot. "Well?"

"Well what?"

"Well, what are you going to do about it?"

"I think we have to see what it is first, honey. If it's a little thing like a bug or something—"

"A *bug*? Who gets bugs tattooed on their body?"

"You'd be surprised. Down at the county jailhouse you'll see tattoos—"

"Don't change the subject. You're her stepfather and a policeman—"

"Should I arrest her?"

She stepped up close and surprisingly wrapped her thin arms around me. With her mouth an inch from my ear she growled in her deadliest voice, *"I want you to talk to her."*

Dinner that night was no fun occasion. Luckily it was my

turn to cook so I didn't have to endure the lunar silence ema-
nating from the living room. Usually dinnertime was nice in our
house. The three of us gathered in the kitchen and talked about
our day. The radio was always on to an oldies station and when
a great one played, we'd stop what we were doing and dance to
the Dixie Cups or Wayne Fontana and the Mindbenders.

That night, for some ominous reason, both women sat in
the living room five feet across from each other, pretending to
read. I think Magda was there to make believe her daughter's
tattoo didn't bother her a bit. Life as usual. The only problem
was you could see her mouth moving as she thought up one good
zinger after another to say to her errant child. I think Pauline
was there because she was either testing the waters or silently
proclaiming she'd do whatever she pleased now and we'd just
have to accept it.

So long as it wasn't something dumb or obscene, I had no
gripe with a tattoo. I was only curious to see what this strange
young woman would want permanently engraved on some as yet
unknown location on her body. While stirring the mulligatawny
soup, I wondered out loud, "A dragon? Nah. A heart?" Et cetera.
But if I didn't placate Magda on this matter I knew I'd be in
soup deeper than the spicy one bubbling on the stove.

I had an idea. Divide and conquer. I opened the kitchen door
and asked Pauline to come in a minute. She shot a quick glance
at her mother to see if this move had already been worked out
between us, but Magda didn't even look.

No one gave up less when it was necessary. The queen of
the Cold Shoulder, the Zipped Lip, Mum's the Word, Pauline's
mum could shut you out quicker than a slammed door.

Tossing her head, Pauline marched across the room and into
the kitchen. "What?" she demanded in an imperious voice completely not her own.

I smiled at her.

"*What?*"

"Your ma's going to glue us both to her shitlist if you don't at least tell me where and what it is."

She crossed her arms and tightened her lips exactly like Magda. "It's my body. I'll do what I want with it."

"I agree. But we've got to come up with a way to resolve this thing without her going nuclear. Being stubborn is not how to do it."

"What do you want me to do?"

"Where is it?"

She sized me up, stuck out her bottom lip. "I'm not going to tell you. You're trying to manipulate me. I hate that."

"Then *what* is it? At least you can tell me that. Give us a bone, Pauline; give me something I can offer Magda that'll calm her down. *Be* an individual, but remember you're also a daughter. Your mother worries about you. Don't be unreasonable. We're on your side."

"Forget it, Frannie. I don't need to justify what I do. I wanted a tattoo and I got one. If I want to pierce my tongue I'll get it pierced."

I looked at heaven and clasped my hands together like an Italian in prayer. "Pauline, *don't* tell your mother that! Don't even use the word pierced within a two-mile radius. Holy shit!"

"I'm not going to get pierced, but I will if I feel like it!"

I mentioned before that as a kid I was dangerously bad news. For the most part I have disappeared that part of me. But now and then that little shit from yesteryear pops up, usually in the wrong situation. Pauline's voice was so rude and self-righteous that young Fran sprang out of my mouth and went right for her throat. In the most annoying and obnoxious voice I had, I mimicked what she had just said. To further the insult, I tipped my head left and right while I spoke, like some retarded Punch and Judy puppet, ". . . but I will if I feel like it!"

To her credit, my stepdaughter said nothing but gave me a long, disgusted look. Dignity intact, she turned and left the kitchen. I heard her mother call out anxiously, "Where are you going?" Then came the sound of the front door closing.

Magda was in the kitchen twenty seconds later. "What did you say to her? What did you do?"

"Blew it. I made fun of her."

She touched her forehead. "This is ridiculous! I'm sounding exactly like my mother with my sister!"

Magda's older sister was a teenager when she was murdered thirty years ago. A wild girl, she was notorious in Crane's View for doing whatever she wanted. Magda said most of her childhood memories were of her mother and sister screaming at each other.

The front doorbell rang. We looked at each other. Pauline? Why ring the bell to her own house? Maybe she'd forgotten her keys. I put down the soup ladle and went to answer it.

No one was there. I stepped out beyond the range of the porch light to have a look around. Nothing. Kids ringing the police chief's bell and running? As I was going back into the house something stopped me: My nose. Although it was much vaguer, that wonderful fragrance was in the air again. The last time I'd smelled it around here was in the garage when Old Vertue reappeared. Was this his calling card? I wasn't waiting to find out.

Ignoring the cooking soup, I crossed the lawn to our garage and looked in. Someone was sitting in the passenger's seat of our car. I took a few steps toward it and recognized Pauline. Before dealing with her I had to check something out. I already had my keys in hand and opened the trunk expecting I don't know what. Nothing was there. I let out a long slow relieved breath. If that dog's body had been there again at that moment with Pauline in the car I would've . . . I don't know what I would've. But the smell *was* stronger in the garage, no doubt about it.

"Pauline?"

"I want a prime-time life." She didn't move. Simply stared straight ahead and addressed the garage wall.

"Nothing wrong with that. Prime time is the place to be."

"We read this line in class last semester that scared me so much; I can't stop thinking about it. 'How can you hide from what never goes away.' That's why I got this tattoo. Mom thinks it's because I want to be like everyone else, but it's just the opposite. I want people at school to hear about it and say '*Her*, Pauline Ostrova? That stupid little bookworm got a *tattoo?*' I don't want the person I am to be the person I'm going to be when I get older, Frannie.

"I rang the bell just now. I didn't want to be alone out here. I was hoping you'd come find me."

"That's okay. But I wish you'd come back in the house now. Soup's on. Remember one thing too—usually what scares you most makes you do the most work. Ghosts make you run faster than a math test."

She didn't move. "I'm not sorry I did it. The tattoo, I mean."

"You don't need to be sorry. What is it anyway?"

"None of your business."

Life went on. We drank our soup, went to bed, rose the next morning, and walked into the future Pauline was so worried about. Old Vertue didn't reappear, and neither did the Schiavos. The air went back to smelling like it usually does; our car started. Johnny Petangles fell into one of the ditches they were digging by the river and sprained his ankle. Susan Ginnety went away for a conference of small-town mayors. When she returned, her husband Frederick had moved out. Even worse for the mayor, he rented a house four blocks away. When I bumped into him at the market he said she could throw him out of her life but he wasn't going to leave the town he had grown to like very much.

I was surprised. To tell you the truth, Crane's View is not much of a burg. Most people happen on it by mistake or while looking for other more picturesque Hudson Valley towns. Sometimes they stop to eat at Scrappy's Diner or Charlie's Pizza. Sometimes they hang around long enough afterward for a stroll around the one-block downtown while digesting their high-cholesterol meal.

I like living here because I like familiar things. I always put my shoes in the same place before going to bed; I eat the same meal for breakfast most days. When I was younger I saw enough of the world to know I was not meant to live in countries whose postage stamps picture elephants, penguins, or *coluber de rusi* snakes. No thanks. Like others of my generation who went to Vietnam and were traumatized by the experience, I traveled a lot before returning home. I can do without waking in the morning to the sound of a coughing camel sticking its head in my bedroom window (Kabul), or eating fresh mangoes at the outdoor market in Port Louis, Mauritius. Crane's View is a peanut butter sandwich—very filling, very American, sweet, not very interesting. God bless it.

A few nights later the frantic little man who took up residence in my bladder around age forty woke me up, demanding the toilet—right now! Welcome to middle age. That time in life when you learn your body is not the sum of its parts but some of its parts work and some stop.

Magda was wrapped around me in a sweet familiar way. She mumbled a sexy grumble when I untangled myself from her. My first wife slept so far away from me that I had to make a long-distance call if I wanted more covers. Even waking in the middle of the night now, the first thing that came to mind was how much I loved the woman next to me. I kissed her warm cheek and stood up. The wooden floor was cold under my bare feet; one of the small sure signs fall was on the way.

Your home is always more mysterious in the middle of the night. After-midnight noises hide behind the rest of the day. The finicky way the floor creaks, the slippy, wood-sanding sound of bare feet going someplace. The fat fly unmoving on the window-pane, black against the silver-blue light from the street. You smell the cold and dust.

I walked down the hall toward the bathroom. To my surprise the light was on in there. Music was playing quietly. Getting closer I recognized Bob Marley singing "No Woman, No Cry" at two in the morning. The door was cracked open a few inches. I leaned forward and peeked in.

Pauline stood with her back to me staring at herself in the mirror. She wore enough black eye makeup to pass for a crow. She was also completely naked. My first reaction was an instinctive whoops! and a quick pull back. Which I did, but something lodged in my brain like a thrown dart. I'd seen something in there and not just my stepdaughter naked for the first time. I did not want to see Pauline naked—not once, not twice, not never—but I had to go back and look again. Luckily, she was still hypnotizing herself in the mirror and didn't notice the Peeping Fran at the door.

There it was! In the middle of her spine, just up from the start of her ass, was the notorious tattoo. Because of its location, few people besides Pauline and her lovers would ever see the thing. It would have been a nice secret present for them if it hadn't been what it was. About seven inches long, it was a tattoo of a feather. *The* feather I had found at the Schiavo house and buried—twice—with Old Vertue. The same wild colors and distinctive pattern all there beautifully rendered above the girl's nice butt.

I stepped back and away. My alarm at seeing that image again, *there,* was matched by the now-serious need to piss. I would use the toilet downstairs. I was glad for a plan because I was so rattled that if I hadn't had to go, I might just have stood frozen and not moved for an hour. The house around me was no longer cold, my hand no longer numb from my happy deep sleep. Something big and clearly unavoidable kept stepping in front of me wherever I turned now. And there was no end to the variety of ways it had of saying, *Yoo-hoo! Here I am again.*

I imagined Pauline walking into the very upscale "body art" parlor in the Amerling mall and looking through books picturing the hundreds of different tattoos available. Had she opened the fourth book, seen the eightieth picture and thought, "Oh that's nice—a feather. I'll have that one"? Or had magic intervened and forced her to like that one? Had any of it been her choice or had this thing taken charge of all our lives now?

Smith the cat met me downstairs. He's a good guy who keeps to himself, disappears somewhere most of the day, and cruises the house at night. He accompanied me to the toilet, tail swishing back and forth. Before I married Magda and again had someone important to talk to after hours, Smith (the only survivor of my first marriage) heard lots of my stories. I was always grateful for that and let him know it.

While relieving myself, I thought of the women upstairs. Pauline naked at the mirror at two in the morning trying on a black eye identity. Black eyes and a new tattoo on her spine, roles that no more fit her than would a pair of size-thirteen men's clogs. Her mother asleep down the hall, completely unaware of resurrected dogs or the fact her daughter had decided to take a walk in the dark woods on the outskirts of her life.

Ten fluid pounds lighter, I washed my hands. Drying them on a pink hand towel I thought with amusement and the greatest love that I live with pink. I *hate* pink. Never would I have imagined that gross color becoming part of my everyday. But Magda loved it, so pink lived all over our house and it broke my heart. I turned off the light in the toilet and started back toward the staircase.

"Since when do you wash your hands after pissing?"

Street light washed across parts of the living room floor, lighting it that silvery blue of chrome and ghosts. To the right of the windows a person was sitting in my favorite chair. His legs were extended out into the light. I saw the cat's tail flick back and forth—Smith was standing on whoever it was's lap.

"Who are you? What are you doing in my house?" I entered the room and stood near the wall, the light switch there. I didn't turn it on. I wanted to hear more before I needed to see.

"Look at your cat. Doesn't that tell you anything?" Was his voice familiar? Yes. No. Should I have recognized it? Was that possible?

I looked at the cat standing on the guy's lap. Contentedly too, by the fact it was unmoving and the slow twists of its tail. Smith did not like to be held. Smith did not like to be touched. Smith called the shots. If someone picked him up and tried petting him, he'd leap away or if held fast, hunker down and growl. I was the one exception. Because he knew I respected him and his ways, the cat let me pick him up. He usually stuck around a while—maybe even purring now and then.

But more than the cat it was the shoes that did it. Until I focused on the shoes I couldn't, or perhaps didn't want to, put all of the pieces together and recognize who was sitting in my chair with my cat on his lap. But the shoes lit by that sexy light said what I probably already knew.

When I was a kid, boys in our town wore only one kind of shoes—high-top sneakers. Black. The brand could be either Converse Chuck Taylors or PF Flyers, but nothing else. If you didn't go with that flow, you were a no. Kids like to imagine themselves individualists, but no one outside of the military is as strict in their dress code as teenagers.

So when my father came back from a business trip to Dallas and handed me a pair of orange cowboy boots—*orange*—I had to fight myself not to laugh. Cowboy boots? Who did he think I was, the fucking Lone Ranger? I loved my old man, even in my mean days, but sometimes he had no clue. I took the boots into my room and tossed them into the black hole that was my closet. Adios, pardner.

But the next morning I went to the closet for a shirt and there they were, all bright and shiny and still orange. I looked at them. Then I looked at my terminally ratty black sneakers on the floor. Then I smiled, I picked up the boots, put them on, and walked out into a new day. I was the worst kid in town. The baddest. The few people in Crane's View who didn't hate me should have. If I felt like being Roy Rogers with giddyap footwear, not one of my peers in his right mind would challenge or make fun of me to my face because they knew I'd eat them alive. I wore those cowboy boots until there was nothing left of them and was sorry the day I had to throw them away.

The night light through the window fell in a wide stripe across orange cowboy boots. From where I stood they looked

new. I ran my eyes up the boots to the leg, the body, and with
a pause for my mind to catch its breath, I finally looked at his
face. "Son of a bitch!"

"No, ape of my heart!"

It was me, seventeen years old.

"I'm dead, right? I died but didn't know it. All this weird stuff
that's been happening is because I'm dead, right?"

"Nope." He gently lifted Smith off his lap and placed him on
the floor. As he moved forward, the light touched his shirt. My
heart lurched because I remembered that shirt! Broad blue-and-
black checks, I had stolen it from a store on Forty-fifth Street in
the city. I put it on in the dressing room, pulled off all the sales
tags, left my other shirt on a hanger, and walked out of the place.

"No, you're not dead. You're not dead and I'm not dead. I
don't know where the hell I've *been*, but fuck it—the kid's back!
Aren't you glad to see the old ape?"

Ape of my heart. I hadn't heard that phrase in years. Once
my father came down to the police station to get me. When we
were out on the street again he grabbed my neck and shook me.
He was a small man and not strong, but when he was mad he
scared the shit out of me. Maybe because I loved him so much
but couldn't stop disappointing him. Part of me desperately
wanted him to be proud. Most of me stuck its ass in his face
and, by my permanent bad behavior, said he could kiss either
cheek. Why he continued to love me was a source of wonder.

"You're a fucking *ape*, Frannie. You're the fucking ape of my
heart. God damn you."

The word shocked me more than anything else did. My father
seldom cursed and he never used *that* word. He was witty; he
liked metaphors and wordplay—"Getting through to you, son, is

like trying to pick up a penny off the floor." His hobbies were crossword puzzles and palindromes. He memorized poetry; Theodore Roethke was his hero. "Fuck" was as far away from my dad's everyday vocabulary as Bhutan. But now he had said it to me, about me, twice in five seconds.

"I'm sorry, Dad. I'm really sorry."

He still held my neck and jerked me close to his very red face. I could feel the heat of his anger. "You're not sorry at all, *ape*. If you were sorry I'd have some hope. You're young and smart but you're a total loss. I never thought I would say that, Frannie. You make me ashamed."

That confrontation didn't change my life but it stabbed me through and the wound bled a long time. Before that my armor had kept me bulletproof, even from my old man, but not any-more. Afterward I always thought of that phrase as marking the end of something in my life.

"Well?"

"Well what?"

"Here I am after all these years. A fuckin' miracle in the making, but all you do is stand there with your thumb up your ass going *duh*."

"What am I *supposed* to do?"

"Kiss me." He reached into his breast pocket and pulled out Marlboros, that beloved red and white package of death. I had smoked them all my life and loved every single one. Magda wanted me to stop but I said no dice.

"You want one?"

I nodded and crossed the room for it. He shook the pack and a couple slid out. He handed me a dented Zippo lighter. Immediately recognizing it, I smiled. Engraved on the side was FRANNIE AND SUSAN—LOVE FOREVER. Susan Ginnety, now mayor of Crane's View, back then love slave to yours truly.

"I forgot about this lighter. Do you know what happened to Susan?"

He lit his and took a jumbo drag. "No, and don't tell me. Listen, we got to talk about all these things. You want to do it here or outside? It's the same to me." His voice was Joe Cool, but it was clear he preferred going out. I was wearing a sweat suit. I needed some shoes and a coat.

When I was ready I opened the back door as quietly as I could and gestured for him to go before me.

"Don't worry about anybody hearing us. When I'm around, no one'll ever miss you."

"How does that work?"

He brought his two index fingers together and touched the tips. "When you and I are together everything else stops, understand? People, things, the whole works."

I looked down and saw the cat was going out with us. "Everything but Smith."

"Yeah, well, we're going to need him."

I looked at young me one foot away, then at Smith. "Why doesn't this disturb me more?"

"Because you knew it was coming a long time ago."

"Because I knew *what* was coming? You're smiling."

"I'm laughing my ass off. Let's go."

Cat Folding

A fat white gob of spit landed with a loud splat inches from my foot. I stared at it and then turned slowly to look at him. I knew exactly what he was doing and why. "If I knock you out will I feel it?"

His right hand froze bringing the cigarette to his mouth. "Try me, motherfucker. Just try." His voice was all balls and threat. At one time in my history that voice had frightened half the county. Tonight standing there it only made me want to pat him on the head and say now, now, everything's all right, little fellow. You don't need to spit at me to make your point.

"Remember, Junior, I got the advantage here cause I know both you *and* me. You only know you—not what you'll be like in thirty years."

He flicked the cigarette away. It bounced far out in the street, throwing up a burst of gold and red sparks. When he spoke his tone had lost the anger and was only unhappiness. "How could you end up like this? I was sitting in that house thinking, 'This is it?' This is how it'll be for me? Yellow chairs with flowers on them and last week's *Time* magazine? Bill Gates. Who the fuck is Bill Gates? What *happened* to you? What happened to *me*?"

"You grew up. Things changed. What did you think life would be like when you got older?"

He nodded toward the house. "Not that! Not what you got. Not *Father Knows Best* or *The Andy Griffith Show*. Anything but that."

"What then?"

His voice dropped back down to earth and became dreamy, slow. "I don't know—a nice apartment in the city, maybe. Or out in LA. Shag rugs, white leather furniture, cool stereo. And women—lots and lots of women. But you're married! You married Magda Ostrova, for Christ's sake! Skanky little Magda in the tenth grade."

"You don't think she's pretty?"

"She's . . . all right. She's a woman. I mean, she's like forty years old!"

"So am I, bro. Older."

"I know. I'm still wrapping my head around that." Looking at the ground, he nodded. "Hey, don't get me wrong—"

"It's all right."

Walking down my street I tried to see my world through his eyes. How different did it look from thirty years ago? What had changed? Whenever I thought about Crane's View it comforted me that almost nothing ever changed here except some shops downtown and a new house or two. But from his perspective it might have been another world.

Home is where you're most comfortable. But the comfort you know as a teen isn't the same as an adult's. When I was a kid, Crane's View was the diving board that would launch me into the big pool. I jumped up and down on it, checked the springiness, thought about what kind of dive to make. When I was ready, I ran down it and threw myself into the air with all the courage and blind trust I could muster. I was comfortable in the town when I was young because I knew one day I'd be leaving and going on to great things. No doubt about it. Despite the fact I did lousy in school, had a police record and no respect for anyone's rules, I was sure the water into which I'd be jumping would be both welcoming and warm.

"Where's Dad?"

"Died four years ago. He's up in the graveyard if you want to go visit him."

"Did *he* like what's happened to you?"

"Yeah, he was pretty happy with me."

"He thought I was a fuckup." He tried sounding amused but behind it was deep regret.

"You *were* a fuckup. Don't forget—I was there. I was you."

We moved on in silence. It was a chilly night. I felt the cold stone sidewalk through the thin soles of my shoes.

"What's the girl like? Magda's daughter."

"Pauline? Very smart, does well in school. Keeps to herself."

"So what's she doing posing naked in front of a mirror in the middle of the night?"

"Trying on different identities, I guess."

"She's not bad looking. Especially if she grows some tits."

Something big in me twitched. I didn't like that kind of talk about my stepdaughter, especially after the embarrassment of having just seen her naked myself. A moment later I was grinning because I realized it was *me* saying it. Seventeen-year-old me. Then he said something else that took my mind in another direction.

"You're going to have to help me a lot 'cause I don't know anything."

"What do you mean?"

He stopped and touched my arm. It was a brief touch, as if he didn't want to but it was necessary. "I know a few things but not as much as you probably think. Nothing about what's happened here since I left. I know what went on before, like when I was growing up and all, but nothing after that."

"Then why are you here?"

"Look at your cat. He's telling you."

Smith was still with us but walking in his own way: he wove in and out of our four legs as we moved along—as if he was sewing us together with invisible thread. Not an easy thing to do, but as with most cats, he made it look easy.

"I'm here because you need me. You need my help. Take a left here. We gotta go to the Schiavo house."

"You just said you didn't know anything about what's going on here now. How do you know about the Schiavos?"

"Look, I'm not here to trick you. I'll tell you what I know. If you think it's bullshit, that's your problem. Here's what I know about the Schiavos: They're married and they disappeared from here the other day. We gotta go over to their house now because you gotta see something."

"Why?"

"I dunno."

"Who sent you?"

He shook his head. "Dunno."

"Where did you come from?"

"Dunno. You. I came from somewhere in you."

"You're as much help as a tumor."

He turned around and started walking backward, facing me as we went. "Whatever happened to Vince Ettrich?"

"Businessman. Lives in Seattle."

"Sugar Glider?"

"She married Edwin Loos. They live in Tuckahoe."

"Jesus, they actually *did* get married! Amazing. What about Al Salvato?"

"Dead. Him and his whole family in a car accident. Right outside of town."

"How old are you now?"

"Forty-seven. Don't you know that? They didn't tell you?"

He blew out his lower lip. "They didn't tell me shit. God didn't point a finger at me and say *Go!* It wasn't *The Ten Com-*

mandments. Fucking Charlton Heston parting the waters with his staff. I was just someplace one minute and now I'm here."

"That's very informative." I was about to say more but I heard the sound of hammering. It was three o'clock in the morning. "Hear that?"

He nodded. "Coming from down the street." A look in his eyes—a twitch, a dart from left to right and then back to me—said the boy knew more than he was telling.

"You know what it is?"

"Let's just go, huh? Wait till we get there." He kept walking backward but wouldn't look at me anymore.

It was clear he wasn't going to say more so I pushed that topic aside and tried something else. "I still don't understand where you were. You were there and now you're here. Where's *there?*"

"Where do you go when you take a nap? Or sleep at night? Someplace like that. I don't really know. Someplace not here exactly but not far away either. All of who we are and were is always around. Just not in the same room anymore; the same house but not the same room."

Before I had a chance to mull that one over, we were a block away from the Schiavos'. Even from that distance I could see strange things going on down there.

In the middle of the darkness the house was brightly lit from all sides. Circling it was a ring of floodlights, all aimed directly at the building. My first thought was mining disaster. You know what I mean—those pictures forever on TV or in magazines of a mining site somewhere in the world—England or Russia, West Virginia. Miles below the earth something went wrong and there was a cave-in or an explosion. Rescue workers have been digging continually for thirty hours to reach the survivors. The site is as bright at night as during the day. They've brought in ten million candlepower to keep it lit for the workers.

That's what the Schiavo house looked like. It was so strange and surreal against the backdrop of deep thick night that no matter what they were doing there, it looked suspicious.

And who were *they*? Workmen. As we got closer I tried to see if I knew any of the men but not one was familiar. Dressed in no special style or uniform, they were guys in yellow and orange hard hats setting up scaffolding. Around the house they were quickly erecting an intricate system of interlocking pipes, struts, and connectors. When done, it would completely encircle the building, holding it captive like an insect trapped inside some kind of giant metal spiderweb. We stopped on the sidewalk in front of the house and watched them work. You only needed to watch for five minutes to know these guys really knew what they were doing. No wasted effort, no horsing around, no cluster of fuckoffs scarfing donuts and avoiding work. This crew was serious; they were here to do the job and then get out.

What *was* extraordinary was how little noise they made. To fit the strangeness of the scene it would have been better if they had been completely silent, but that wasn't the case. They made noise—metal struck metal, the creak and strain of things being fitted, bolted, erected. With all the activity and workers on the site it *should* have been a hell of a lot louder. But it wasn't. You heard things, sure, but not enough to believe it was somehow real—how could all this go on so quietly?

"They're making no noise."

The boy rubbed his nose. "I was thinking that. The whole scene's got like a muffler on it."

"What are they doing to the house? What's with the scaffolding? Why are they doing it in the middle of the night?"

"Beats me, Chief. My job was just to get you here."

"Bullshit." I didn't believe him for a minute, but it was useless arguing. He'd tell me only what he wanted and I'd have to figure out the rest.

I walked to the house and asked a worker where the foreman was. He pointed to a tall dark man who looked Indian passing a few feet away. Taking a few fast steps, I caught up with him. "Excuse me? Could I talk to you a minute?"

He looked me up and down like I was an eggplant or a whore he was considering buying.

"My name is McCabe. I'm chief of police in Crane's View."

Unimpressed, he crossed his arms and said nothing.

"Why are you here? Do you have permits? What are you doing to this place? Where are the Schiavos?"

He remained mute until a small smile twitched on at the edges of his mouth. As if what I had said was funny. I ran the tape back in my head but nothing on it sounded funny to me. "I asked you a question."

"Dot does nut mean I have dee an-suh." Sure enough, he spoke with the kind of thick Indian accent where the tongue never moves in the mouth, as if it were a cow lying in the middle of a road and words had to drive around it to get out.

"You wanna explain that?" The boy stepped in toward the foreman and got up so close they could have touched. His voice was one hundred percent disagreeable—a verbal shove in the other's chest.

"I explain nothing. I'm working! Can you not see I'm busy?"

"You won't be busy after I kick your ass, Gunga Din."

The Indian's eyes widened in disbelief and rage. "You little fuckah—"

Whomp! The kid kicked him in the balls so fast and hard that the sound filled the air. Gasping, the man fell down holding his nuts. As soon as he hit the ground, the boy kicked him in the face—boom boom boom—like trying to kick in a door. With both hands on his crotch the foreman had no chance to cover his head before the kicks rained down.

The boy smiled and stretched his arms out like wings, like he was doing the Greek "sirtaki" dance. Zorba the Greek on your head, bam bam bam. The viciousness and speed of his assault was brutal. The kid went from zero to a hundred, from chat to blood, in a second. And that kid was me.

Seeing him attack, part of me shouted *Yes!*

We lose it, it disappears, evaporates. The edge, the courage, the black madness and abandon of the young. The dazzle of living one hundred percent in the minute. It goes away, leaks out of us like water through cracks. Cracks that come from growing older. They start when you buy whole-life insurance policies and mortgages, or hear the results of not-so-good physical checkups. They start when there's a need rather than a desire for warm baths. Safety over spontaneity, comfort over commotion. Part of me hated it. Not the growing older, but becoming tame, upstanding, predictable, halfhearted, skeptical about too much. A good-sized chunk of me loved this flipped-out kid stomping a man for no reason other than a shitty attitude, a dismissive look in his eyes. That part of me wanted to join in on the beating. Am I ashamed to admit it? Not at all.

I grabbed the boy and dragged him away from the Indian. His body felt like electricity through steel; he was all high voltage and tensile strength. I am *very* strong but didn't know if I could handle him.

"Stop! Okay, stop. He's down, you win."

"Get off me, asshole!" He tried throwing another kick but was out of range.

"Enough!"

"Don't tell me—" He twisted around and threw a punch at

my face. I blocked it and in the same motion, grabbed his arm and twisted it up around his back in a hammerlock. Then I put my other arm around his throat in a chokehold.

No good. With the heel of his cowboy boot he stomped down hard on the top of my right foot. The pain was like fire. I let go. He jumped away and hands up, started dancing around like a boxer throwing jabs, ducking and weaving. Who was he fighting? Me, the Indian, the world, life.

"Who the fuck do you think you are, huh? You think you can beat me? Think you can take me? Come on, try it!"

I stood like a flamingo on one leg, holding my throbbing foot and watching him taunt me. The Indian lay on his stomach, hands under him, moaning. Teen me kept dancing around, doing Muhammad Ali routines. A group of workers had gathered to watch our festivities. While I held my foot, one of them stepped out of the crowd and whacked the kid on the head with a board. Afterward the guy just stood there with the two-by-four in his hand, looking stupid, like he was waiting for someone to tell him what to do now.

The kid was suddenly on the ground on all fours, head hanging low. Someone was helping the Indian up. I tested my foot to see if it still worked. It hurt, but I'd survive. "All right, that's it, everything stops. Who's in charge, who's the construction company, where are your permits? I want to see everything *right now."*

"Frannie?" A familiar voice said my name. Still down on the ground, the boy looked up slowly because it was his name too. Nearby Johnny Petangles stood holding a large bottle of club soda. He stared at me with impassive eyes. "What're you doing, Frannie?"

I looked from him to the house, the workers, to little Fran on the ground. It felt like every one of them was staring at me but none made a sound. And then the idea arrived. I pointed at the house. "What do you see, Johnny? What do you see over there?"

He tipped back his bottle and took a long drink. Lowering it he burped and clumsily wiped his mouth with the back of his hand. "Nothing. I see a house, Frannie. You want some of my club soda?"

I limped through the crowd of workers to the house. The air smelled of freshly cut wood, burnt metal, and gasoline. It smelled of hammered nails and power tools just turned off, sweat in a flannel shirt, coffee spilled on stone. It smelled of many men working at hard physical jobs. I took hold of one of the long steel bars in the scaffolding and shook it till things rattled. "What's this, Johnny? Do you see this?"

"I told you, it's a house."

"You don't see the scaffolding?"

"What's that?"

"Metal bars wrapped around the house. Like what they put on when they're fixing it, doing construction?"

"Nope. No cat folding. Just a house." He said those three words as if he were singing—da dee da—and gave one of his rare Johnny smiles.

I pointed to the boy on the ground. "Can you see him?"

"Who?"

"Johnny can't see me, I told you. No one can see any of this but you."

"Why?"

The boy flickered—was there, gone, there again like interference on a TV. Then he began to fade. The construction workers too, as well as the metal spiderweb around the house. All of it began fading, growing dimmer, changing from solid to transparent to gone.

"Why only me?"

"Find the dog, Frannie. Find it and we can talk again."

I tried to step toward the kid but used the bad foot. The pain that flew up my leg almost buckled me. "Which dog? The one we buried? Old Verture?"

"Who you talking to, Frannie?" Johnny had his mouth over the bottle hole. He blew into it and made the low, sad toot of a boat leaving the harbor.

Everything had disappeared. The Schiavo house was no longer encased in a metal web. There was no sign of a construction site, workers, anything out of the ordinary. No bent nails on the ground, wood shavings, tools, electrical cords, discarded Coca-Cola cans. Just an empty house on a well-kept lot on a quiet street at three in the A.M.

Petangles blew into his bottle again. "How come you're out here tonight, Frannie? I never see you when I'm out walking." He tooted once more.

"Gimme that stupid bottle!" Snatching it out of his hand, I threw it as hard as I could. But even that disappeared, because wherever it hit, it didn't make a sound. I started walking home. He followed.

"Johnny, go home. Go to bed. Don't follow me. Don't come with me. I love you, but don't bug me tonight. Okay? *Not to-night.*"

Bill Pegg turned into the school parking lot while I looked out the car window. When we stopped I reached down and flicked off both the siren and flashing light. After the motor died, we sat there a moment gathering strength for what came next.

"Who's the kid?"

"Fifteen-year-old girl named Antonya Corando—new student this year. Eleventh grade."

"Fifteen in eleventh grade? She must be smart."

"I guess not *so* smart."

Bill shook his head and reached for his clipboard. I got out of the car and checked my pockets to see if I had everything I needed: notebook, pen, depression. Ten minutes after I entered the office that morning, we got the call from the principal at Crane's View high school saying they'd found a body in the women's toilet. She was sitting on the can and was discovered because the syringe she'd used was on the floor in front of the stall. Some girl saw it, looked under the door, and ran for help.

We walked into the high school and, as always happened when I went there, I shuddered. This had been the worst place in the world for six years of my life. Now a lifetime later—way past the Himalayas of youth and down onto the plains of middle age—I still got the creeps whenever I entered the building.

The principal, Redmond Mills, was waiting for us in the entranceway. I liked Redmond and wished there had been a principal like him when I was a student at the school. The high point in his life had been attending the Woodstock Festival. He wore his sixties sensibilities like too much patchouli, but better that than the old fascists who ran the place back in our day. Redmond cared a lot about the students, his teachers, and Crane's View. I often bumped into him at the diner across the street from the school at ten at night because he had just left work and was getting a bite to eat before going home. Today he looked stricken.

"Bad news huh, Redmond?"

"Terrible! Terrible! It's the first time it's ever happened here, Frannie. The news is already all over the school. That's all the kids are talking about."

"I bet."

"Did you know her?" Bill asked gently as if the dead girl had been the principal's daughter.

Redmond looked left and right as if about to say dangerous information and didn't want to be overheard. "She was a *nebbish*, Bill! Homework was her middle name. Her essays were always ten pages too long and she was supposedly cataleptic if she didn't make the high honor roll. See my point? That's what I don't understand about this. She carried her books against her chest like she was in a fifties TV show and was so shy she always looked down when teachers talked to her."

He turned to me and his face went cynical. In a loud, resentful voice he said, "I've got kids at this school who are devil worshippers, Frannie. They've got swastikas tattooed on their necks and their girlfriends last took a bath when they were born. *Them* I could see killing themselves. But not *this* girl, not Antonya."

What immediately came to mind was an image of Pauline in the bathroom last night wearing only eye makeup and an attitude. Who knows what Antonya Corando did behind her closed doors when everyone thought she was doing calculus homework? Who knows what she dreamed, what she hid, what she pretended to be? What on this earth did she hope to gain from sticking a needle full of heroin in her arm while sitting on a toilet?

"You didn't move her?"

"*Move her?* Why would I do that, Frannie? She's dead! Where am I going to put her, in my office?"

I patted his shoulder. "It's okay. Take it easy, Redmond." His eyes had crazy in them by then, but he was a gentle man. Why shouldn't they after what he'd seen that morning?

We walked down empty, silent halls. In contrast, through small windows in the classroom doors, I could see the bright, buzzing life of school everywhere. Teachers wrote on black-boards, kids in white aprons and plastic goggles worked over Bunsen burners. In a language lab two boys were horsing around until they saw us and disappeared fast. In another room a beautiful tall girl dressed in black stood in front of a class reading aloud from a large red book. When she tossed her hair I thought, Oh boy, Frannie from last night would love her. I looked in another room and recognized my old English teacher. The old bastard had once made me memorize a poem by Christina Rossetti, which to this day I couldn't forget:

> *When I am dead, my dearest,*
> *Sing no sad songs for me—*

Fitting for what we were about to see. Redmond stopped at a door and took a key out of his pocket. "I didn't know what else I should do, so I locked it."

"Good idea. Let's have a look."

Pushing it open, he held it for us to go first. The light, that false, bright, terrible light of a public toilet, made everything grimmer. Nothing could hide here—no place for shadows, everything was on display. There were six stalls but only one of the doors was open.

For her last day on earth Antonya Corando wore a gray Skidmore College short-sleeved sweatshirt, a black skirt, and a pair of Doc Martens shoes. That made me wince because they were the brand hip kids wore. Pauline said dismissively that anyone who wore Docs was only trying to be cool. Poor square Antonya who always did her homework—buying a pair of those shoes had probably been a very large gesture for her. And it must have taken courage for her to wear them when she knew how closely kids check out each other's clothing. Maybe she first put

them on in the secrecy of her bedroom and walked around checking herself in the mirror to see how they looked, how she walked
in them, how she came across as a Doc Martens girl.

But the worst part was her socks. They were fire-engine red
with little white hearts all over them. Her skin above the socks
was a different white and so transparent you could see a swarm
of fine blue veins just below the surface.

I am only a policeman in a small town. But over the years
have seen enough violence and death both here and in Vietnam,
where I was a medic to vouch for this—most times it is the
small, irrelevant things that burn the horror into your heart. The
dead are only that—finished. But what surrounds them afterward, or what they brought with them to their final minute,
survives. A teenage girl overdoses on heroin but what flattens
you are her socks with white hearts on them. A man wraps his
silver car around a tree killing him and his whole family, but
what makes it unforgettable is that that song you love, "Sally Go
Round the Roses," is still playing on the radio in the wreck when
you get to it. A blue New York Mets baseball cap spotted with
blood on a living room floor, the scorched family cat in the yard
of the burnt house, the Bible the suicide left opened to Song of
Solomon on the bed next to him. These are what you remember
because they are the last scraps of their last day, their last moments with a heartbeat. And those things remain after they're
gone, the final snapshots in their album. Antonya went to her
drawer that morning and specifically chose the red socks with the
white hearts. How could that image not crush you, knowing
where she would end up three hours later?

Redmond began to cry. Bill and I looked at each other. I
motioned him to take the principal out. There was no reason for
him to be in the bathroom anymore.

"I'm sorry. I just can't believe it."

My assistant Bill Pegg is a good man. A few years ago he lost his daughter to cystic fibrosis and that ordeal turned him into a different person. He now has a special manner with the shocked or grieving; a way to keep them balanced in the first unbearable minutes after real horror has entered their lives. When they're trying to understand the new language of grief, as well as cope with the loss of gravity, the *weightlessness* that comes with desolation or great suffering. When I asked Bill how he did it he said, "I just go there with them and tell them what I know about it. That's all you can do."

After they left and the door hissed shut I went over to Antonya. I got down on one knee in front of her. If someone had come in then how silly it would have looked—like I was proposing to a sleeping girl sitting on the toilet.

One arm hung straight down at her side. The other lay across her leg. I assumed she had been right-handed, so I looked at her left arm to see if I could find the needle mark. Her head rested against the white tile wall, eyes closed. The needle mark was a small red welt just below the crease lines in her left elbow. I unconsciously felt for a pulse. Of course there wasn't one. Then I reached up and touched that mark.

"This is where you died, stupid kid." Holding her elbow in my hand, I ran my thumb tenderly over the mark and whispered to her, "Right here."

"I'm not stupid."

Empty-headed, refusing to believe, I automatically looked up from her arm upon hearing the soft, slurry voice.

Antonya's head rolled slowly from left to right until it faced me. She opened her eyes and spoke again in that same, not-quite-there voice. "I wasn't supposed to die."

"You're alive!"

"No. But I *can* still feel your hand. I feel your warmth." Her voice was a halting whisper, a trickle. Her tap had been turned off but some water was still left in the pipe, a dribble. "Tell my mother I didn't do this. Tell her they did it to me."

"Who did it? Who's *they?*"

"Find the dog." Her eyes stayed open but emptied. Every trace of life oozed out, into the air, back into life. I saw it go. Nothing specifically happened, but I knew exactly what was going on. Life left her and then she *was* gone.

Still on one knee I stared, willing her back, willing her to come back and help me understand.

"Frannie?" Bill stood in the doorway, holding it open with an arm. "The ambulance is here and I've called the girl's mother. I'm going over there now. Is that okay?"

"Yeah."

"Fran, you okay?"

"Yeah. Listen, tell Redmond I want to look in her locker. And if she had a gym locker, in there too."

I waited there while they got the body ready to move. They took their time. I was making notes when one of the ambulance guys said, "Whoa! Check this out!"

Looking up, I saw him holding a feather—*the* feather I had already seen too many times. I took it out of his hand and had a closer look to make sure. "Where'd this come from?"

He gave a dirty chuckle and raised his eyebrows. "Fell out from under her skirt! Do you believe that? What's she doing with a feather up her dress?" he leered.

"I'll keep this." I put the feather between the pages of my notebook and closed it.

From the expression on his face the guy thought I was joking. He whined, "Aw come on, Chief, I want it."

"Finish up and stop *fuckin' around!*"

Smiles fell off their faces and they were done in five minutes.

I followed the gurney as they rolled it down the hall. Classes were still in session, so luckily we didn't have to go by a slew of gawking kids.

Passing the principal's office, I stopped and went in. His secretary immediately handed me a slip of paper with Antonya's locker number and combination written on it. The woman said none of the kids were given permanent gym lockers anymore because the school was too overcrowded now and there weren't enough to go around.

At the top of the paper, a bright pink Post-it note, was written number 622. An instant later it hit me like a stubbed toe: the same locker number I'd had as a senior at Crane's View High School. The number below it, the lock combination, was also the same as thirty years ago.

"This is right? This is correct?" My voice bounced all over the place.

Puzzled, she nodded. "Yes. I just copied it out of her file ten minutes ago."

"Son of a bitch!" I'd planned to ask Redmond more questions but not anymore. I had to look inside that locker *now*. I was no longer confused, no longer at a loss. My wife says watch out for Frannie when he knows who the enemy is. Antonya said she was murdered. Rushing out of the office, the horrible thought struck me that she might have been killed for no other reason than she had the same school locker as I once did. Old Vertue, teenage me, the Schiavo house, Antonya. Who was doing all this and what did they want from me?

A bell rang to mark the end of class. The big Bap! Bam! Bap! of doors flung open and hitting walls rang out everywhere. Kids flooded into the halls with the manic, jailbreak energy that comes from being held prisoner in algebra class for forty-five minutes. Cliques gathered like metal filings pulled by a magnet, bodies bumped or crashed into each other on their way to anywhere. Shouts and whistles, crazy laughter came from all over. Three minutes of freedom. Lovers met for intense head-to-heads before the next class, like an undertow, pulled them apart and shoved them back into Yawnsville for another forty-five.

I remembered all of it. How could you ever forget being sixteen and full of equal measures of hope and shit?

"Hey, Chief."

"Hey, Mr. McCabe!"

I recognized a few of the students. Some bad boys looked away as soon as we made eye contact. I gave a wink and two small "hi there" waves to other kids—nothing else. Those who greeted me didn't want more. I knew how this worked: proper high school etiquette. No matter how well we knew each other outside the building, this was their turf and their rules. I was an adult *and* a cop. Read "outsider."

I slowed a little on realizing I was doing one of those weirdo speed walks you see on the summer Olympics. That is, right before you switch the TV channel to anything more interesting than a bunch of adults walking like ducks in Nikes. It made no sense hurrying to Antonya's locker because I couldn't open it until the kids were gone again. There was no telling what was inside, and I didn't want others around for any more ugly surprises.

About twenty feet away I caught sight of Pauline. She stood off to one side of the hall talking to some girls. She didn't notice me until I was almost past.

"Frannie! Is it true about Antonya Corando?"

I stopped and nodded hello to her pals, who were watching me with a mixture of interest and distrust. "What do you hear?"

"That she's dead."

"It's true."

The girls looked at each other. One put a hand over her mouth and closed her eyes tightly.

"Did you know her, Pauline?"

"A little. Sort of. Sometimes we were in the computer lab together. We'd talk."

"What was she like?"

"Intense. I heard she was a good artist, that she could draw really well. But I almost never saw her because she was always studying."

One of the other girls said in an accusing voice, "Sounds familiar!" as if Pauline was guilty of the same crime. The class bell rang again. As they were walking away, one of the girls said way too loudly, "Your stepfather's cuuute."

"Don't be perverse!" Pauline's voice was outraged.

I stood looking out a window until the halls were empty and quiet again. Down in the parking lot the ambulance was pulling out onto the street. I imagined the girl's body on the gurney, Doc Marten'd feet open in a *V*, arms crossed on her chest. There was that small red bump on the inside of her left arm. *Tell my mother I didn't do this. They did it to me.*

Years ago after Magda and I first became lovers, we spent an especially frenzied afternoon in bed. When we were done and shiny wet—sated, finished, *filled*—her face four inches from mine—she looked me ten miles deep in the eye and said, *"Remember me like this*, Frannie. No matter what happens, no matter how long this lasts between us. I want you to remember me like this, the way I look right now."

Antonya? I would remember her head against that white tile wall, the dead eyes opening slowly to tell me her last fact. *I didn't do this.*

Locker 622. I'd once kept a loaded pistol in there for two weeks. A pistol, then a deadly brown recluse spider in a Jif peanut butter jar, a homemade Molotov cocktail I whipped up in shop class and dropped in the window of a teacher's car. Later I hid the stolen grade-book of my American History teacher in that locker and a signed first edition of Isak Dinesen's *Seven Gothic Tales* our English teacher had brought in to show the class. As a teenager I stole everything because I thought everything I wanted should belong to me.

Instinctively I put my thumb against the lock and my other fingers behind it. Turning the wheel back and forth, I put in the combination. After the last number in the sequence, the lock gave a slight click. I slid up the handle and swung the door open.

A kid's school locker is her inner sanctum. In it she builds a shrine to her dreams, her everyday, her wannabe image of herself. Antonya Corando's was no exception. Inside the door was taped a black-and-white Calvin Klein ad torn from a magazine. On it a handsome guy wearing extremely white underpants stared at the horizon. Maybe he was looking for the rest of his clothes. On the walls inside the locker were many other pictures—puppies, fashion models, bad Polaroid snapshots of family and friends looking pleased or silly. Nothing special, everything sad now in light of what had just happened. Who would take these pictures down, her mother? I imagined the poor woman opening the door, seeing this sweet little world and staggering for the hundredth time since learning the news of her daughter's death. Would her mom know why each of these pictures had been important to the girl? Would she save or throw them away because they were radioactive with her Antonya?

The same thing had happened to Magda's mother thirty years ago after *her* daughter was murdered. The woman saved everything. Only after she died was I able to convince Magda to put her sister's stuff in boxes and store it far away from our house and our life.

Geometry textbook, world history, jazzy blue calculator, a comic book called *Sandman*, gym clothes (nothing flashy or expensive), almost too many pens and felt-tip markers. Two CDs: Willy DeVille and Randy Newman—interesting taste in music.

"What's this?" Lying way in the back of the locker was a large black ring binder. Sliding it out, I assumed it was Antonya's class notebook. But wouldn't she have carried that with her? Why was it here? I opened the book and the first few pages were only that—class notes. In careful italic handwriting were extensive notes (with important passages highlighted in yellow) on Plato, Sophocles, the Hellenic Empire, yada yada. I almost stopped flipping pages because it all looked like Greek to me and who cared?

At the bottom of the next page was the drawing. Like an afterthought, a doodle, a two-minute mind nap during class was an absolutely terrific pencil sketch of Old Vertue. What's more, he was sitting in the same pose I had seen in the painting George Dalemwood showed me at his house. What's more, on the ground in front of the dog was *the* feather.

I turned the page.

The Hangman's Shove

"They're absolutely amazing."

"George, I'm glad you like them. But what the hell do they mean?"

As usual my good friend ignored me, not even looking up from Antonya's notebook when I spoke. He wore his square Clark Kent reading glasses—the ones with frames so thick and black they resembled two small TV sets joined over his nose.

"And she said *they* killed her?" He stared at a detailed colored-pencil drawing of Frannie Junior and me looking at the Schiavo house wrapped in its metal spiderweb scaffolding. Everything about that night was in the drawing, even Smith the cat at our feet.

Antonya Corando's loose-leaf binder contained six pages of meticulous notes about the rise of the Greek Empire. Another twenty pages were her drawings depicting what had recently been going on in my life. Later I spent a long time trying to find if she had done other relevant drawings. After searching everywhere it appeared these were the only ones.

To this day I cannot tell whether those pictures were any good. George thought they were the work of a prodigy, someone on par with other great naive "outsider" artists like Henry Darger or A. G. Rizzoli. I wouldn't know. To me they seemed more like explosions on paper. Looking at them, you knew whoever drew these things was seriously troubled and maybe even insane.

Old Vertue was doorman to Antonya's warped kingdom. In the first illustration, at the bottom of a page of notes on Greece, the dog sat in that familiar pose with *the* feather in front of him. Startled I mumbled, "What're you doing here?" and turned the page.

The second drawing was of him lying in the parking lot of the Grand Union market. It took a moment to remember that's where he'd been found the first day I met him. What set Antonya's drawings apart was at the center of each was a careful likeness of something literal and easily recognizable—Vertue in the parking lot, Frannie Junior and me looking at the Schiavo house. But everything *else* in her pictures was from Antonya Corando's outer limits.

Her "Vertue in the parking lot" was a perfect example. Around the outside edges of the paper, like a Hieronymous-Bosch-meets-R-Crumb designed picture frame, dancing razor blades held hands with pieces of popcorn which were shitting lizards with human heads. Immediately inside *that* frame was a second: cabbages with smiley faces bleeding gobbets of bright red blood from hatchets and knives buried in their heads. Androgynous angels flying overhead pissed down on them. Giant words were black-crayoned across all of the drawings. Words like "smegma," "abscess," "Hi, Mom!" as well as obscure phrases like "Jesus Soup" or "manus maleficiens." George explained that was Latin for "the hand that knows no good."

He slid his glasses down his nose and over until they hung precariously off his right ear. "When did this all start, Frannie?"

"The day I buried Old Vertue."

He nodded and flipped pages in the book till he came to Antonya's drawing of me putting the dog in the ground. "Did you notice this?" He pointed to a small detail in the picture. I couldn't see it clearly so I leaned forward.

"What?"

"The black shovel. There are three things that appear in every one of her drawings—that shovel, lizards—"

"And me."

"And you, that's right."

"What am I supposed to do with that, George? Shovels, lizards, and me? No, wait a minute—I also buried my father with that shovel. You think that has anything to do with it?"

"Let's assume it does. What about the lizards?"

"What about them?"

"Do you like lizards? Are they important to you?"

"Are you nuts?" I jabbed a finger at the middle of my forehead to emphasize the point. "George, forget the lizards, willya? I'm confused enough."

"All right. Then the best thing now is to go see if the dog is still buried in the yard."

"That's what I was thinking. Have you looked back there since we put him in?"

"Yes. Nothing was different."

"That doesn't mean anything. I wouldn't be surprised if he'd resurrected and was sitting on my front step."

George put down Antonya's notebook and slowly laid his glasses on top of it. He paused, sighed, ran a hand through his thinning hair. "I'm nervous about this, Frannie. I think I'm afraid to look."

"Nothing wrong with being afraid."

His eyes fell to his lap. "Are you ever afraid?"

I made to say something but stopped. George knew me too well. It was useless to lie. "No, not very often."

He nodded as if he'd known that all along. "You were never afraid. As long as I've known you I've never seen you afraid."

I reached into a pocket and brought out my knife. "Fear is like this knife, George. It serves one purpose: it cuts into things. Keep it folded in your pocket and it can't hurt you."

"How do you do that?"

"You create your fear. It's not out there like an infectious disease. Mostly it comes from love. When you love something so much you can't bear to lose it, then fear's always nearby. I've never loved anything enough to worry about losing it. That's my fuckup. Magda says it's the most pathetic thing about me. She's probably right."

"You don't love your *wife* enough to fear losing her?"

I shook my head.

"Do you really mean that, Frannie?"

I wouldn't look at him. "Yes. Let's go."

Chuck the dog led the way. He's a silly little guy who thinks he's king of the world. The moment we stepped outside he disappeared. It was so abrupt and ridiculous that we just stopped and froze. He was walking three feet in front of us with the confident waggle dachshunds have. From one moment to the next he was gone—zoop!

George took a step forward and said uncertainly, "Chuck?"

The yard was small and well kept. There wasn't a place he could have gone without being seen. But George still hurried to a far corner and, bending way down, searched the grounds.

My cell phone rang. Instinctively I knew something else was wrong.

"Chief?" Bill Pegg's deep voice came through, completely wired.

"Yeah?"

"The Schiavo house is on fire. It's a meltdown. Somebody had to've set it. It's going up like gasoline."

"I'm on my way." George scurried around uselessly looking

for the dog. I flicked off the phone and called out to him. "Forget it. Whoever disappeared him is playing with us. You won't find him now."

He glared at me. "Don't say that!"

"He's gone. Come with me. Someone set fire to the Schiavo house. Everything is connecting up, George. He might even be over there."

Eyes closed, he shook his head. "No, I have to stay. He might be here somewhere."

I went over and took his arm. "The minute we're going to dig up Old Vertue I hear the *Schiavo* house is on fire. Is that a coincidence? You don't think somebody's messing with our heads? We're not supposed to do this now."

"Maybe we are. Maybe that's exactly what you're supposed to do, Frannie! Dig up your dog right now."

I stopped and realized he might be right. But what was I supposed to do? The chief of police has to be where there's trouble. At that moment trouble was burning five blocks away. "Look, I gotta go over there now. I'll be back as soon as I can."

He looked frantically around. "What's happening, Frannie? What's going on?"

"I'm going to find out."

"Ooh, baby, baby, you fucked up this time!" The boy stood on the burning deck . . . or rather this familiar boy stood in front of the burning Schiavo house, his back to the fire, hands in pockets. Next to him was a black man of indeterminate age. Neither paid any attention to the blaze. They seemed intent on watching me approach.

"What are you doing here?" I said.

Behind them the Crane's View Volunteer Fire Department

worked hard to control the flames. Those guys knew what they were doing, but the fire was roaring and it took everything they had.

The black guy stepped forward smiling and put out his right hand. "I came to see you, Mr. McCabe. My name is Astopel."

Warily, I shook with him. The kid stood with arms crossed and a strange, anxious expression on his face. What did it say?

"You're only a few inches from the hangman's shove, Mr. McCabe. That's what necessitated this visit."

As if for dramatic affect, the roof on the house chose that moment to collapse in an explosion of sound, flying sparks, and debris.

"Is this your calling card?" I pointed at the house and tried to sound cool.

Junior cringed and mouthed, "Don't!"

"Haven't you seen enough wonders recently to convince you life has changed?" The man barked a short cough and tried repeatedly to clear his throat. "No, that isn't my calling card, but if you'd like, I could turn you into a wood louse. Or perhaps a spine-tailed swift, the fastest bird on earth. Would you rather suffer from a hideous rare disease for five minutes? Lesch-Nyhan Syndrome? Opitz Disease? How about Alien Hand Syndrome?"

"I always wanted to be Elvis—"

Little Frannie threw up his hands in exasperation. "You're a retard! Do you know who this is?"

"Apostle."

"*Astopel*, Mr. McCabe, Astopel. My name is not an anagram. I am no apostle." For the first time his expression changed. He looked amused by his remark. "The fire, by the way, is not my doing. In fact it's your fault. If you had been quicker about things, this house might have been saved."

I waited. He waited. Little Fran looked back and forth between us like he was watching a tennis match. Or two gunfighters about to draw on each other.

Finally I'd had enough of the standoff. "Look, I'm just from planet Earth, okay? I don't understand how a TV works, much less the fucking universe. So let's skip Alien Hand Syndrome and get to the point. Obviously I've been missing something here. So call me stupid and let's get on with it. Tell me what I'm supposed to do. You don't have to show me more dead girls, dogs, midnight construction crews . . . Burn this house down—I don't give a shit. Just say what you want me to do!"

He nodded. "I will. I'll even give you two choices. You can find it forward or backward. I will accept either."

"Explain."

"Forward means you can continue to search for the answers the way you have been. Obviously that hasn't worked so far but that doesn't mean it won't in time. The only problem is 'you have no time. One week, to be precise. You have one more week to figure out what is going on in Crane's View, Mr. McCabe, and how it applies to you.

"The other possibility is to figure it out backward. I will send you to the last week of your life with only the knowledge you have now. From that vantage point you will have to work backward to again decipher what is happening to your town."

"How do I know when that last week would be?"

"You don't. That's the risk of that choice. You might die next week or in forty years. What you discover could be reassuring or depressing. You take your chances."

"When you say one more week, does that mean to live or to figure this out? Because if I'm going to die tomorrow anyway—"

He looked at his watch. I looked at it too and did a double take because it was a white-gold IWC Da Vinci. I know because it is rare, costs a fortune, and was exactly the same watch I wore. Instinctively I looked at my wrist. My watch was gone. I always wore my watch. He was wearing my watch. I was so instantly sure that I didn't need to ask to see if a long thin scratch ran across the back.

"That's my watch."

"And a very beautiful one too." Raising his wrist, he turned it slowly back and forth.

Fran Junior saw it coming before I even knew it was in me. He shouted, "Don't!" But it was too late. Nothing stops my anger when it comes. Nothing.

"Don't! Don't! Don't!"

But I was already throwing the punch as Astopel admired my watch. Starting up high, I dropped it down just enough to give him the full pop on the temple. Bull's-eye. He fell where he stood.

Little Fran froze. Squeezing his eyes shut, he slapped both hands over his ears, as if preparing for a big boom to follow. Because I was watching him, I didn't see what was going on with Astopel. I'd assumed he was out for a while. Wrong. When I looked down, he was staring at me with the same warm smile we'd begun with.

"Give me back my watch."

"Excellent choice!" Undoing it, he handed it up but he was looking at Little Fran and not me. I took the watch and turned it over to check the back. The scratch was there, but so was a date engraved in thick gold numbers that had never been there before.

"What's this?"

"A reminder, Mr. McCabe. You have one week. One week from the date on that watch. Incidentally, I *was* planning on returning it to you. But your reaction does make things so much simpler. A quick question—how's your German?"

I didn't remember what day it was so I looked at the watch again. I saw the date and a moment later—my hand. Liver spots. My hand was covered with cantaloupe-colored liver spots. And half of the pinkie on my right hand was missing. The skin was very wrinkled and looked much too big for the bones it covered. A child's bones in an adult's hand. Shocked, I lifted the other to see the same—an old man's hand.

And the pain! Both hands felt like they were five fingers of fiery ache. I could barely hold onto the watch.

"You know, Frannie, I asked that dentist why should I pay for an expensive crown when all I use my teeth for these days is eating hamburgers and suckin' up soup."

An old man stood nearby wearing a god-awful golf cap that looked like it fell into a plaid factory and couldn't escape. The rest of his outfit made things worse. A shiny green short-sleeve shirt about two sizes too big and—help!—plaid pants that not only didn't match his hat but were at war with it. Large gold glasses magnified his eyes into pool balls and a smile so full of yellow teeth they might as well have been bamboo.

I gave him the once-over glance and then returned to looking at my hands. I saw something else wrong. My eyes slid down to my shirt and pants, both of which were—red. I was wearing red clothes? But I mean *really* red—clown-nose, Coca-Cola-sign red—baggy red shirt and pants on top of a pair of brown suede Hush Puppies. Had I changed into an old golfer? Shriveled hands, Hush Puppies, and red pants? Holy shit! It wasn't bad enough growing hair out of your ears and nose when you got old; apparently you grew serious bad taste too.

"What do you think, Fran? Think I should get the porcelain or the gold?"

When I could finally stop gawking at my hands, pants, and this old windbag in his plaid cap, I slowly looked around. We stood in the middle of a wide walking street. Every sign on it was in German. I remembered Astopel's last question, "How's your German?" Now I knew why he asked.

It was a beautiful street, but one glance told you it was not America, much less precious old Crane's View.

"What's your name?" I asked Mr. Plaid. My voice was another shock—it was much higher than I knew, and all the words came out a whine.

He looked at me strangely. I had to get some kind of hold on reality before I flipped out. Almost without my realizing it, my whole body started to introduce itself. I had to take a fierce piss. Little pains announced themselves all over me. My knees cracked when I moved, my back sang ouch! when I turned to look behind. I discovered I couldn't turn very fast even if I had wanted to. Although my body felt lighter, there was no energy to move it.

"Whatsa matter, Fran, had too much of that schnapps at the restaurant last night?"

"Where are we? Where is this?" I tried moving my head around to take in our surroundings. But something cracked viciously in my neck and paralyzed me for a moment.

"I *guess* you had too much! Wien, buddy, do you believe it? The old Blue Danube's just down the way. Remember we walked this street last night to get to the boat?"

"What boat?"

He smiled like he thought I was kidding. "Boat around the city. Remember how you said it was so loud? But you spent most of your time at the bar with Susan so I didn't think you was listening too hard." He let out a laugh that sounded like a braying donkey. Hee-haw hee-haw.

"Susan who?"

"Susan who, the man asks. Well, how about Susan your wife?"

"Uh-oh. Fucked again." I looked around again and only then did it slowly begin to seep through my cracks what had happened. Astopel had flung me forward to the last week of my life. Which took place a long way from home. The word *Veen* came back to me. That's what Mr. Plaid said. Where the hell was Veen?

I looked at him again and was about to ask, but the expression on his face shut me up. The guy was angry.

"What's the matter?"

"I told you about that language, Fran. I'm not a man who likes hearing profanity from no one. We've talked about this before—"

I stepped in close and grabbed his throat with an aching right hand. "Don't give me any shit, Droopy. Who are you, where are we, and please answer *whatever* questions I have right now. Or I'll knock your teeth so far down your throat you'll have to stick a toothbrush up your ass to brush 'em!"

Droopy grabbed my hand and gave it some kind of karate twist. Suddenly my arm was up behind my back in a hammerlock and he was breathing old-man breath over my shoulder. "Don't be a dumbbell, Fran." He gave my arm a sharp push up my back and even more pain flooded me. I thought I'd pass out.

"Please let him go, mister! He gets senile sometimes and doesn't know what he's doing."

I recognized the voice but couldn't move to see if it really was whom I thought it was.

Behind me, Droopy said "You know him, young fella?"

"Yes, sir, he's my grandfather. Grandpa McCabe."

My arm was released but stayed where it was. For a moment

it felt like I'd never be able to unbend the damned thing again. It just sort of stayed up behind my back like a bent chicken wing.

"You better tell your granddad to behave himself or he's gonna get into big trouble with that kinda talk."

"Yes, sir. I'll keep an eye on him. *Thank you*, sir!" Frannie Junior's voice came out sounding like the worst kind of suck-up, sycophantic, brown-nosing ass-kisser. He came from behind and took me gently by the other arm.

I snatched it away. "What the hell are *you* doing here?"

He looked at Droopy and rolled his eyes in exasperation. "Don't you remember, Gramps? I came this morning to surprise you."

"Yeah? Some surprise." I tried to march away but my legs felt like hot rubber bands. "I'm old! What the hell am I doing old?"

"You should be happy! Now you know you're going to live a long time. That's what you get for punching Astopel."

"The guy stole my watch!"

"Yeah but you weren't exactly diplomatic taking it back."

I shook my head. "You would've done the same thing! What about the guy you hit at the Schiavo house?"

"That was different." He crossed his arms to indicate *that* discussion was finished.

"My grandson! If I had a grandson like you I'd move to Sumatra."

"If you were my grandfather I'd buy you the ticket."

"So are you fellas catching up on family business?" Droopy came up and was all smiles again.

"What's your name?" I had to start somewhere and knowing who he was might lead to something.

"August Gould, Gus to my friends; pleased to make your

acquaintance. *Again.* You want to shake hands now and make it official?"

"Gus Gould."

"That's right, sir." He was smiling like a carved Halloween pumpkin.

"Gus, my memory is a sieve today. Tell me exactly where we are and what we're doing here."

"We're in Vienna, Austria, Fran. This is a two-week tour of Europe and we got one more week to go. After here we go to Venice, Florence, Rome, Athens, and then home."

"Where's home?" I almost didn't want to ask for fear he'd say some place like Yanbu, Saudi Arabia.

"Yours is New York. Mine is St. Louis."

"Crane's View, New York?"

"No, the city. Manhattan."

The kid looked at me. "That's cool. I wouldn't mind living in the city. But what happened to Crane's View?"

I shrugged and turned back to Gus. "And you say my wife's name is Susan? Not Magda?"

"Come on, Fran, now you are pulling my leg! You can't not know who your wife is, for crying out loud. If your memory was *that* bad she'd have to lead you around on a leash." He sighed like my little game with him had gone on too long. "Susan Ginnety. That's her name as far as I know. Although I don't think I'd be so happy having a wife that didn't want my last name when we got married."

Both the kid and I yelped in disbelief the instant we heard her full name spoken. Susan Ginnety? I had married Susan Ginnety? The kid was so overwhelmed by the news that he jumped away from me, grabbed his head, and did an agony dance right there on the spot.

"Susan Ginnety?! Eeyow! You married that spaz? First Magda Ostrova out of tenth grade and then Susan Ginnety? What happened to your brain? No, what happened to *my* brain? You killed it!"

"Cut it out! I know as much about this as you do. Susan's already married! She's—Uh-oh." I suddenly remembered right before all this happened she and her husband had separated. "We gotta find her. We gotta talk to her. Gus, where is she? Do you know where Susan is now?"

He glanced at his watch. It was a strange-looking thing. Appeared to be more a black rubber bracelet than a watch. And from what I could see, the numbers on it made no sense, watchwise. He brought it close to his mouth and said, "Call Susan Ginnety."

The kid let fly a low whistle. "That's a *phone?*"

Gus raised his eyebrows but said nothing, obviously waiting for some kind of response from his phone. Suddenly he began talking. "Susan? Hi, it's Gus Gould. Yeah, I'm keepin' an eye on him and that grandson of yours. What? Yeah, your grandson. No wait, wait. I got Frannie right here. Says he wants to talk to you about something." He smiled at me. I frowned. "Well, Fran, go ahead, talk to her."

"What do you mean?"

He pointed to my wrist and for the first time I saw/realized I was wearing one of those bracelets; the kid too. Hesitantly I brought it up toward my face but didn't know how far away I was supposed to keep it when I spoke. From afar it must have looked like I was afraid the bracelet was going to bite me. "Susan?"

"Hi, Frannie. What's up?"

Her voice was crystal-clear, but how the hell was I hearing

it? I felt around and inside both ears but nothing was in either. "How am I hearing this? How does this work?"

Gus announced authoritatively, "Linear matrix tubing."

"Say what?"

"Linear matrix tubing. There's a deliberated fiber-optic conduit bleached through an open-end ekistics feed—"

"Forget it! Susan, where are you? We gotta talk right now."

"At the café, Frannie. Don't you remember? You and Gus said you wanted to go—"

"Yeah yeah, forget it. You and I gotta talk *immediately*."

She was silent too long and then sighed like a martyr giving up the ghost. "I hope you're not going to complain about this trip again. I really don't want to hear another rant—"

"I ain't going to rant, Susan, and what I've got to say is not about the trip. I just gotta ask some things." I could hear my voice going weird and desperate. If it went any higher, pretty soon I would sound like a teakettle whistling.

"We're at the café. But you know that."

"No, Suze, I don't know that. I didn't even know where I was until about five minutes ago, but I won't dwell on that one. What café?"

"The Sperl."

"The Squirrel? You're at a café called the Squirrel?"

"*Sperl*, Frannie, Sperl. Turn your hearing aid up, dear."

"All right, I'll find it. What do you look like now?"

She chuckled in her trademark way. I'd heard it often enough at our weekly meetings when we discussed the goings-on in Crane's View. "What do I look like now? Well, like I did this morning, in case you forget. Byyyye!"

Gus Gould thought that was *the* funniest thing and again his annoying heehaw laugh broke out of the corral. I'd forgotten he could hear both sides of our conversation. "I'll point her out to you, Fran."

"Yeah, great, thanks. Where is this Café Sperl, Squirrel, whatever?"

"Right near our hotel." Gus gestured for us to follow him and strode away.

I looked at the kid. "*Our* hotel? What hotel? I have no idea what the hell is going on here. What's wrong with this picture?" I started walking.

"It didn't have to be like this. It's your fault! If you hadn't been so stupid and hit Astopel—"

"Change the channel willya, sonny? You already said that nineteen times. If you're expecting an apology you're not getting it. Anyway, you still haven't said what *you're* doing here."

"I don't know. One moment I'm living my own life, minding my own fucking business, then *whoomp*, I'm in yours, and now I'm here."

"I don't believe this. Plus if we're so far in the future, how come things don't look different?"

Which was true. If I was now somewhere between seventy and eighty years old, at least three decades had passed. But from what little I'd seen of the surroundings, the world hadn't changed much. Stores were stores and cars rolled by on streets, not in the air à la *Back to the Future*. Most of them looked sleeker and more aerodynamic, but they were still cars.

Junior interrupted my thoughts. "It was the same for me. When I got to your time I thought what's so different? Same kind of clothes, a TV's still a TV—"

"Who sent you up to my time?"

He shot me a quick, sneaky glance and looked away real fast. Then he started walking away at a frightfully *brisk* pace. The little fucker was trying to make a fast getaway. Hobbling after him, I managed to catch up and touched his shoulder. He shook me off.

"Astopel! It was Astopel, wasn't it?" I must have said the magic word because he moved away so fast that if he had been a car his tires would have laid down a patch of rubber thirty feet long. Watching him and Gus Gould go, the truth suddenly dawned on me. "Because you hit him too! You hit Astopel too, *didn't you?*"

The boy didn't answer, but I knew I'd hit the bull's-eye. *That's* why the boy had been so worried about how I'd react to the black guy when I first met him. And that's why he'd started hollering when I knocked Astopel down. Because he knew what was going to happen! Because he'd done *exactly the same thing* and ended up being shot into his future, just like me.

"Why didn't you tell me?"

He kept moving.

"Hey, asshole, why didn't you tell me what would happen if I hit him?" People standing nearby stopped to stare at the old crazy fart in red, shouting down the street at a kid who was obviously trying to ignore him.

"I'm talking to you!"

Gus was watching now, as were half the people on the sidewalk, but not Junior. If I'd had any legs under me I would have sprinted over and—Stopping, he put his hands on his hips and turned slowly. His face showed only disgust. "Don't you get it yet? I can't do anything for you! You think I wouldn't have said something if I could? You think I want to be here? Are you really that stupid?"

"Then why *didn't* you tell me?"

"Be-cause-I-can't!"

We shouted at each other across that wide space. Sooner or

later a cop was bound to appear and it was sooner. Police in Vienna wear green uniforms and white caps that make them look more like crossing guards than police. This dude was husky, wore a matching husky moustache and an attitude you could smell in five different languages. He chose to interrogate me. The prick— he had to pick on an old weak man. In red.

"Na, was ist?"

"What's the problem, officer?" Probably because I answered in English and didn't hesitate looking him in the eye, his expression downshifted to sullen and confused—a bad combination if you're on the receiving end with a cop.

He responded in limping, phrase-book English. "Why do you screaming? It is not allowed to scream so in Wee-ena."

"I'm not. I'm calling my grandson." I pointed at Junior. I hoped the cop would see the family resemblance. The kid shrugged. The cop pursed his lips and moustache hairs went up into his nose. Out of the corner of my eye Gus Gould came hotfooting over toward us. He must have thought I was completely bonkers.

The cop's nametag said Lumplecker. I paused a moment to digest that and stop myself from laughing out loud. "Officer Lumplecker?"

"Ja?"

"What year is it?"

"Bitte?"

"The year. This year, now. What's today's date?"

Lumplecker shot me a lumpy look, like I was trying to pull a fast one on him. "I do not understand you. My English is poor. Here is your friend. You may ask him your questions."

"Come on, Frannie, we gotta get to the café." Gus nudged me with his hip while smiling a lot of old yellow teeth at patrolman Lumpy. Some bystander in leather shorts and green knee socks nearby said, *"Was ist mit ihm?"* The cop turned his annoyed attention at this unsuspecting Fritz and started shouting at him in machine-gun German. Gus and I drifted off without saying so much as an *auf wiedersehn.*

"What's the matter with you this morning, Frannie? Are you on drugs? Did you take something?"

My father used to ask me that question when I was young and permanently in trouble. "Are you *on* something?" was his way of putting it. He hoped I was so there would be a valid excuse for my detestable behavior. And if he could somehow get me "off," I'd return to normal again. Fat chance. At the time the only drug I was on was me.

"Wait a minute! How come you can see him?" I pointed at Junior ten feet away.

Gus unwrapped a piece of gum and put it in his mouth. "How can I *see* him? Why wouldn't I?"

I walked to the boy. "Why can he see you now? Back in Crane's View you said no one could see you but me and the cat."

"Because we're both in the wrong time slot now. Neither of us belongs here."

It was spring. Girls passed in sherbet-colored summer dresses, their perfumes wiggling come-hither fingers at your sense of smell. I might have been old as hell but my nose still worked. Couples strolled slowly from here to nowhere enjoying the warm weather. Street musicians played everything from classical guitars to musical saws.

Vienna. Austria. Mozart. Freud. Wienerwald. Sacher Torte. I'd not gone there even when I had the travel bug because I'd never had the slightest curiosity about the city. London, I'd spent some time in. Paris. Madrid. Other exotic places too, but Vienna meant opera, which I hated, those Lippizaner horses that hopped on their back legs depressed me, and the town was where Hitler got started being Hitler. Who needed it? Plus George Dalemwood had visited and returned to say that generally speaking, the Viennese were the most unfriendly, unpleasant people he'd ever met. What the hell was I doing here in my dotage? Married to Susan Ginnety, no less.

"There's the opera house. I thought it would be bigger. It sure looked bigger in the pictures."

As we approached I saw the celebrated building but felt nothing. Of course a heart is supposed to surge forward on seeing certain famous sites—the Grand Canyon, Big Ben, the Viennese opera house. But my heart usually went into reverse at those moments just because it doesn't like being told what to do.

"Don't forget, Frannie, we're supposed to take a tour of the place this afternoon."

"Uh-huh. How far is this café?"

"About another ten minutes."

"Jesus, that far?" My body felt like lead, like paste, stone, wood, double gravity, it felt like shit. So *this* was what it was like to be old? Forget it! I wanted to trade me in on a new model. Immediately. How did old people put up with it? How did they lift their unbendable, hundred-pound legs and put one in front of the other day after day? My hands were lava-hot with arthritis; legs cold with I had no idea what. It seemed like every person whizzed past us as if they were all on rollerskates; but they were only legs connected to younger, healthy bodies they took for granted. I wanted to move faster, to stop, and to weep in frustration all at the same time. "Guys, wait a minute. Hold it—I gotta rest."

Gus and the kid exchanged looks but stopped. I wanted to kill them both. How could they keep going while I felt like a boulder was sitting on my head?

"Are you okay, Frannie?"

"No I'm not okay! Just wait a minute, willya?"

"No problem, partner."

"Is that a hot dog stand? What's a wurstel?" The kid pointed to a small kiosk nearby that had different pictures of hot dogs taped to its windows. "I'm hungry. I'm getting one."

Between gasps, I asked if he had any money.

"Nope. You got any?"

Without a sliver of surprise, my hand slid over a bunch of cards in my pocket. I took them out to see what they were.

Gus said, "Use your Visa card."

"They take credit cards at a hot dog stand?"

He made a face that said I couldn't be *that* dense. "Are you going to pay with a five-dollar bill? When was the last time you saw paper money?"

"I got a card too. I got one of those. I had it all along." Junior waved a shiny pink card and moved toward the stand.

I could not catch my breath. My entire body felt outraged at having had to walk so far so fast. Yet I knew we hadn't come far at all. Besides all the other shocks whirling around like multiple cyclones, I couldn't believe this was me inside me—an aching, whining, grumpy, exhausted, old . . . shithead.

"So tell me about your grandson, Frannie. He's a good-looking boy."

We watched good-looking boy buy his hot dog, with much pointing and nodding until the seller understood what he wanted. It had been so long since I was in a place where I didn't speak the language. Now suddenly I was in two simultaneously—Austria and Old Age.

While concocting some piece of nonsense about my "grandson" to tell Gus Gould, I heard a huge high sound. Instinctively I knew what it was because I'd made the sound myself many times on my Ducati—the high ripping whine of a downshifting motorcycle. Turning from Gus toward the street, I saw the last thing I would ever see: A most beautiful silver and sleek motorcycle, airborne, was sailing straight at me.

The End.

Holes in the Rain

The next thing I knew, I was staring at my hands. They were holding a strawberry milk shake in an old-fashioned fluted glass. They were "my" hands again—no liver spots, bread-dough skin sagging in tired layers, no knuckles the size of walnut shells protruding from beneath. Instead, the skin was a healthy color, not the patchwork quilt of sickly hues and spots it had been in Vienna.

Slowly, I curled one into a fist and was thrilled as a child to feel no pain slither up through it. But before I got too excited, I uncurled the hand just as slowly to see if it worked the other way too. Success. Was I back? Was I me again? Putting the hand flat down on the red Formica counter, I felt the cool of the plastic beneath my reborn palm. I slid it back and forth across the smooth surface. Then I lifted my hand a few inches and had the fingers do a little dance to celebrate our return.

"Are you going to drink that milk shake or are you trying to hypnotize it?"

I knew it was too good to be true. I knew the voice and did not want to see the face it came from. But against the advice of every atom in my body, I turned the rotating stool to look.

I was in Scrappy's Diner in Crane's View. Scrappy's is never empty from the minute it opens at six in the morning until it closes at midnight. But the joint was empty now. That is, except for me and good old Astopel sitting way down at the other end of the counter. Watching me, he smiled like a son of a bitch.

"Couldn't I just have had thirty seconds of happiness alone before I saw you again? Isn't there a law against too much you in one lifetime?"

"You can have all the time you want, Mr. McCabe. But your clock is ticking."

My throat was dirt-dry so I sipped the milk shake, which tasted as good as sex at that moment. In fact I couldn't stop sipping, which turned into glugging until the glass was empty. Even my throat felt younger, it was so happy and eager to belt the sweet stuff down.

I wiped my mouth with the back of my hand. "All right, *what* clock is ticking?"

"How did you like your death? It's certainly dramatic."

"Is that really how I'm going to die?"

"Yes, a motorcycle in the head."

"I'll be killed by a motorcycle in the head in Vienna when I'm a hundred years old and so worn out and cantankerous that I should have died years before. Now that's something to look forward to."

"Not quite one hundred, I'm afraid."

"How old?"

"I cannot tell you. You must find out all those things yourself. But at the rate you're going, you won't even find that out before your time is up."

"Explain."

He slid off his stool and went behind the counter. He walked toward me, picked up my glass, and poured more into it from a metal shaker. He placed it in front of me. "Strawberry, right? That's the flavor you prefer?"

"You made this? It's good."

"Thank you. 'Consider the last of everything and then thou wilt depart from the dream of it.' Do you know that line? It's from the Koran." He drew a glass of Coke from a machine and to my astonishment, put it in a microwave oven. Setting to its highest temperature, he waited till it pinged seconds later. Removing the glass, he took a sip of what must have been six-hundred-degree Coca-Cola and smacked his lips in delight.

"Astopel, tell me you didn't do that. Is your tongue asbestos? Or are you the devil? Is that what all this is about?"

"You keep looking for easy answers, Mr. McCabe. Unfortunately there are none. Perhaps you should find a better way of looking."

"Yeah? Well, a moment ago I was too busy being traumatized as an old man and wearing a motorcycle for a hat."

"That's a pity. Because you only have four more chances to go back to your future before the week is over. *When* you return is up to you, but you have only these six days—"

"What do you mean, six? You said seven. You said I had a week."

"Look outside."

It was pitch-black out there. "Today's over?"

"Today is over."

"Today is Tuesday."

"Was."

"I have until next Tuesday either here or in my future to figure this out?"

"Correct."

I tapped the edge of my glass on the counter. "Or else?"

"Well, remember what Antonya Corando told you."

"She said she didn't kill herself. Said someone else did it to her."

Astopel nodded. "And not only your own well-being is at stake now. A great many others' as well. You have seven days because you have seven days. You can spend your remaining time trying to understand why, but I think that would be a waste.

"Perhaps it will comfort you to know there are others in the same situation as you right this minute, Mr. McCabe."

"Who have to do the same thing as me?"

"Yes."

"They're in Crane's View?"

"No, all around the world."

I drank the last of the strawberry shake. It didn't taste so good this time.

"Two other things to know, Mr. McCabe. You can return to your future whenever you want this week. Say the phrase 'holes in the rain' and you will go. Once there, however, your return to the present is out of your hands—it will simply happen.

"The second thing to know is when you visit the future, it will always be to the day previous to the one you experienced. So your next visit will be to the day before you died."

"This is completely crazy."

"Hopefully it will eventually make sense to you." He finished his drink and came around the counter. Without looking back, he moved toward the door.

"Wait! One more thing: Why did I marry Susan Ginnety? Did something happen to Magda? *Will* something happen to her?"

He raised his head and looked at the ceiling. "Something happens to everyone, Mr. McCabe." And then he left.

The streets of Crane's View were empty and still as I trudged home from the diner. Night keeps its own sounds to itself because most of them come from the other side of silence. Because there is so little noise after midnight, your ears perk up and strain to hear anything in their neighborhood. So used to being flooded with everyday white noise, they don't know how to relax. Ears are not happy with hush; it's not their domain. So they turn up the volume on the single-engine plane flying by far overhead, or the lone car moving its way across the night five blocks away.

And when those were joined by the screech of a cat being humped at that quiet hour, it was the sound equivalent of a pair of scissors jabbed into your ear. But all of them came from here and now, this moment, not the future—now. I welcomed them and wished there were more to reassure me I was back in the time where I wanted to be.

As often happens when I'm confused, I started talking to myself. It's a helpful habit I developed in Vietnam while trying anything to keep from going crazy in that hell.

With the utmost concern I asked myself, "Are you all right?"

Pause. Scowl. "All right? I'm alive. That's it. I'm alive and don't know what the fuck to do. What the fuck I'm *supposed* to do. I know zero but am still supposed to figure all this stuff out in a week. Or else. Good luck, daddy-o."

Looking around at the quiet familiar surroundings, the combination of rancor and confusion for what had happened to me, combined with the love in my heart for where I was almost made me dizzy. "That's what this whole thing does—it makes me dizzy!"

I needed a lot of Crane's View to regain my balance that night, so I took the long way home despite the late hour. I purposely passed the Schiavo house just to see if anything else had happened there. What was left of the burnt-out ruin was dark and silent. A few minutes later I stood in front of George Dalemwood's place. As usual the downstairs was lit up because George doesn't like the night. He says lit bulbs keep him company. I would have loved to knock on his door and gone in for a long talk about everything but didn't. I knew that before I spoke with him again about any of this, I needed to think things through carefully. I was sure sometime in the future I'd want his help, so presenting the details to him clearly and calmly was essential. George was a patient, open-minded man but hearing what had happened to me that night, especially if I told it the wrong way, might make even my good friend reach for a butterfly net.

I sighed/said, "Go home, Fran. Go home to your family."

Smith sat like a statue on the top step of the porch to our house, looking as if he had been waiting for me to return. I was so tired I didn't even say hello. Reaching down, I just stroked his head a few times and then opened the front door.

Home sweet smell. The Dutch have a line that goes something like the sound of a clock ticking is always nicest at home. Even better are the smells of home. One whiff and the soul knows where you are before the mind does. I stood in the front hall and, closing my eyes, simply breathed home for a little while. After what I had been through, it was God's perfume. My life was on that air. The people I lived with, the objects we owned, the cat, popcorn someone had made earlier, Pauline's CK One cologne; even the dust smelled familiar.

Upstairs the two women would be asleep—Magda in sweatpants and one of my Macalester College T-shirts, her body sprawled across as much of the bed as possible. Pauline in a nightgown huddled on an edge of her bed as if she were afraid of taking up too much space. Unlike her mother, she slept lightly, she had bad dreams; her closed eyelids always fluttered.

I was exhausted and empty as a dead man's mailbox. The thought of slipping into the warm bed beside my wife was almost as gratifying as the act itself. But as soon as the word "wife" trotted across my mind, the next thing that followed was a picture of Susan Ginnety who, x years in the future, would be Mrs. F. McCabe. Thinking about that deranged union snapped my eyes open.

The cat purred at my feet. Without warning, he raced across the room, leapt in the air, and threw himself full force against a window. There was a squeaky squawk and a bird sprang off the outside windowsill and fluttered away. Two large white feathers drifted lazily down and out of sight. I watched and thought— feathers. So now that feathers were on my mind, up came a picture of the one tattooed on Pauline's spine and then the one I'd found and buried with Old Vertue and . . . Like a bomb bursting in my brain, I remembered something from my future. It made me so excited that without thinking I said, "Holes in the rain!" Because I had to return to find another feather I'd seen up there that might be the answer to everything.

I was naked. I was naked and in bed. I was naked and in bed with a woman. Who was naked. And old. And not my wife Magda. And she had her hand on me, clearly trying to bring Old Horny to attention with her busy fingers.

I stood straight up on the bed and covered myself, but not before noticing she had been semisuccessful with her hand jive.

An old Susan Ginnety smiled up at me with a triumphant leer. "I told you I'd get you up, Frannie! Get back down here now. Stop being silly."

Sixty years earlier, this woman and I had had sex in every position two eager teenage bodies could manage, not to mention using every one of our nooks and crannies to fullest effect. But now, towering above her on wobbly old man's legs, I felt as modest as a nun in the boys' locker room.

"Cut it out, Susan! Are you crazy?"

That got her up. She stood on the side of the bed with hands on her bony hips showing me a naked body I did *not* want to see. "I have been very patient until now, Frannie. But I am a woman. I have *needs*!"

If I played this wrong, I'd never get any answers out of her.

"Look at me, Susan. You want to make love to *this* body? I look like a Dead Sea Scroll!"

She was unmoved. "Why did you marry me if you knew this would happen?"

Before I could stop myself, I blurted out, "That's a good question."

She punched me in the knee. Thank God I stood on a bed because I collapsed sideways and my head bounced like a Ping-Pong ball on the mattress.

"Bastard! You proposed to me! Why did I ever say yes? Why did I ever think it would work?"

World War Knee had my full attention while she ranted. Even when the pain dropped back below the danger zone, I kept rolling around and groaning. As if I'd been kneecapped by the Mafia rather than punched there by an old woman.

Two sharp knocks on the door froze us. We stared at each other like we'd been caught doing something bad. A short pause followed by three more knocks. I pulled the blanket up to my chin. In no hurry, Susan wrapped herself in a green terrycloth robe that had been slung over a chair.

For the first time since I'd "awakened" here, I looked around. It was one of the most beautiful hotel rooms I'd ever seen. It should have been occupied by a head of state, or at least someone with their own Gulfstream jet fueled and waiting at the airport; definitely not a room for the Crane's View chief of police. My first wife (First? Now I was apparently on my third!) loved the caviar life, so I had spent time in many plush hotel rooms. But those were railroad waiting rooms in Upper Volta compared to this palace. How the hell had I ended up here with a geriatric nymphomaniac? More importantly, who was paying for it?

"Hi, Gus," she said glumly.

It wasn't the Gus Gould I'd seen the day before. This gentleman looked like the head of state that belonged in this fancy room. He wore a dark suit so perfectly cut and understated that one glance told you it had to have come from a tailor who required four fittings before his work was done. Snow-white shirt, cuff links, and thin black tie with a narrow gleam off the silk. I raised up on an elbow to look at his shoes. They immediately spoiled the picture. Nice though they were, they were still black snakeskin cowboy boots.

"Why are you kids still lying around in bed? We got a whole day ahead of us and things to do!"

"My *husband* and I were having a chat." Susan flicked me a look that would have fried the snakes on Medusa's head.

"Well, better get up now. You know Floon doesn't like it when you miss a meal."

"Who's Floon?"

"Don't be stupid, Frannie." Susan sashayed into the bathroom, closing the door behind her a lot too hard.

"She's a fine-looking woman, Frannie. You're a lucky man."

"Uh-huh. I'll trade her to you for a few answers."

"What do you mean?"

"Nothing."

Gus walked to one of the large closets and opened the door. He reached for something and pulled out a suit exactly like his—dark, rich, beautiful. A fortune in cloth. "Here, I'll help you on with it. We gotta get moving. You got the shirt and boots somewhere?"

"We're wearing the same thing?"

He looked at the suit, briskly brushed the front, and pointed to it. "Frannie, I never imagined a man's suit could cost ten thousand dollars. That is, until this trip when he gave us this one." He held up a foot. "And John Wayne wore Lucchese boots like these. If Floon wants me to wear these clothes today, I'll do it. He paid for them but we get to keep them when the trip's over."

I got out of bed naked. What else could I do, hold a pillow in front of my package? "Gus, my mind is a little unreliable today, so forgive me if I ask some dumb questions."

"Will do. Here's your undies." He held out a brown box.

Opening it, I pulled beautiful lime-colored tissue paper aside, and stared. "I don't wear boxer shorts."

"Today you do, buddy. That's how Floon works—everything down to the last detail. Those undershorts probably cost more than my first automobile."

Unhappily, I slid them on. Next came the white shirt, black cashmere socks, and *the* suit. Luciano Barbera. I'd always wanted to own one of his suits. Yes, I was an old man but could still feel the quality of the material sliding across my skin. "This suit really cost ten thousand bucks?"

"Yeah, and Floon bought twelve of them for the men. I don't want to even guess what he paid for the women's clothes. Know what he told me? That he paid for them all in ngultrums."

"What's that?"

"Bhutan money." He went back to the closet and took out my cowboy boots. The last pair I'd seen were the orange ones worn by teenage me. At least these were black. Turning one over in my hand, I had to admit that if you had to wear a pair of lizardskin boots these were the ones.

Dressed, I checked myself in a full-length mirror. "We look like rich Texas Rangers."

"I don't know what Caz has planned today, but you can bet it'll be interesting."

"Caz? Caz Floon? What kind of name is that?"

"Caz *de* Floon. He's Dutch. Frannie, if you don't remember

this guy's name, you *are* having memory problems. Susan, are you ready in there?"

"In a minute!"

That minute turned into quite a few more, but when she emerged, my third wife looked great. She wore a sleeveless blue summer dress that made her appear years younger and sort of sexy, for an old woman.

"What are you wearing, Susan?" Gus's voice was not friendly.

"Don't be a bore, Gus. I don't like the dress Floon sent. It makes me look like a palm reader at a cheap carnival. Madame ZuZu. I am going to carry the handbag though. It's very nice."

His mouth tightened and he took a deep breath before speaking. "Please don't do this, Susan. You know what's going to happen."

They locked eyes. Neither backed off or looked away. You could almost hear the sound of their wills crashing head-on.

"Forget it. I like *this* dress. Caz de Floon is on an ugly power trip. He has to control everything. He invites his so-called friends to go on little trips with him, but then dresses them up in clothes he chooses and moves them around like they were Barbie and Ken dolls. I don't like it. At first I thought it was okay but it's not. It's perverse. He's perverse."

"Yes, but you know what Floon will do when he sees you're not wearing what he wants. Why create a fuss? It's not a big deal."

"To you it isn't but it is to me. I'm not a puppet. I'm tired of his whims and fits and furies. Everything always has to be his way. When it isn't, he sulks like a twelve-year-old. God, you'd think being one of the most powerful men in the world would have matured him a bit. I never would have gone on this trip if I had known how he was going to behave."

"But Susan, Floon's paying for everything. He gave you women all the same dress because he doesn't want anyone being jealous of anyone else. That makes sense, doesn't it? Plus the fact we've been living like gods on this trip."

"Little gods." She adjusted a shoulder on her dress. "Floon's little gods who he bosses around as if he were Zeus. Going on this trip was like selling our souls to the devil. Sure you see everything and eat well, but you also have to do exactly what he wants or Floon gets mad. I can't believe his 'friends' go along with this craziness. Screw his power trip—I don't want to play anymore. Frannie was right—we never should have come. I made him, but now I know it was wrong."

What I remembered from my last time in the future was Susan scolding me over the phone to stop griping about the trip. Today she wished she hadn't come. Tomorrow she'd tell me to stop complaining. What happened between today and tomorrow to change her mind? More importantly, what happened today— period?

Who was Caz de Floon, besides one of the most powerful men in the world? How did he fit into my equation? And where was that feather I knew so well? I knew I had seen it up here. I was certain of that.

Downstairs in the lobby Floon's merrymakers had assembled. The world is full of people standing around. We all do it and we're used to seeing it. But now and then you see someone standing around looking so damned odd that your brain slams on its brakes and leans on the horn as hard as it can.

Downstairs in the lobby, Floon's merrymakers were not only dressed identically, but because they came in various shapes and sizes, my first sight of them standing together was a picture that will stay with me until that motorcycle takes off my head.

Of course there was a midget. Or maybe he was a dwarf.

Definitely, a little person, or whatever they are calling themselves these days. His suit fit him perfectly but the cowboy boots made his already-odd walk odder. When he saw me coming out of the elevator he gave a big wave like we were best buddies.

The fortune teller dress Susan had complained about was all over the lobby. The majority of women who wore it were old. This dress might have worked on a twenty-year-old girl with perfect skin, body, and bedroom eyes that melted your underpants. But on these fat and thin white-haired birds, it looked tasteless at best, a cruel joke at worst. I later said to Susan these women looked like the chorus from an old age home's production of *Carmen*, God forbid.

"How are you this morning, Frannie?"

I slid my eyes from the fossil gypsies to another man standing a couple of feet away wearing the suit of the day. "Are *you* Floon?"

He liked that. He opened his mouth and laughed—I guess. It looked like a laugh but he didn't make a sound. "No, I'm Jerry Jutts. Remember we talked last night. Jutts Desserts? Caz is over there yakking with that big blond."

The woman he pointed to looked like a sumo wrestler. Easily two hundred round pounds, not including a Grand Ole Opry hairdo that rose up off her head in a frozen yellow cyclone.

I whistled long and low. "Man, you'd need a *wrecking ball* to knock her down! Is that Floon's bodyguard? She looks like a female Odd Job."

"She's my wife," Jerry Jutts declared in a huff, and marched away.

I wanted to check out Floon before going over. But Astopel said I had no control over when I would be returned to my own time. Which meant I couldn't waste a minute staking this guy out, knowing I might be flashed back home before even having had a conversation with him.

He looked normal enough. About sixty, he was middle everything—height, weight, a face you thought you might have seen before but couldn't be sure. My first impression of Caz de Floon was businessman, well groomed, hands that he used constantly while speaking. They rose, circled, and swooped; the fingers pinched together and dropped like an Italian explaining anything.

Jerry had joined his gigantic wife. The two of them listened, rapt, to whatever Floon said. The incident that tipped me off to him was small and would have been easy to miss if I hadn't been watching them so closely. Neither Mr. nor Mrs. Jutts opened their mouths while Floon spoke. His hands moved continually, his face was very animated. He smiled often—a nice one, open and showing lots of teeth. However, it left as quickly as it came. Nothing that looked like it actually meant real warmth. His audience leaned forward to catch every word.

When he finally finished, his shoulders relaxed and he slumped a bit. Some seconds passed but none of them said anything. Then Mrs. Jutts spoke; her face bright with the kind of anticipation you see on a person before they say something they think is very smart or witty. Both men listened with full attention. She couldn't have said more than three sentences—it took no more than a few seconds. When she finished it was plain she thought she'd said it just right. Jerry's smile said the same thing. He was proud of the missus.

I cannot lip-read but I read Floon's when he said to her, "That's very stupid." He mouthed the words slowly, dragging out "very" so that it became "verrrrrrry." Mrs. Jutts' face collapsed like a tent when the center pole is pulled away. Her husband looked quickly away. Floon said nothing more and neither did his expression. He drove the final nail into the coffin of her self-esteem by patting her shoulder and walking away. Looking stricken, the couple watched him cross the lobby—as if his leaving had been their fault.

"What a dick."

I was about to follow him when a man in my suit came up and held out a folder. "Here are the plans for today."

I took it, flashed a quick "thanks" smile, ignored the folder, and searched again for Floon. Perfect—he was standing alone by a leafy potted plant looking at the crowd. For a moment I thought of Jay Gatsby standing at the top of the stairs of his Long Island mansion watching his party guests. But those people wore what they wanted to Gatsby's and behind his carefully created facade he was a nice man. Having seen what Caz de Floon just did to Mrs. Jutts, I knew instinctively that he was not a nice man, no matter what people said about him.

He appeared content to stand alone and watch. Once in a while he smiled at someone or raised a hand to wave, but the aura around him said stay away. No one made any attempt to approach. I started looking around the room to see how his guests responded to him from a distance. It was easy to distinguish us from the other people in the lobby because we all wore the same clothes. The silliness of the idea of the outfits became dark and perverse when I thought of how he had humiliated the fat woman. Most of the people kept sneaking glances at him. Some seemed eager, others simply curious to know where he was. When he greeted someone, their face lit up like they'd been blessed. If his eyes passed over someone and they saw, it was a blow, a moment's small defeat. They wanted him to know they were there. His small waves gave them stature, when they received one they lit up like torches.

It was only a matter of time before our eyes met. When that

happened, I felt my heart clench like a cramp in my chest. I
didn't know the man but his gaze still jolted me. I pushed on a
smile and raised the folder in my hand in greeting. Out of the
corner of my eye I caught sight of the front page. Cramp number
two hit. Embossed on a shiny white background were two
things—the name FLOON in large black letters. Below it was a
painting of *that* feather.

My mind snapped its fingers and all at once I remembered
where I had seen this image before in this time: while walking to
the café with Gus to meet Susan, I had seen a large poster on a wall
amidst a bunch of others. On it was printed FLOON and below it
the feather. That's all—no tag line like "Where do you want to go
today?" or "It's the real thing!" Just that strange last name and
the rainbow colored feather on an otherwise empty white poster.
Seeing it hadn't registered on me then because I was simply too
thunderstruck by everything else happening at the moment.

"*Terrytoon Circus.*" That was the first thing Caz de Floon said
to me when the flashbulb burn of recognition faded from my
head and I realized *the* man was now standing next to me.

"Excuse me?"

"*Terrytoon Circus.* Who was the emcee?" Now his smile was
authentic. I had no idea what he was talking about.

"Sorry, Caz, but you're going to have to create a context for
me on this."

The smile evaporated and his mouth set in a thin grim. "Play
fair, Frannie. I admit you won last night with Cocoa Marsh and
Mighty Manfred the Wonder Dog but give credit where it's due.
I think *Terrytoon Circus* is a great one. So tell me who was the
emcee." He spoke with the faint accent of a European who's
lived in America a long time. "Terrytoon" came out sounding like
Terror Ton.

"Are we talking old television shows here, Caz?"

"TV shows, advertisements, anything from the fifties and sixties. You know it's my passion so answer the question."

He was messing with the wrong guy. As a kid I must have
watched four hundred years of television combined. My TV ca-
reer started back in the days when there was no color and no
remote control. A rabbit-ears antenna sat on top of a set. When
the picture was bad you fooled with those ears or smacked the
side of the box with your hand. There were only seven channels,
all in black-and-white. Every day programming began with a U.S.
Army propaganda show called *The Big Picture* and ended with a
religious one called *Lamp unto My Feet*. I know. I was there.

"Are you serious, Caz? You really want to go one on one
with me about old TV shows? You'll lose."

"You're stalling for time. Answer my question." His voice
had a strange ability to sound mean and joking at the same time.

"Okay. Claude Kirschner." Now I was relaxed. I could play
this game asleep and still beat his ass. "That's too easy. How
about this—who sang the theme song to *Wyatt Earp*?"

He tossed one busy hand in the air. "The Ken Darby Singers.
Who was Yancy Derringer's sidekick?" People were watching us.
Floon was playing to them.

"Pahoo. What actor played the part?"

"X. Brands. Who played *the Cisco Kid*'s sidekick?" I crossed
my arms.

"Leo Carrillo."

Smug. Smug. I wanted to slap him in his smug smile. He
didn't need mountains to climb—he could have rappelled off his
own ego. At his suggestion we moved from TV to sports trivia
of that time. He was damned good at it. When we'd come up
even on baseball, football, and basketball, I decided to raise the
trivia stakes. "How about pro wrestling, Caz? Back in the days
when Ray Morgan was announcing at Uline Arena?"

Floon opened his arms in a sweeping, theatrical gesture for me to begin.

"Name the Fabulous Kangaroos."

"Roy Heffernan and Al Costello."

"Who was Moose Cholak's tag-team partner?"

"The Mighty Atlas. Please, Frannie, give me some credit."

"Skull Murphy's?"

"Brute Bernard."

"Where was Skull from?"

"Ireland."

The questions and answers got faster, our voices louder. I'm sure we looked and sounded ridiculous: Two old men in identical ten-thousand-dollar suits yelling at each other about Skull Murphy, Haystacks Calhoun, Fuzzy Cupid. This nonsense went on until he introduced Corn Bob.

I smirked at the stupid name. *"Who?"*

Mr. de Floon wasn't used to being ridiculed. His mouth did a little tight dance. His hands stopped dancing altogether. "Corn Bob. He had a submission hold called the corncob."

Usually I like liars because they make life more zippy, but Floon had already rubbed me so much the wrong way that he could have passed for a piece of sandpaper. "You're full of shit."

Our corner of the universe suddenly got exceedingly quiet. Floon's eyelids flared but he said nothing. The only thing in my mind was how was I going to discover anything here if I keep pissing people off?

He rubbed his nose. "You don't believe there was a wrestler named Corn Bob?"

"No."

Silence.

"Do you know why I like you, Frannie?"

"Why?"

"Because you're the only one who talks back to me. The only one who has the balls to do it."

The tension went out of his voice and out of the air. People in our group who had heard looked at me with either admiration or envy.

"What was the name of Buster Brown's dog in the shoe ad?"

He wasn't going to quit, but I'd had enough. "Tyge. Look, I've got a question about something else—where did this feather on your logo come from? I see it everywhere."

"Ha ha. And I'm supposed to address that question seriously?"

"Yes, I'd like to know."

"You'd like to know where the Floon feather comes from?" He waited long enough to realize I was serious. "Frannie, you're kidding, right?"

"No."

To my surprise, instead of answering he snapped his fingers a few times to catch someone's attention. Quickly a very pretty young woman in the gypsy dress appeared. "Nora, I think Mr. McCabe is feeling a little floaty this morning. He's having some trouble remembering. Perhaps you can help. Frannie, you've met Nora Putnam? She's our resident doctor on this trip."

"Do you feel dizzy or light-headed, sir?"

"Floon, answer my question: Where does the feather come from?"

"You *know* where it comes from."

"Remind me."

Dr. Putnam reached out to touch me but thought better of it and dropped her hand. "We can go right over there and sit down, Mr. McCabe. The Viennese *fohn* wind is blowing today and sometimes that affects people physically in strange ways."

"Leave me alone. Floon—"

Seeing something over my shoulder, everything about him

went rigid. It was astonishing. From sweet concern to whole-body fury in two seconds. "What is she doing?"

Both the doctor and I turned to see what had him in such a twist. We had to—his anger was beyond belief. I saw the same flock of people moving around and talking in the lobby. What was Floon's problem? As I was about to turn back to ask what the hell was going on, I caught a glimpse of Susan in her nice blue dress walking toward us.

"Where is her costume? Why isn't she wearing it?"

"She didn't want to."

"Didn't *want* to? That's interesting. Susan didn't want to wear my dress?" Floon spat this at Dr. Putnam, who winced and looked like she wanted to run far away. Next he gave me the X-ray glare. "I owe you a great deal, Frannie. Without you my life would have been very different. But you're here and so is your wife. You accepted my invitation. All that I asked in return was that you do a few things for me in the proper spirit. This is *not* the proper spirit."

"Good morning." Susan arrived smiling and it didn't change when she saw Floon's flaming look. She wore a nice perfume that lifted me.

"Where is your dress, Susan? Is there a problem with it?"

"No, Caz, I just don't look good in it. I didn't think you would mind."

"I mind very much."

"I'm sorry."

"You can still go put it on. We have time."

"I don't want to put it on, Caz."

"Sure you do, go ahead. I'll hold breakfast for you."

"She doesn't *want* to put it on, Floon, so why don't you drop it?"

"Thank you, Frannie." It was the first time Susan had smiled at me.

"I don't think I want to wear this either, come to think of it." I took off the suit jacket and dropped it on the floor. Then I began working the knot of the tie loose.

"What are you doing?"

"Taking off my clothes. Taking off *your* clothes." The knot wouldn't come undone. I tugged harder. When it wouldn't budge I said screw it and reached down to the belt buckle. I liked the idea of standing naked in front of Caz and his guests. Susan in her taboo blue dress, me in my wrinkled birthday suit.

Floon bellowed "Gus!" and out of nowhere Mr. Gould appeared.

"Can I help?"

"Get them out of here. Out of my sight! I will not let them ruin anything. This is my trip! I've planned it for too long."

"Now Caz—"

Floon shook his head once and walked away. I warbled "Bye!" to his back.

Susan laughed. "Do you think he'll write a note to my parents?"

Gus didn't think any of it was funny. "This is not good, Susan. You made a really big mistake."

"I don't think so. Come on, husband. Looks like we have a free day together in Vienna."

I picked the jacket up off the floor. "Let's go for a walk."

Gus tried to stop us. "Please don't go. Maybe if I talk to him we can work this out—"

Susan took my hand. "I don't want to work it out, Gus. I'm not guilty of anything. Dinner tonight is on that boat cruise around the Danube, right? And we can wear what we want? So we'll meet you down there. I think Frannie and I need some downtime from Floon and this whole trip." She started us toward the revolving front door.

Dr. Putnam asked, "But Mr. McCabe, I thought you were feeling ill?"

"I'll survive. The only thing I'm sure of is today I don't have to worry about dying."

We walked down a beautiful, wide tree-lined street for a long time without talking. It was a nice day. The trees were in full bloom, and even the many cars passing nearby seemed more quiet than usual when there's a lot of traffic. Susan had her arm linked in mine. I figured it was best to keep quiet until she spoke.

I kept busy looking for signs of what life would be like thirty (?) years on. Clothes looked more or less the same, although occasionally someone passed wearing an outfit like the costumes kids wore in the futuristic music videos Pauline watched on MTV. Cars were sleek and generally small—I rarely saw a big honker like a Mercedes or a BMW. When enough had passed, I realized they were so quiet because no exhaust was coming out of the tail pipes. There *were* no tail pipes. Without thinking I said to myself, "Electric."

"Hmmm?"

"Nothing."

"Frannie, what did that woman mean when she asked if you were feeling ill?"

A man walked by wearing a black plastic helmet over his entire head. And there didn't seem to be any place for him to see out the front. But he walked straight ahead and didn't bump into anything.

"What's with that guy?"

Susan gave him only the briefest glance. "He's studying."

"*Studying?* With a bowling ball on his head?"

"Don't change the subject, Frannie. Aren't you feeling okay?"

Ding-Dong! The whole solution came to me in a flash. I knew exactly how to find out what I needed to know. "Can we sit down a minute?"

Park benches were conveniently placed along the way. We walked to the next one where I sat down slowly and heavily, giving out a midsized groan for added effect. After a few beats I took her hand. "Susan, I have to tell you something. It's the real reason why what happened this morning—"

"You mean in bed?"

"Yes, that's part of it. I didn't want to tell you because, well, because it scares me and I didn't want it to scare you too. Especially while we were on this trip."

"What, Frannie, what is it?"

"I can't remember things anymore. Big things or small things—it's all the same. All of my head is empty. I think I might have Alzheimer's disease. I'm scared shitless."

"So?" Her voice was calm; her face said so what?

"*So?* Is that all you can say? Memory is leaking out of me like air from a balloon and you say so?"

"We'll go to a drugstore and get you some Tapsodil. What is the problem?"

"What's Tapsodil?"

"It's medicine for Alzheimer's disease. You take it for three days and you're cured."

"Shit." I made a sour face.

"What?"

"They can *cure* Alzheimer's now?"

"Of course. I had it two years ago. It's not a big deal, Frannie. You don't even need a doctor's prescription."

"But . . ."

"But what? Is that all you're worried about?"

I couldn't think of another thing to say. My brilliant plan to trick all the info I needed out of Susan had come and gone like a breeze. Stumped, I watched another person go by with a full-head helmet on, only this one was yellow. "What the fuck is this, the Pod People? Look Susan, until I get some of this espadrille—"

"Tapsodil."

"Tapsodil. Yeah, whatever, you have to help me. I don't like walking around in my own life bumping into walls, not able to remember the layout. So just for now answer a few questions. Okay?"

"Okay."

"Who's Floon? What is that feather logo he uses?"

"He owns the largest pharmaceutical company in the world. They make Tapsodil, among hundreds of other drugs. The feather is the company trademark. You really don't remember this?"

"No. But why that feather?"

"You gave it to him. You and George."

"George Dalemwood?"

"Yes."

"Where is *he*?"

"My God, Frannie, you don't remember that either?"

"Nothing. Where is George?"

She looked at her hands in her lap. "He disappeared thirty years ago."

"What do you mean?"

"Just that. He disappeared from Crane's View and no one knows what happened to him. You tried to find him for years but never had any luck."

"Disappeared? *George?*"

"Yes."

I had given Floon the Old Vertue feather? And George—dependable, sedentary George Dalemwood disappeared never to be heard from again? This was my future? While trying mentally to swallow those two lumps, I heard someone singing Aretha Franklin's "Respect." Two voices sang, one of them sounding distinctly weird. That was because the voice came from a dog.

A man in faded jeans and a green T-shirt that said DROPKICK MURPHYS walked next to a Rottweiler. The man moved quickly while the dog trotted next to him looking up at his master occasionally as if waiting for a cookie. But the two *were* singing "Respect" and they weren't half bad. The dog's voice was gravelly and rough, sort of deep and sort of not. I don't know what I'm saying—how the hell do you describe a dog's singing voice?

I whipped around to Susan and saw she was looking the other way. I elbowed her hard and she cried out. "Susan! Susan!"

"What? Why did you do that? It hurt!"

"Look! Look!"

"So what? Why did you hit me?"

The singers passed us singing R-E-S-P-E-C-T . . .

"That dog is singing!"

"Yes, and?"

"When did they teach dogs to sing?"

She rubbed her arm. "Years ago. I don't know when. Ask Floon. They invented the stuff."

"What stuff? To make dogs talk?"

She must have remembered I had Alzheimer's because she stopped looking angry. "No. But you can give them stuff that makes them learn things. Like how to sing or say certain phrases."

"Jesus! Why would you do that?"

"For fun. I don't know. I hate dogs."

As a kid I used to eat as fast as I could. My parents would say slow down, slow down or you're going to throw up. But there was always someplace important to go or someone to see and food was only fuel to get me there. As a result I often ate so fast I'd get a stomachache that lasted hours. Sitting with Susan on that bench in Vienna, in a world where Rottweilers sang Aretha Franklin and people passed with bowling balls on their heads I had the same feeling; only this time the ache was in my head and not my guts.

"I wanna go home."

Susan nodded and sighed. Little did she know to what home I was referring.

"When did you and I get married?"

Wrong question to ask. She didn't answer and only when I turned did I see she was crying.

When she finally spoke, her voice was bitter. "I thought everything would now finally work out. Stupid me, eh? Stupid me! Do you realize I have loved you my whole life? My whole damned life you've been stuck in me like a piece of meat between my teeth I can't get out. But finally *finally* I thought we were home free. I waited my whole life for you. I fought and I was patient and I never gave up hope because I just knew one day I'd prevail. I honestly believe life makes sense if you're patient. And I was, Frannie! All those years I waited for you like the girl in a corner waiting to be asked to dance. When you asked me to marry you—"

"I *did*?"

"Yes you did, damn it! Please don't tell me you forgot that too. I think I've been humiliated enough for one morning. When you asked, I thought: fifty years too late but why the hell not? I've loved the idiot all this time so why not finish the party with him? One great last hurrah before . . .

"I'm going back to the hotel and lie down. Go to a pharmacy

or whatever they call them here and ask for Tapsodil. I'm sure they'll have it." She stood up and rubbed her arm some more.

"Don't go, Susan. Let's have this day together and be happy. Everything's my fault and I apologize. We'll do the town." I moved to stand up but my lower body promptly reminded me I was an old geezer. My legs were uncooperative. Cursing quietly, I rocked back and forth twice to gain momentum and only then was able to rise. "I'm not good at being old."

"You still look pretty cute to me, husband. And I want to tell you a secret. Do you know what made me love you most of all? I always had a thing for you, sure, but the thing that really hooked me?"

"Tell."

"How wonderfully you cared for Magda when she was dying. I'd never seen that side of you, Frannie. I never thought you had it in you."

Hearing those terrible words, hearing that my Magda died was as bad as if it had just happened. What immediately came to mind was the conversation I'd had with George when I told him I had never loved anyone enough to fear losing them. But now, in this strange no-man's-land time, I realized I had never been more wrong about anything in my whole life. Knowing Magda would die before me was unbearable.

"When, Susan? When did she die?"

She made a worried face and moved to go. "We have to get you those pills."

I stepped in front of her. *"When?"*

"On my forty-eighth birthday. I'll never forget it."

Magda would be dead in less than two years.

What happened next almost saved me and the rest of my life a lot of trouble. Almost. We found an *apotheke* and Susan bought some of the Alzheimer's medicine for me. I didn't watch the transaction because I was too busy looking around the place, trying to familiarize myself with a world thirty years my senior. This drugstore looked pretty typical except for some futuristic gadgets on display that did God only knows what to repair and improve human life. If they'd spoken English there I'd have asked, but my German vocabulary consisted solely of *ja* and *nein*. Walking out of there, we almost bumped into another Pod Person— this time wearing white.

"All right, what the *hell* is he learning with that thing on his head?"

"White is for memory recall. It allows you to relive any part of your life that you choose in perfect detail. It's mostly used by psychologists in therapy; and by the police in criminal investigations."

My mind went *hooray!* I'd hit the mother lode, the bull's-eye, and the way home with one question. I could barely keep the excitement out of my voice. "You put that thing on your head and you can remember your life? The whole thing? Everything that happened?"

"Yes. But I wouldn't want to do it."

"I would! Right now! Where can I get one?"

"Frannie, if you take these pills you'll be fine in a few days. Your memory will return, I promise."

"I don't want an old man's memory—I want my whole life! Where can I get one?" I couldn't believe my good luck. All I had to do was strap that stupid-looking ball over my head and I'd have all the answers I needed. Then when I was sent back to my time I'd know exactly what was going on and what to do.

"They sell the white ones at Giorgio Armani stores."

"*Armani?* The fashion designer?"

"Yes."

"They sell a machine at a clothes store that brings back your memory? Why there?"

Susan thought, shrugged. "I don't know."

"This is a weird-ass time! Maybe memory's considered a fashion accessory. Who cares—let's go."

With lots of questions, shrugs, and hand gestures, we eventually found someone who spoke English and knew the way. They directed us to a small side street off one of the main drags. There, behind a door guarded by two men in what appeared to be Kevlar vests, was the Armani store.

"Are those guys cops or private security? Why are they wearing protection?"

"There have been so many attacks and bombings, Frannie. I didn't think it would be as bad here as in America. You take your life in your hands when you go shopping. Forget going to a mall anymore. Those are war zones. Remember what happened in Crane's View?"

The guards came to attention as we approached. Susan lifted her arms from her sides like wings and gestured for me to do the same. One guy ran a wand around our bodies like security people do at an airport when your pocket change sets off the alarm. I couldn't believe it. All this because we wanted to shop? When the electronic frisk was done, Susan took what looked like a credit card out of her pocket and handed it over. One guard inserted it in a small black box he wore at his waist. At once a small peep peeped. He moved out of the way, allowing us to enter.

Once inside I kept staring at them through the window. They were not your typical rent-a-cop chubsters. Both men looked fit enough to wrestle alligators and win.

I was about to bombard Susan with more questions but a saleswoman came up to us. She spoke perfect English and actually bowed slightly when asked if she had a "Bic white."

I waited till she was gone before asking. "Bic white? That's what they're called?"

"Red, white—you ask for the color."

"But it's really Bic, the makers of the cheapo pen? The throw-away razor?"

"Yes, it's the same company."

"Is it disposable too?"

"No. They cost about a hundred dollars." Susan wandered off to look at clothes. I watched the guards through the window. Brave New World. Brave cheap world. Here you could resurrect a whole life of memories for the same price as a good floor fan in my time. While I pondered away on that one, something bumped my foot. First I kicked it away, and then looked to see what it was. A small brown machine like a round hassock moved off without a sound. It took a while of staring to realize it was a robot vacuum cleaner. The damned thing was terrific. I wished there were some way I could bring one back to Magda, who absolutely hated cleaning the house. That thought brought back what was going to happen to her. I shuddered. Wasn't there anything I could do to stop it? Take her to the hospital as soon as I returned and have them run every test . . .

But by using this mind machine, I was about to have all of my memories back. I could learn what actually happened to my wife. Maybe knowing the details would help me to figure out what to do.

I was thinking about this and watching the vacuum cleaner whiz around when the saleswoman said, "Have you ever used a Bic before, sir?"

"What? Oh, no, I haven't."

"It is not difficult, but you must try it on. This is a large. Perhaps it is best if you sit down?"

After I sat in a nearby chair she handed me the helmet. It was strangely light. "What do I do?"

"Put it over your head and say 'face focus.' The computer will create the adjustments if they are necessary."

"It has a computer in it?"

"Yes, sir. Just put it—"

"I heard you, dear." The moment of truth had arrived and, sure, my soul gave a small shiver. What would happen to me in the next minutes? Unlike the drowning man, the life I was *going* to lead was about to flash in front of my eyes. But I didn't hesitate because too much was at stake.

Slipping the helmet over my head, I was pleased by what felt like the softest leather sliding across my cheeks. I could see nothing at all. Everything was pitch-black. It was like putting my head inside a leather glove. How could anyone see out of it? How could you walk down a street and not bump into everything? Maybe when the thing turned on

"Now what?" I asked.

"You say 'face focus'—" Her voice came through clear as a bell, which was reassuring.

"Oh yeah, right. Okay. Face focus!" I felt my hot breath spread back across my face when I spoke.

The helmet came on with a fast click-click. Next there was a whirring sound. It stopped. Then a pause. Then a big green flash and something inside the helmet exploded, knocking me out of the chair onto the floor. Onto the vacuum cleaner rather, which tried to drive away with me lying on top of it. But valiant little fellow that it was, I outweighed it by a hundred and fifty pounds so it could only jiggle beneath me making desperate noises. I flailed at my head trying to get the helmet off, petrified by a nasty smell of burning metal inside.

"Help!"

"Sir, sir, please wait, sir."

"Get it off me!"

Someone pushed me over, quickly undid the helmet and pulled it off with a pretty hard fucking jerk. The first thing I saw was the vacuum cleaner lying on its side nearby. One of the security guards held the helmet and looked at me with a big smile in his eyes but not on his mouth. The saleswoman stood next to him wringing her hands.

"This has never happened before! Never!"

"Lucky me. What the hell happened?"

"I don't know, sir."

"You don't know. You sell a product that microwaves my head, then tell me you don't know why? Face focus, my ass!"

"Frannie, are you all right?"

Before I had a chance to answer, Susan's wristwatch beeped. She bit her lip. "That's the emergency. I should answer it— something must be wrong."

"Yeah, my head!"

She raised her wrist to her mouth and mumbled something. While she spoke, the saleswoman meekly asked if I would like to try again with another Bic. I glared at her. Later I realized the whole catastrophe was my fault. The helmet blew up because my brain shorted out the computer's circuits. How could the Bic restore memories of a life I hadn't lived yet?

"Frannie, it's Gus Gould. He says Floon is wild that we left. Apparently he had a big surprise he was going to give you at breakfast but then we disappeared."

While she spoke I warily touched my eyebrows and discovered both were badly singed. "We disappeared because he's an asshole. I don't want any more surprises."

"But it's *George*. Caz found George Dalemwood and brought him here. He's at the hotel waiting for you."

I looked at my fingertips, which were sooty-black and covered with tiny bits of eyebrow. But hey, tomorrow a motorcycle was going to kill me. Who needed eyebrows?

"How old am I, Susan?"

"Seventy-four." Her face showed only love and concern.

"How did Magda die?"

"A brain tumor."

"Jesus God!"

"Frannie, Floon specifically said to tell you he found Vertue. He has it with him, whatever that means."

"I know what it means. Let's go."

I couldn't wait to get back to the hotel, but there were no taxis around and my fossil legs could only go so fast. Thirty years after mysteriously disappearing, my best friend turns up in Vienna with a resurrected dog hundreds of years old? Damned right I couldn't wait to get back. And the way he phrased it: "He had found Vertue" led me to believe there was more here to be reckoned with than just man with old dog.

On seeing the hotel I felt my spirits lift. This was it. I only had to somehow brush Floon off and get George alone in a corner. He would answer my questions. I might even tell him exactly what had happened to bring me here because George would understand. Where had he been for thirty years? What had he been doing? What had made him leave Crane's View and disappear for eleven thousand days? And had he really found the dog?

These questions and so many others took off and landed in my head as if it were a busy airport. I didn't know what to ask first. I wanted to know everything at once. There was the hotel.

Walk faster, old man. Somewhere inside was George Dalemwood and the answers. It wouldn't be long now!

The street was jammed with people so it was not surprising that I did not see him as he approached. Susan had already asked me twice to slow down but I paid no attention. George might even have an idea of how I could save Magda—

"I'm sorry, Mr. McCabe, but you can't go to the hotel."

"Astopel! Why are you here?" I looked around to see if Frannie Junior had accompanied him. He was alone, and without any warning so was I with him. Without any warning we were suddenly the only animated objects in a world that had become a still photograph. Somehow Astopel had frozen the world around us, including Susan. She was looking worriedly at me and reaching out a hand.

"You cannot meet George."

"*Why not?*"

"Because you must find out the answers for yourself. I told you that before. You can't just ask another person questions. It must be your doing, Mr. McCabe."

"You let me burn my brain in that goddamned helmet for no reason at all, but now I can't ask my friend a few questions?"

"No, you can't."

"What if I go anyway?"

"You'll find this." He gestured at the frozen world around us.

"Astopel, if I lose my temper at you again, I won't be able to *find* it! All I've discovered here are dead ends. You said go find the answers in the future. Now I think I have, but you stop me. What am I supposed to do? I've only got a week!"

"Five days."

"Five days, all right. I have five days. Tell me what am I supposed to do?"

"Perhaps it would be better if you went back to your own time. Maybe you could find it there."

"I want a favor. You have to give me this one favor. I don't know what the hell else I can do."

"What is it?"

"Let me see George now. See what he looks like physically. I know that'll help. Can I? Will you let me?"

"Yes."

Although surprised at how quickly he acceded to my request, I still made a fist and punched it triumphantly into the air. "Yes! Let's go." I started again toward the hotel.

"We don't need to walk there, Mr. McCabe—unless you want to."

"Are you kidding? The less I use these bum legs the better."

"Good." He looked at the sky. I looked too. Abruptly I was no longer looking at the blue Viennese sky but at a white sconce on a ceiling. My eyes rushed down to find George in this room, wherever that was. I was sure once I saw him

On a large bed covered with a gold-and-white spread was Old Vertue, alive. No question about it. Like everything else, the dog was frozen—in a sitting position. But its eyes were open and looked alert. I couldn't help smiling at the old son of a bitch. I had grown even fonder of it after what we'd been through together. Now here it was yet again, brought back this time by my friend. Where had it been all these years? Where had George found it? I felt a great urge to go over and pat its nondead head, but first things first—where was George?

The room was large and elegant, similar to the one Susan and I occupied, only this one was much grander in every way. I walked around looking for any sign of life—a book by the side of the bed, an open suitcase, a wallet or passport on the dresser. But there was nothing—no sign of anyone, much less George

Dalemwood. Other than Old Vertue perched on the bed, this room gave the feeling it had been empty a long time. It held the smell of old suitcases and laundered sheets, room freshener was somewhere in there too.

I walked into the bathroom but it felt even emptier. No kit bag sat next to the tub. The water glasses were all unused and turned upside down on the shelf above the sink. No toothbrush/paste laid out, no shaving things all in a row. On a hunch I touched the towels. None was damp. Each was neatly folded and evenly spaced on the stainless steel drying bars.

I lowered the toilet seat lid and sat on it. I put my elbows on my knees and my chin in my palms. For some inexplicable reason my gums began to ache, and I was again reminded of how old and ornery my body was. Looking through the door at the dog on the bed, I tried to figure the whole thing out. On first realizing the room was empty, I thought George must be with Floon. Both were waiting somewhere for us to return. Why then would Astopel bring me here? What was the point if George wasn't here? My view into the bedroom included Astopel's foot sliding back and forth over the carpet near the door. He'd been silent since we materialized here but that hadn't struck me till now. I started touching my singed eyebrows again.

His foot stopped. "Are you ready to go?"

My hand stopped. "What do you mean?"

"Is there anything else you'd like to do here?"

"Yes—*see George*." My voice, whining, echoed off the walls.

The pause that followed was a long one. "Could you come in here a moment, Mr. McCabe?" Astopel's voice was patient and earnest, as if he were a father having to slow down a lesson so that his young child could understand.

"Oh my God!" I said to myself, to the walls, the sink, and the silence of that empty room. The bathroom floor was made up of row after gleaming row of black and white ceramic tiles. They played tricks on your eyes when you stared at them too long. I closed mine and made tight fists in my lap.

What was going on had abruptly come clear to me and now I was stalling for time. I tightened my fists until both arms shook. When I returned to the other room I would confirm what I already knew. The moment that happened, my world would become an entirely different place. Magda's mother used to say life is short but very wide. For me it had just grown about as wide as *this* human's mind could stand. But stand I did and walk out of there because I had to see for myself.

His back to me, Astopel held a gold curtain aside and stared out the window. Over his shoulder, blinding sunlight reflected off the glass facade of a building across the street. The glare made me glance away. I looked at the dog. Mistrust took over and I thought Old Vertue was smiling. At what? Because he was glad to see me? Because of how things had turned out? At the fact I'd finally gotten the point?

"Did you do this?" I asked Astopel's back. Silently I willed him to turn around and acknowledge me. He didn't.

"No, Mr. McCabe. I'm only here to show you things, not interfere."

"It's George there, isn't it? That dog is George."

"That's right."

"Can you tell me why?"

"He and Mr. Floon recently collaborated on an experiment with a new drug they invented in one of Floon's laboratories. You see the results." He let the curtain drop but did not turn around. "Does that make things any clearer?"

The Wooden Sea

When I awoke I was in bed with Magda. The sun was streaming in the window, which meant it was early morning. Our bedroom faced east, and Magda, who was very much a morning person, liked to say sunlight was the alarm clock in this house. She lay with her head turned toward me on my outstretched arm. She was smiling. My wife often smiled in her sleep. She also gave me kisses in her sleep but when she woke up said she didn't remember doing it. I was home. I was with my wife who was alive and smiling. Another day had passed. I had five left.

My last memory of the other place (as I came to think of it) was reaching out to touch Old Vertue/George Dalemwood on its frozen-in-place head. But at the last moment I hesitated because I was afraid. Yes I, Mr. Courageous, was afraid to pet a dog. I'd asked Astopel if it was all right to do it. Not even bothering to turn from the window, he said only "Why not?" His tone of voice sounded more like "Who cares?"

I reached out to pet the dog but stopped. Then I felt something heavy on my arm. Then I was back in bed with my wife and my life and all this confounding strife.

Normally I loved to lay in bed in the morning, barely awake, letting my still-sleepy brain simmer. Loved to lie next to Magda McCabe and watch her sleeping smile and smell her. She was the sweetest-smelling human being who ever lived. I could never get enough of her odor. Even when she was hot and sweaty after a ten-mile bicycle ride in the middle of August this woman smelled delicious. What is more gratifying than to lie next to your partner in your own bed mornings, thoughts just beginning to take shape, sharp-edged early light coming through the window and warming a patch of floor where your shoes are mixed with hers from the night before? What is more fulfilling than waking to your own satisfying life with someone treasured next to you? What more could we ask for and not be ashamed?

But that morning I shot up out of bed like I'd been launched by a catapult. I had so much to do and no idea of how to do it. Or even where to begin. And I was ravenously hungry. Atomically, tidalwavedly hungry. Never in my life had my stomach felt emptier. Was it because of what had been happening to me? Did time travel use up more calories than a day of normal clock time?

I walked toward the kitchen wearing nothing but a pair of boxer shorts, assuming my stepdaughter wouldn't be up for hours, as was her habit. I was thinking scrambled eggs and many pieces of bacon, cold tart orange juice that stung the tongue and enough hot coffee to float my eyeballs. I was thinking hot cinnamon buns—when the doorbell rang. I looked at my watch but saw I wasn't wearing it. They had thought of everything, whoever they were. I always took off the watch before going to sleep. I was certain if I returned to the bedroom now and looked at my night table it would be there. The watch Astopel had taken from me. The watch that meant absolutely nothing anymore because time was no longer a highway going from A to B, but rather an amusement park with too many nauseating rides.

The doorbell rang again. I guessed it was about six A.M. Even in normal times I would have beheaded anyone who rang my bell at that hour. Without thinking about the effect of appearing at the door in my underwear, I appeared at the door in my underwear and opened it. And groaned.

"No, not you again! Please, enough for one lifetime!"

"Step aside!" he said in a perfect imitation of Moe Howard from *The Three Stooges* Frannie Junior elbowed me out of the way and once again in his orange cowboy boots entered into my house uninvited. He stood in the hallway looking everywhere but at me. It seemed like he was searching for something or memorizing the surroundings.

"What do you want? Go away and leave me in peace."

"You'll be in pieces, all right. Anyway, everything looks okay here. And let me tell ya, bub, that's a fuckin' relief!"

"Look, before we go even deeper down the rabbit's hole with this, can I get some breakfast? I haven't eaten since I was seventy years old."

"Breakfast sounds good. I'm hungry too." He grinned like an evil wolf in a cartoon, all long teeth and menace. I didn't have the energy to spell out I hadn't invited him to join me.

"Why don't you make some scrambled eggs with Worcestershire sauce and curry powder?" His request startled me because that was exactly what I had planned to cook.

"Why don't *you* sit down and put a cork in it? You'll eat what I make."

"Bite me."

I was opening cupboards. "I'd get food poisoning. Sit down and be quiet."

He sat down but wasn't about to be quiet. "Where've you been?"

"Guess." I took down my favorite frying pan.

"Up in the future?"

I nodded while taking things out of the fridge I needed to make our breakfast.

"So you don't know yet?"

I began cracking eggs into a bowl. "Know what?"

"I think we should eat first and then you can shit your pants."

"More surprises?"

"The word surprise is not part of this vocabulary, man; it's all just one long nightmare. Wait'll you go outside and see what's happening today. Hey, by the way, who's Mary J. Blige? I was watching this MTV before and *that* is a ring-a-ding-ding woman!"

I was about to comment on his obsolete compliment when I remembered where he came from—the years when Frank Sinatra and his Rat Pack were the coolest guys around, cigarettes and roast beef were okay to ingest, and James Bond was still Sean Connery. In those days a "ring-a-ding-ding woman" was one hell of an endorsement.

"Don't put too much curry powder on it. You always put too—"

"Be quiet."

"Howsabout some coffee while we're waiting?"

"Howsabout my hands are full and maybe it'd be nice if you got off your ass and made it."

"Fair enough. Where's your pot?"

"We don't use a coffeepot. The machine's over there."

"What machine?"

"That silver one on the counter. The espresso machine—the one on the counter with the long handle. It says 'Gaggia' on the front?"

Sliding his hands into his jeans pockets he *tsk*'d his tongue in utter teenage know-it-all disgust. "Espresso? I'm not drinking Italian faggot coffee. That stuff tastes like burnt tires. Where's your coffeepot and the Maxwell House? That's good enough for me."

"There is no pot. That's what I've got—faggot coffee or nothing. Drink water if you don't like it."

Crossing his arms, he didn't say another word until I put a full plate down in front of him. I couldn't resist a final verbal pinch. "I put a little foontageegee on yours."

His shoulders stiffened. "Foonta—what?"

"Foontageegee. A spice from Morocco. It's very . . .

hmmm . . ." I swishily put a hand on my hip, two fingers to my mouth and said, "*Robust.*" I stretched out the *s* as far as it would go and finished on a very hard *t*.

He shoved the plate away and actually wiped his hands on his pants. "That's it! I ain't eating. Foontageegee. Holy shit."

"Eat the goddamned food, willya! It's a joke. I was kidding. It's bacon and eggs the way I always cook it."

Not believing me, he took the fork and poked everything on the plate slowly and suspiciously as if testing for landmines. Only after he'd bent down and sniffed things did he give in. Eating in silence, the boy didn't let the foontageegee get in the way of a crocodile's appetite. He kept his head low over the plate so he could shove more in faster. I was going to say something about it until I remembered he was me and that was how I had eaten when I was his age, God forbid.

"Hi, Frannie. Who's he?" Pauline stood in the kitchen doorway wearing a thin green nightshirt that didn't cover much. She must have stepped outside to get the morning newspaper because she held it in her hand. She was staring at Junior with grave interest.

Instead of answering her question, I grabbed his elbow and pulled him toward me. "She can see you? You said only I could see you here."

"Leggo my arm, man. Can't you see I'm eating? I told you, everything is screwed up today. Wait till you go outside and have a look. That's why I came back here now. You're going to need someone to protect your ass."

"This is insane! How am I supposed to know what to do if the rules keep changing?"

"There are no rules, man. Get used to it. Why do you think I'm here, eating your eggs?"

"Frannie?" Normally shy Pauline's voice had a sharp, demanding edge to it while she continued staring at him.

"Oh yeah, Pauline, this is my second cousin's son, uh, Gee-Gee. Actually it's Gary, uh, Graham, but we've always called him Gee-Gee." Shocked that she could see him now, the only word I could think of was the ridiculous Foonta . . . geegee, so that's who he became. He looked at me as if I had just pissed on his head.

"Hi, Gee-Gee. I'm Pauline."

He gave her the patented McCabe million-dollar smile I knew very well. When it overwhelmed her enough to make her look away, he hissed just loud enough for me to hear "Gee-Gee?"

"Frannie never told us about you. I didn't even know he had a second cousin."

The new Gee-Gee nonchalantly twirled his fork around his fingers in a complete circle. A very cool little trick my friend Sam Bayer had taught me when we were thirteen. "Yeah well, you know Uncle Frannie."

"Uncle? That's what you call him? Where are you from?"

"LA. California."

"I know where LA is," she chided him but attached to that was a coquette's smile that tipped the balance in his favor. Remember that this was the girl I had nicknamed Fade because from what I could see, she spent most of her life trying to. Yet now she spoke to Gee-Gee in a voice I'd never heard her use before. I would never have thought Pauline even capable of such a voice: It was coy and sexy. More than that, it was very knowing and that was the wildest part. Pauline? The too-timid computer-head was suddenly flirting like a bad blond actress on a TV sitcom. Not even getting into whom she was flirting *with*. For an instant I wondered if I would have liked this girl when I was his age? No, I would not.

But Gee-Gee sure seemed to like her. He patted the chair next to him to encourage her. "You wanna sit down and have some breakfast with us, Pauline?"

"I don't eat breakfast, but I wouldn't mind some coffee."

"What are you doing up this early, Pauline? You never get up at this hour."

"I know, but I heard voices downstairs so I came. Anyway, my tattoo was hurting and I guess that's what woke me."

Thoroughly impressed, Gee-Gee gave a long low whistle. "Whoa, you got a tattoo? I don't think I ever knew a girl who did that."

I corrected him. "Pia Hammer had a tattoo."

He shook his head. "Yeah, but Pia's a fuckin' lunatic. She also counts her breaths. I'm talking about a sane human female."

Pauline's eyes moved slowly and seductively from me to Gee-Gee. I couldn't believe her performance. I couldn't believe it was she. Pausing for just the right amount of time for full effect, she hit him with the important detail. But her blasé tone of voice said it was no big deal. "I got my ass tattooed. Or, just above my ass. You know, on the spine?" She stopped and checked to see how I was registering this new fact. Fortunately I already had seen her arsework so I was able to stay expressionless. When she saw I wasn't going to fly out of the chair and spank her she continued. "Sometimes it still hurts. Anyway, I'm going to get dressed first but then I'll be back. Would you make me an espresso, Gee-Gee?"

"Sure." He got right up and went over to the machine. "Hey, you got a Gaggia. They're the best machines around for espresso."

Pointing at me, Pauline rolled her eyes. "It's Frannie's. He's the world's biggest caffeine snob. I'm completely happy drinking regular coffee but he's got like this obsession about it."

"Yeah well, once you taste good espresso it's hard to go back to that canned shit," Gee-Gee said while he fiddled with the machine, pretending to know what he was doing. I had to swallow a laugh watching him work to impress my normally shy-as-a-snail stepdaughter.

"Whatever," Pauline said and left the kitchen, but not before one last long look over her shoulder at guess who.

When she was gone I put my hands behind my neck, crossed one leg over the other and crooned, "Check out Gee-Gee on that Gag-gia."

"Fuckin' Gee-Gee! What kind of name is that?"

"Short for foontageegee."

Even he had to laugh. "That was quick thinking. But it makes me sound like that French movie *Gigi* with Maurice Chevalier.' "

"I don't think anyone is going to mistake you for Leslie Caron. You want me to show you how to work that?"

"You gotta. I don't want Pauline to think I'm a retard or something."

I couldn't resist asking in a tone of voice that was too dubious, "You *really* like her?" And then because I was embarrassed, I hurried to a cupboard for the coffee beans and grinder. Opening the bag of beans, I took a long, deep whiff. Ecstasy.

"Yeah, I like her. She really got a tattoo on her ass? Wow, I'd never do that. What happens if you change your mind in a few years? Or your taste in pictures? But she's got to be gutsy to do it. And not bad looking. You don't think so?"

I was both uncomfortable and embarrassed. How did I tell teenage me that I thought Pauline was extremely plain and I never would have been interested in her, tattoo or not. Yet he was me and vice versa, so why didn't I understand his attraction to her?

"Show me how you make coffee on this thing. Hurry up— she might be back any minute."

He was incredulous but I think also secretly impressed with

all the preparation it took to make a single cup of black coffee. Along the way to its completion, we had three separate arguments. Why didn't I buy preground beans and save myself the trouble? Why buy a machine that only made one cup at a time? When I deliberately told him how much it cost he almost had a convulsion. Don't forget he was used to 1960s prices. The last round of our battle started when he asked why I was such a perfectionist about something so (fucking) trivial. I started out answering his questions calmly because I thought he was interested. But he didn't listen to my answers—he only wanted to reinforce his own opinion about the silliness of what I was doing. When I refused to agree, he got short-tempered and belligerent. He was a thug with a temper and a nasty tongue. I remembered all too well what we had done with both over the years. Why had my parents put up with me? "Ape of my heart" was what my father had called me. Gangrene was my name for this rude twerp.

When I was finished and the holy smell of fresh coffee smoked up out of the small white cup, Gee-Gee took a sip. "It's good, but too much trouble to make. Let me do the next one."

I left for the bathroom while he ground more beans. A nice moment passed when I took a quick look at him as I was leaving the room. He had a handful of the beans pressed to his nose, his eyes were closed and he was smiling. I remembered! I remembered at his age never admitting to liking anything too much because any high emotion expressed in capital letters was uncool. Back then the overriding first male commandment was Always Keep Thy Cool. Show approval only with a shrug or at most a two-inch smile. Give nothing away, especially your emotions. Let girls go ahead and show their love, but you pretend you can't be bothered. If you ever do anything nice for a girl either deny doing it or brush it off as no big deal. Commandment number two was never let anyone know you care too much about any-thing.

But seeing that secret smile on Gee-Gee's face when he thought no one was looking was the clue to what later saved him, or rather saved *me*. For years he thought life's goal was to be cool. One very important day he realized being curious was much better.

That's what I was thinking when I turned a corner and saw Pauline's bare ass again in the bathroom mirror. Rather, I saw some of her ass because she held her nightshirt hitched up with one hand, her panties pulled partway down with the other. Tee-tering awkwardly on tiptoe, she arched to look over her shoulder and see her back in the mirror's reflection.

She saw me in the mirror. "Frannie, come here! Come here!"

I looked at my shoes. "Pauline, put your nightshirt down."

"No, you have to look. You have to see this. You have to tell me you see it too and I'm not crazy."

I stepped forward, eyes still averted. "See what?"

"My tattoo. It's gone. Everything is gone, even the bandage covering it. How's that possible? I didn't touch anything. I just peeled the bandage off a little to look, but then I put it back really carefully. But now it's all gone. Everything."

"Let me see."

It was true. The other night when I'd seen her standing naked, there had been *that* feather, bright, swollen, and colorful tattooed at the base of her spine. Now there was nothing—only perfect teenage skin.

"This is exactly where it was." She touched the place and her skin dimpled. "Right here, but now it's gone. How's it possible, Frannie?"

I touched her to feel if there might be any tactile proof or indication that something had happened there. I slid my finger across her skin hoping for an abrasion, a cut, any roughness to prove how a large amount of multicolored ink injected under this girl's skin less than three days before had disappeared.

Nothing. Rather than stay there trying to explain to Pauline something I could not explain, I pushed her out of the bathroom, did my bit there, and returned to the kitchen. Earlier Gee-Gee had said that things were different outside today. Now I was beginning to know what he meant. I needed answers, and he was the only one around who might have some.

When I got to the kitchen, Pauline was pointing through her nightshirt to the spot on her back where the fugitive tattoo had been. As I walked in Gee-Gee said in an innocent voice, "So show me."

I slapped him on the back of the head. "Cut it out. Come with me, doofus. Pauline, we'll be back in five minutes."

As we were leaving he touched her shoulder and said, "Don't move, you. I'll be right back and I want to see where that tattoo was."

"Okay, Gee-Gee," she warbled.

"If you so much as touch Pauline—"

"Cool it. What are you, my chaperone? And why hit me in front of her like that? I didn't do nothin'!"

"No, but you're planning to. 'I want to see where your tattoo was.' Ha, what a terrible come-on line. You must have graduated from the Fred Flintstone School of Seduction, Gee-Gee. Sub-tle. Real sub-tle."

He shoved me. "Where are we going?"

"You said things were different today. What did you mean?"

"Open the front door and see for yourself, mud-brain."

The man who lives across the street from us drives a white Saturn. He always parks it directly in front of his house and gets pissed off if anyone else uses that space. When I opened my door

I saw a gleaming black Jaguar Mark VII parked there instead of the Saturn. A rare and expensive car when it was made back in the 1960s, today it is very rare. I know because my father owned one. His one great indulgence, Dad bought a used Jaguar that he loved even though it was an indisputable piece of shit, your classic lemon. From the moment he brought it home until he later sold it for a whopping loss, that car broke down almost continually, costing him untold money and trips to an expensive "foreign car" mechanic in a neighboring town. No one in our family but Dad liked that automobile. But he could never be convinced the previous owner had cheated him.

Anyway, that morning parked across the street from my house was a black Jaguar identical to the one my father had owned. A landslide of memories thundered down my head as I stared at it. But there were things to do, so I only pointed it out to Gee-Gee and said, "Looks just like Dad's Jag, huh?"

"It *is* Dad's Jag, pal. I saw him get out of it before."

Before I could answer, a forest-green Studebaker Avanti drove slowly by. There was a woman at the wheel. Although dark in there, from what I could make out of the driver she looked familiar. I hadn't seen an Avanti in twenty years. This one looked like it just came off a showroom floor.

Two kids slouched down the sidewalk toward us. Around sixteen, they had shoulder-length hair and their sloppy clothes were all tie-dyed. Hippies thirty years too late. In front of the house, both flashed us the peace sign and said, "Hey, McCabe!"

Both Gee-Gee and I said hey. Then we looked at each other. Then the hippies looked at each other but kept on truckin' along like stoned characters in a R. Crumb comic strip. Happy at the site of these living anachronisms, it took another moment for me to realize who they were. "Was that Eldritch and Benson?"

"No other, brother."

"How is it possible?"

Gee-Gee's voice was all sarcasm. "Well, let's think about this a minute. There's Dad's Jaguar across the street. Eldritch and Benson just passed. Andrea Schnitzler drove by in her Avanti—"

"That was Andrea?"

"No other, brother."

My father was dead. Andy Eldritch died thirty years ago in Vietnam. Andrea Schnitzler moved from Crane's View after our junior year in high school and was never heard from again. Her father owned a green Avanti. We used to talk about which we desired more—Andrea or her car.

"It's the sixties? We're back in the sixties?"

"Yup."

I thumbed toward the house. "But back inside, Pauline and Magda are—"

"Exactly, back *inside* the house. Out here it's the sixties. Welcome to my world." He hopped up and perched himself on the wooden railing that went around the porch.

Before I could say anything, a door slammed across the street. My father came down the walk toward his car. He was in his forties again and still had some hair left. He wore a beige summer suit I remember going with him to buy. He always wore a suit to work, always wore a tie. Usually it was one solid color—black or maroon. Stripes or crazy designs weren't him, ever. For his birthday I'd once given him a tie designed by Peter Max with Day-Glo-colored elephants and spaceships on it. He dutifully wore it to please me, but it was plain he was mortified. This man dressed like he didn't want to be seen, like the less the world noticed him the better. When I was Gee-Gee's age I loved my Dad but had little respect for him. We may have lived in the same house but not on the same planet.

This was in the sixties. We wore buttons on our jean jackets that announced (idiotically) never trust anyone over thirty. Or really anyone who had a regular job, wore a suit, carried a mortgage, believed in The System . . . I was never a hippie because I thrived on violence, selfishness, and intimidation. Pacifism would have deprived me of fun and opportunity. But I sure did like the drugs and free sex that were such an essential part of the movement. Which predictably made matters geometrically worse between Dad and me. Only later, after being to Vietnam and seeing people like Andy Eldritch get their heads blown off, did I realize how much of what my father said and lived was correct.

Gee-Gee shouted out, "Hey, Dad! Over here!" as the Jaguar passed. But the driver, a man I had buried with my own hands, didn't look our way, although it was definitely him—Dad. Alive again.

We watched the car until it was out of sight. I turned to the boy and asked, "What the hell's going on?"

"My guess is someone fucked up. Astopel or one of the people he's with."

"Meaning?"

He pulled out a pack of cigarettes and lit up. "Meaning someone needs Frannie McCabe to do something for them. You've got a one-week time limit to get it done. But for whatever reason they can't tell you what it is. So first they start off by giving you hints—the buried dog coming back, the feather, the empty Schiavo house . . ."

"And Pauline's tattoo, which was a picture of the feather. But now even that's disappeared. Wait a minute—she had the newspaper in her hand. She must have stepped out here this morning when things were changing!"

He blew one smoke ring and nodded. "Which exactly fits into what I'm thinking. None of those hints got you to do what they wanted. So I bet they got desperate and brought me here to help. If grown-up Frannie can't do it, bring in Frannie the kid. But that didn't work either so they pushed both of us to the future."

I took the cigarette from him, had a puff, handed it back. "Who're *they?*"

"I got no idea. That's the sixty-four-thousand-dollar question. But it almost doesn't matter. We know how powerful they are. They can mess around with time and parts of our life and other stuff. But so far they haven't been able to make you do what they want. So how powerful can they be? If they were God they'd just say, 'Do that!' But they don't because they can't."

"Maybe they're small gods," I mumbled, thinking out loud.

Stubbing out the cigarette on the bottom of his boot, he flicked the butt into Magda's mums. "Small gods, that's right. But look around, man—they really screwed up this time. You were in the future and were supposed to return to your time. Instead you came back to both yours *and* mine at the same time."

"Gee-Gee? Where are you?" Pauline's voice floated out of the house.

He slid off the railing and started for the door. I caught his arm and asked, "How did you figure this out?"

He undid my fingers. For the first time his voice became soft and vulnerable. "It's the best I could come up with. You think I might be right?"

"I think you probably are right."

He brightened and encouraged, leaned in close to tell me his next brainstorm. "And you know something else? I think they brought me back because whatever it is they need, you can't do it by yourself. You need me along because otherwise you're going to blow it."

"Why do I need you?" I asked too loudly.

The bad boy voice, attitude, everything slipped instantly back into place. "Because you been tamed, Chief McCabe. You dry your face with pretty pink towels and don't even realize it 'cause you're used to it. But me? I'm still the caveman version of Frannie McCabe. I kick ass and piss out the window. I swing on vines in the jungle. I hunt with a club on the fucking *veldt*."

I had to have a look. No matter how little time remained to figure out what "they" needed done, I had to call a short intermission and see Crane's View rewound thirty years. I went back into the house for a pair of pants and shoes. Gee-Gee and Pauline were in the kitchen talking and laughing. They ignored the old guy in the boxer shorts as he passed. It was a pleasure to see Pauline looking so happy, even if it was due to Mr. Hot Pants and his sleazy ways.

In a pair of jeans and a T-shirt I went out the door again and down the porch stairs. As I began walking toward town I stopped and looked across the street. Why was my father coming out of that house so early in the morning? I tried to think back to who had lived there three decades before but came up blank. I would have to ask Gee-Gee later.

What I did remember was that as he grew older, Dad had increasingly bad insomnia and used to go out walking or driving around at all hours. My mother and I grew used to his coming and going at the strangest times. Once Mom even said the Jaguar and the insomnia were the two things that made him different from every other Tom, Dick, and Harry. My father's name was Tom.

Walking toward town I remembered a terrible story she told. Right before they were married, they made a date one day to meet in New York under the big clock at Grand Central Station.

Mom was a few minutes early and waited eagerly for her fiancé to arrive. After some time she saw him walking toward her so she moved to greet him. It took many steps (her phrase) while staring straight at the guy to finally realize it wasn't Tom McCabe but a complete stranger. Shocked at her mistake and then relieved she hadn't made a fool of herself, she slunk back to her place under the clock.

A few minutes later she was *sure* she saw Tom. Again she moved out to say hello. But God forbid, it happened again— only a few less steps this time to recognize this second stranger who also looked so much like the love of her life wasn't him. She laughed when she told the story, but Mom never told it when my father was around. We both knew it was funny but sad as hell too. Because it was the truth—throw a stick at a bunch of commuters waiting at any Westchester County train station at seven any morning, or during coffee break in a Manhattan office building, and you would have hit six guys identical to my dad. That's why his showy car and insomnia pleased her so. They were his only distinguishing characteristics.

Walking along, I enjoyed seeing great old cars that in my time were like extinct animals—a Corvair and a MG-A parked on opposite sides of the street. Passing Al Salvato's old house, there was his father's dogshit-brown Ford Edsel. The car with automatic transmission buttons in the middle of the steering wheel. Salvato's father enjoyed seeing us kids sit in the Edsel when it was parked in their driveway. Al always encouraged me to sit in the driver's seat, but that was only because he was afraid. All my pals were afraid of me and for good reason. I loved fighting, stealing, lying, and hurting. My favorite sport was knocking people out, preferably with an iron bar or anything hard. I thrived on being everything your parents warned you against. I was the delinquent, the crud, the bad apple, and the criminal they knew would one day go to hell, to jail, to no good end. And I wore that charge proudly. I passed the little blue house where the assistant high school principal had lived. When he suspended me from school for stealing a teacher's book, I set his car on fire. Down the block in an ugly split-level had lived the head of the Crane's View branch of the Veterans of Foreign Wars. One night I broke into their meeting hall and stole every gun they had on display. Et cetera.

But was Gee-Gee right? Had things like Magda's pink towels and a happy life declawed me? More important, did I care? Did it matter if I had left him, *that* Frannie, behind years ago? What do you see when you look at old photos of yourself, besides bad haircuts and tasteless clothes you gave away to the Salvation Army twenty years ago? Was that strutting punk back at the house really me, or had we only lived in the same body, like an apartment, at different times?

A small dog trotted by, looking self-important and full of plans. "Jack!" Hearing its name, it stopped and checked me out. I slowly offered my hand, which it sniffed but no wagging tail followed. This was my friend Sam Bayer's dog. A pooch I had liked very much when it was alive. Which didn't stop me, however, from pissing on it and Johnny Petangles one day years ago while Jack sat on Johnny's lap, but that's another story.

Since I was no more than a stranger with an empty hand, Jack walked away. I realized he was probably going back to my house because that's where the Bayer family had lived when we were kids. I had always liked that house, and when it came on the market a few years ago I bought it. What would the dog find when it got back there? The Bayer family circa 1965, or teenagers Pauline and Gee-Gee still flirting over their cups of Italian coffee? What if it *was* the Bayer family? What if I was to follow the dog home and find that everything I knew as an adult had disappeared into thirty years ago? What if I had been sent permanently back to the world I had inhabited as a sullen, mean-hearted semipsychotic teenager?

"Shut up and get going," I said out loud because if I didn't nudge myself along, I could easily have stood there waiting for Godot or anyone to come along and tell me what I could do to get out of this fix.

Something did save me, something unexpected—my stomach. It let loose a grumble that sounded like a small lion's roar. I still hadn't eaten. The hunger that had been there since I awoke was becoming urgent. But that was all right because I was near Scrappy's Diner. I'd go there for a whopper breakfast, and while eating I could think some more about what to do. A plan. I finally had a plan and that made the rest of the walk to town pleasant.

Climbing the diner stairs, I looked down at the last one. I'd broken off a large piece of that step one night when I threw a sledgehammer at my then-girlfriend. Thank God it missed her by a mile but knocked off a large chunk of the slate step. Scrappy Kricheli, who was such a cheapskate that he would have recycled his farts if he could have made money on them, didn't replace it for two years. Luckily he never discovered who broke it. Untold numbers of customers tripped on it and threatened to sue him. I think the guy enjoyed watching them fall down. Ultimately someone did sue the cheap bastard and Scrappy lost a bundle.

There it was again under my adult foot, looking like someone had taken a jagged bite out of the stone. So they even had that detail down too, whoever they were. Walking into the diner I wondered how many times I was going to have to refer to them as "whoever they were."

Inside, the first thing I saw was Scrappy Kricheli sitting behind the cash register with a toothpick in his mouth, reading a copy of *The National Enquirer*. Today Scrappy looked to be in his forties. He would die of a stroke sitting in that same seat just after his sixtieth birthday.

Behind the counter, wearing a red waitress dress that barely contained her amazing body, was his daughter Alice. Both looked at me indifferently. I sat on the ninth stool facing the counter, the same place I always took here. That made me smile. When I looked up Alice was staring at me with a "What's your problem?" look in her eyes.

I wanted to say something but what? Instead I reached for a menu. As usual, three of them (turquoise with thick gold lettering) were stuck behind each jukebox selector down the counter. When I was finished ordering breakfast, I wanted to see which hot tunes Scrappy was stocking on his box that day.

"You want coffee?" Scrappy's family lived in the Bronx and they all spoke with a heavy accent. When Alice said the word it came out sounding like "coo-woffee."

"Yes please. And I'll have scrambled eggs, hash browns, and bacon with that."

She nodded while pouring me a cup of smoking brown coffee. Yes, brown. It also smelled like dishwater and I knew that's what it would taste like because that's what coffee always tasted like here. Scrappy's Diner was a greasy spoon that catered to cops and truckers and high school kids who ate anything so long as it was a hamburger and french fries. Ask for an espresso here and, like Gee-Gee, they would have thought that you were a soft ice creamer.

I was admiring Alice's behind when I sensed him first and then heard his soft voice next to me.

"Excuse me? I'm sorry to bother you, but I just gotta. Do you mind?"

I turned and there was my Dad two feet away gaping at me.

I rotated the seat around so as to give him my full face. "Yes?" Up that close I realized we were about the same age. My father and I were today both in our late forties. I got so many shivers going up and down my spine that it almost fell off.

"I don't know how to say this and it sounds crazy but . . . Would you mind if I sat down?"

"Please—have a seat." I pointed to the stool next to mine.

That suit. I remembered so well the navy blue suit he was wearing.

"I just walked in and when I saw you I couldn't believe it. Because I have a son, he's seventeen? And well, you look exactly like what I think he'll look like when he gets older. It's uncanny."

I poured sugar into the coffee. "He must be a handsome boy."

My father was a very uptight guy and incapable of saying anything funny. But he was a wonderful, appreciative audience. The moment those words were out of my mouth he laughed so hard he started coughing.

"Sit down before you collapse." I almost, *almost* ended that sentence with, "Dad."

He sat and I slid him my glass of water. He slurped a swallow and shook his head. "You took me off guard. I'm Tom McCabe."

When he put his hand out to shake I said, "Bill Clinton."

"Nice to meet you, Bill. But I can't help thinking I should call you Frannie. That's my son's name."

I nodded, smiled, sipped the coffee, and almost choked. "Sorry I can't help you there, Tom. I'm Bill, married to a woman named Hillary and we have a daughter named Chelsea."

He drank more water. "Yes, but the likeness is still amazing. Do you mind if I ask what you do?"

Looking down at the counter, I nodded mysteriously and said after a pause "Politics."

"*Really?*" He was impressed. My father loved politics. He often read to my mother from the *New York Times* about the bullshit going on in Washington. Invariably he had a comment on it. "That's just amazing." He chuckled and rubbed his face hard with both of his hands. "My son will be lucky if he stays out of jail. Frannie is a mess."

It felt like he'd stabbed me in the heart. But why? I *ran* the jail now! All these years later I knew I'd succeeded and that before he died, Tom McCabe had been very proud of me. I'd become the kind of upstanding citizen he'd always hoped for. So why did his remark hurt me? Simple: Because no matter how old you are, the relationship with your parents is like a dog being walked on one of those retractable leashes. The older we get, the further we wander. Years later we're so far away that we forget we're on their line. Predictably, though, we do reach the end, or they press the rewind button for some reason, and a second later we're back at their side with a bad case of whiplash and once again hoping for their approval. No matter how strong or distant we are, Mom and Dad still have that power over us and never lose it.

"Maybe you're being too hard on your kid, Tom." I couldn't look at him.

"You wouldn't say that if you knew my Frannie."

"But maybe as a kid I was enough like him to know what I'm saying."

"Bill—"

"Here you go." Alice put my plate down with a thump. "Anything else you'd like?"

The eggs' weak yellow contrasted the bark-brown bacon. Haute cuisine a la Scrappy.

I looked at her and smiled. She didn't smile back. "Anything wrong?"

"Yes, I asked for some hash browns with it."

"No you didn't."

My father piped right up. "Yes he did. I heard him order hash browns."

Alice frowned and put a hand on her hip that in no uncertain terms said, "You wanna make something of it?" I remembered when I was younger we used to call this girl who we all lusted after "the bitch with the tits." That is, once upon a time before the world became politically correct. But I also remembered something else about Alice that was far more important.

Waving away the potatoes I said, "It doesn't matter. They'll just make me fat. But do you mind if I ask you a question?"

Her hand didn't come off her hip. "That depends. What?"

"Do you know this man's son? Do you know Frannie Mc-Cabe?"

Her whole face slowly lifted into a great wide smile. "Sure I know Frannie. He's a nice kid."

"Nice? How? In what way?"

"Don't you know him? You kinda look like him." She checked Dad to see if he agreed.

"We were talking about him and wondered what other people who know him think."

"I told you—Frannie's nice." The brick was coming back into her voice. I felt like launching my scrambled eggs into her cleavage but couldn't because she had something I needed at the moment. If I pissed her off I wouldn't get it.

"So that's all, he's just nice?"

The young waitress squinted across the room to see what her old man was doing. He was still nose-deep in his toilet paper, which gave her the green light to keep talking to us.

"When Frannie comes in here with his friends he acts tough and plays the bigshot. But when he's alone he's sweet and sometimes does real nice things."

Bull's-eye! Come on, Alice—tell Tom the story.

It looked like she was going to leave it at that so I goaded her on. "Nice? Like what?"

"Like me and my boyfriend have troubles, right? Like we're not exactly Ozzie and Harriet. Well, one night in here we had this bad fight—" Again she looked up to see what the boss was doing. "And I really lost it. Luckily the place was pretty empty so when I started crying like a hysteric, nobody but Frannie really noticed. But he was so nice. He was here alone, like I said, and we talked for like two hours about it. He didn't have to do that. He wasn't playing Mr. Tough Guy or nothing, just being nice. And what he said was smart too. He said things about people, you know, in general which I thought about a lot after. Then the next day he came in? He gave me a copy of this record I said I like, *Concrete and Clay* that we both said we liked. He didn't have to do that either. He's okay, Frannie." She said that looking straight at Dad.

I gave a satisfied hum. "Good story, Alice. Could I have my hash browns now?"

The warmth in her eyes snapped shut like sprung mousetraps. "What did you say?"

Leaning forward, I spoke loud enough so that Scrappy could have heard even if he'd been dead. "I said I want the hash browns you haven't brought me yet, dear."

"Wutz da problem?" said a voice like an incoming bazooka shell lobbed at us from behind the cash register. It launched our waitress double time toward getting my potatoes.

In the meantime I began eating the unwholesome food in front of me and it tasted great. After a few mouthfuls, I pointed the fork at my father and said, "Don't always judge a thug by his cover, Tom. Sometime if you sneak into his room at night, you'll probably catch him reading under the blankets with a flashlight."

He grinned at the silliness of the image. Public Enemy Number One reading under a blanket? But something in it must have wrenched him too because the next moment he looked like he almost believed what I said might be possible.

We were quiet then but it didn't matter because it was enough to be with my old man again, drinking weak coffee at Scrappy's Diner. And morbid as it sounds, I appreciated him so much more knowing what life was like when he was gone. However long this lasted, this dream or nightmare or whatever it was, there was no other place on earth I wanted to be. Sitting at the counter in this dump, convincing my skeptical father his son had good stuff in him and would eventually prevail.

Although more people came and left, the diner stayed relatively quiet. We didn't talk much while I ate. Alice brought my potatoes but sailed them down the counter at me as if they were a Frisbee. Dad ordered a blueberry muffin and a glass of orange juice from another waitress. When they came he ate very quickly. I was pushing a last piece of toast around the bare plate to sop up whatever last tasties were left. When I was done I looked to the left and saw her coming toward us.

Her name was Miss Garretson. Victoria Garretson. She taught music at Crane's View Elementary School. Always a little hefty and rosy-cheeked, she had a 24/7 unflagging enthusiasm for her subject and job that invariably turned most of her students off from the force of its wind machine. For three years she had been my music teacher. You couldn't hate her because kids only hate teachers who literally hurt or diminish them in some ugly way. We just couldn't stand Miss Garretson's arm-waving, cheek-puffing glee as she conducted us through Stephen Foster songs, or tingled triangles, shook the maracas. Thanks to her, if I never hear or see another maraca in my life that'll be just fine. What did she look like? Like a youngish woman who sold bed sheets

in a department store and talked about them for too long. Like
a secretary in a failing real estate office. She looked like a picture
of someone's aunt.

"Tom! What on earth are you doing here this early?"

Tom? Miss Garretson knew my father? Knew him so well
that she called him by his first name?

"Vicki! Hey there! I should ask you the same question."

Vicki?

She simply stood with her hands held in front of her, staring
at me. She had big lips and wore too much dark lipstick. It took
me a few moments to realize she was either waiting to be introduced or for both of us to stand and show we were proper
gentlemen. Eventually Dad stood up but I didn't.

"Vicki Garretson, this is Bill Clinton."

I nodded and gave her a midrange smile. She gave me an
unsubtle once-over with her eyes. It sent me back forty years to
the days she used to give me another kind of visual once over:
to check if my seven-year-old zipper was open or if there was
breakfast jam on my Mickey Mouse Club T-shirt.

"Vicki is a teacher at our school."

"Music theory and choir." She said proudly and dishonestly.
The only theory this toots taught was take your finger out of
your nose, child, and read the notes. I loved it though—Miss
Garretson was lying to impress me.

"And what do you do, Mr. Clinton?"

"Bill's in politics," Dad chirped, full of admiration.

"How interesting. May I sit down?"

"Sure, of course, Vicki." He gestured to a stool where she
proceeded to rest her not-small can.

We talked for a while about nothing. Miss Vicki was boring
and self-involved. It was plain she liked the sound of her own
voice and the trivia of her life. But my mind was only half on

what was being said because I was mesmerized watching the body language going on between them. It didn't take long to read between their lines. When I had, I started grinning like a lunatic and I'm sure acting strange. Because it was clear Tom McCabe was parking his skin Pinto in Vicki's garage. Their conversation was full of in-jokes, references, secret sexy looks, and a casual history of things they'd done together. Not to mention the serious electricity bouncing back and forth between them. Dad was screwing my old music teacher! They spoke to each other in an intimate unguarded way because who was I? A stranger they met in a diner who neither would ever see again. Some guy who sits next to you on a plane or you strike up a conversation with in the station while you're both waiting for an overdue train. The only thing that gave me a little distinction was I looked like Tom's son who Vicki had had as a student years before.

After *that* egg hit the heated skillet of my mind and started sizzling, another dropped right after it. Why was Dad coming out of that house across the street earlier this morning? Did he have another lover over there that he visited on his insomnia rounds? The secret life of Thomas McCabe. My father—Mr. Drip Dry, cap-toed oxford shoes from Florsheim, Robert Hall suit, one whiskey before dinner and never more. Always paid his taxes on time, his dues, his respects. My mother couldn't pick him out of a crowd. But now here he was doing the Wa-watusi with my elementary music teacher and maybe others too. Yee ha! Isn't life wonderful? I wanted to take him in my arms and dance a jig. I've heard people say that one of the worst experiences of their life was discovering their parents betrayed each other. I was thrilled. I wanted to know details—every iota in Cinemascope and Dolby Surround. Crane's View was small; the walls had eyes and ears. Did this odd couple sneak off to the Holiday Inn in Amerling with a bottle of cheap champagne, a collection of Rod

McKuen love poetry, and a transistor radio that played Ravel's "Bolero"?

I wanted to hug Dad. Or at least pat him on the back, but in these circumstances that was out of the question. I loved what I had discovered and I loved him. Even more oddly it made me love my mother more for being so totally 180 degrees wrong about her beloved partner. Ma, he's a *hound!*

"Tom, I've got to hit the road. But it has been a pleasure." We stood up and shook hands. I remembered he didn't give a very strong shake and there it was again after all these years. Tears came to my eyes. Shaking hands with your father. If you love him, there's nothing greater. And I did love this man. Silently I thanked and blessed him for having had so much loving patience. For putting up with a terrible, frustrating son who had made him suffer and worry for almost twenty years. I wanted to say to Tom McCabe, I'm your kid, Frannie the thief, the good-for-nothing you should have hated but didn't because you're a good man. But I'm all right now. I survived, Dad, and I'm fine.

Instead I smiled at Victoria Garretson (Vicki—never in my life would I have addressed the woman by that name) and turned my back on Thomas McCabe for the last time.

"Bill? Excuse me, Bill?" I was on my way to the cash register when he called my name.

"Yeah, Tom?"

"Could I pay for your breakfast? I'd really like to do that."

"Why?" Here came my tears again. I looked at Scrappy.

"Because of what you said about my son. Because maybe you're right and I just worry too much. Because, I don't know, it's a nice morning and meeting you was an unexpected surprise."

I handed him the check. "You're a prince, Tom."

He made a strange face. I asked if anything was wrong.

"Frannie says that sometimes. 'You're a prince, Tom.' But when he says it he's always sarcastic."

I tried to sound cool and offhand. "Well, you said we looked alike. Pretend for a minute I am him and am saying it for real. You *are* a prince, Tom. Have a good life."

"And you too, Bill."

I couldn't resist. "Vote for me when I run for president."

He laughed and went back to his lover.

How does weird get weirder? I'll tell you. Feeling pleased and lifted by what had just taken place, I left the diner smiling and cheerfully blissed out. That lasted maybe five minutes. Out the door and turn left toward the heart of downtown Crane's View—all one block of it. Curious to know what would be there, I tried to remember what Main Street had looked like then. My town, thirty years ago. How much had they charged at the Embassy Movie Theater for a ticket? How much had a box of Goobers chocolate-covered peanuts cost at their candy counter? What were the names of the different candy they sold? Charleston Chew, Zagnut, Raisinets, Good & Plenty, Fifth Avenue . . . Retarded Johnny Petangles knew every one of their television ads and would recite them ad nauseum. The theater had been torn down two years ago and was replaced by a Blockbuster video store, which I thought was ironic. Trading the big screen for the little one. Let's keep walking down McCabe's memory lane. Back then the Embassy Theater stood next to Dan Pope's Bar and Grill. It was where we all had our first legal drinks the day we turned eighteen. In my mind I could still smell the place—boiled cabbage and cigarette smoke. Next to Pope's was—

A man wearing one of those helmets that had kebab'd my

brain. The learning helmets from my last days in Vienna. That's right—walking down Main Street in 1960-something Crane's View, New York, was a guy wearing a black full-head helmet. Slapping a hand over my mouth, I made some kind of strangled uh-oh sound. It felt like someone had spilled cold raw egg down my spine. What's more, there were people around but none of them paid any attention to him. Brian Lipson in his Crane's View varsity letter jacket stood talking to Monica Richardson in front of the town library. Helmet Head walked right past them. They both looked, no expressions changed, they went back to their conversation. My town is conservative and changeless. Always has been that way. Anything new is instantly noticed and discussed endlessly. Whether it was Crane's View today or thirty years ago, if someone walked down the street wearing one of those goddamned goofy helmets people would notice. Watching these two kids glance but turn away indifferently meant they were used to the sight. That gave me the big bad creeps. Everything was possible now—chaos reigned. Back when Lipson and I sat in geometry class and I cheated off his exam papers, I never saw any helmet heads go by. If I had, I sure as hell would have told the world about it.

I decided to follow this guy. See what happened when other townspeople caught sight of him. See if—

"Hey, Frannie!" said teenage Brian Lipson looking right at forty-seven-year-old me.

"Hello there, Frannie McCabe" echoed scrumptious Monica Richardson but with a smile dirty enough to melt any fellow's underpants.

If I had been a cartoon character at that moment you would have heard all around me the sound of car brakes screeching and seen smoke billow up from the bottoms of my shoes.

I stopped so abruptly that I really needed a moment to regain my balance. "You know me?"

They looked at each other. Lipson snickered. "Why wouldn't we, Frannie? I mean we sit next to each other in geometry class."

"Yeah but—"

Down the block I watched Helmet Head disappear around a corner. But I had to let him go because this was ground zero for the moment.

"You know me like this?"

Monica gave her head a cute little twist to the side like a dog hearing a harmonica for the first time. "Like what?"

"Like I am now, like this!" I pointed to my chest, my face, to McCabe almost fifty years old.

"Well sure, why wouldn't we?"

"I gotta go."

"Don't forget tomorrow night, Frannie; Dionne Warwick." Monica crooned, like a siren luring me to her rock. And then the memory *hit* me like a rock. Junior year in high school I had been trying every way I knew to get Monica Richardson to do the dirty deed with me. But she was cleverer than I was. Whenever I thought I had her, she slipped out of my paws. Finally I decided to give it the full-court press and spend serious money on her, which I proceeded to steal from my mother's purse over the course of three weeks. The plan was a Dionne Warwick concert in White Plains and a Surf'n' Turf dinner at Dick's Cabin restaurant. Everything went great until I took her home. I had never been to Monica's house. When she invited me in that night I thought for sure I had won. As we were going through the front door she said offhandedly, "My parents might be awake, but that's okay. They're cool. We'll just say hi and go up to my room."

They were sitting in the den. Mr. Richardson had a pipe in his mouth and held a newspaper in his free hand. Mrs. Richardson was knitting a yellow sweater. Both of them were stark naked. I was so stunned by the scene that I basically ran out the door back into the comforting night. After that, whenever I saw Monica at school I didn't know what to do. And I was so embarrassed by what I had seen that I never told a soul. That's why it was only years later I learned her parents were nudists.

Looking at her now and remembering that moment at her house, I didn't hear the car come up behind me and stop. Both of the kids looked over my shoulder and their mouths tightened.

"McCabe!"

The car was black with a single red light on top. That's all— no deck of high-speed blues that strobed and flitted nervously back and forth across your eyeballs as it approached. No metal grate between the front and back seats to keep the human animals at bay when you were bringing them in. No shotgun rack bolted to the dashboard because in the 1960s guns were either on the cop's hip or stashed safely in the trunk of the car. The trunk of a Chevrolet Biscayne because the Crane's View police department only used Chevrolets. The chief of police was brother-in-law to the only Chevy dealer in town.

"Pee-Pee!" I was so happy to see him that for a moment I forgot who I was/where I was/when I was, etcetera. I simply walked across the sidewalk and made to shake hands with patrolman Peter Bucci. This guy and I went back a long, long way. When I was young, Crane's View had three full-time cops and two part-time. Pee-Pee joined the force right after high school and for the first few years he was a bullying, lazy bum. But somehow he managed to meet and marry Camille, a great woman who turned him completely around and gave him a happy life. When I returned to town after Vietnam and became a cop, we got to be good friends. It was a hard blow to both the town and our police force when he died so unexpectedly three years ago of a stroke. But like my father a few minutes before, here was Pee-Pee again, looking young and strong and, best of all, alive.

He grabbed my face in an iron hand and squeezed my cheeks so hard I had to open my mouth. "Always the wiseguy aren't you, McCabe? You criminal piece of shit! Always got the mouth going. Well guess what, smartass? You're going to jail. Say bye-bye to your playmates and get in the goddamned car."

"Pee-Pee—"

He still held my mouth and squeezed harder. In a minute my teeth were going to see stars. "Don't call me that. Only my friends call me by my name and you're not even an acquaintance. You're shit on the bottom of my shoe, McCabe. You're green snot I hawk up on the street. Get in the car."

What must that have looked like: a squat twenty-five-year-old butterball in a badly fitting uniform squeezing the face of a tall middle-age man who could have knocked Patrolman Bucci into next week if he had chosen to.

But I didn't. Like the good law-abiding kid I'd never been, I just got into the patrol car and stared straight ahead. He came around to the driver's side and got in with a grunt and a slide around on the seat in search off a comfy spot for his fat ass.

"I'll call your dad for you, Frannie!" Brian yelled too loudly. I was only five feet away from him. I nodded.

"But what about Dionne Warwick, Frannie? What do I do if you're still in jail?"

"Tell your father to get dressed and take you."

"What?"

We drove away before I could elucidate.

———

"You're fucked now, McCabe. You're going to reform school for sure this time. It's the gray-bar hotel for you." Pee-Pee looked at me with a piranha grin.

I said nothing. The drive to the police station took five minutes. We could have walked there but I think he liked the whole routine of taking me in the proper way. When he pulled up in front of the building he turned off the engine but made no move to get out. When I reached for the door handle he barked, "I'll tell you when to move, McCabe."

I put my hand back in my lap. "What'd I do?"

"What did you *do?*" He was enjoying this little time before he had to bring me in. I belonged to him for a while. He was going to milk it for all he could. This was Pee-Pee Bucci pre-Camille; Pee-Pee at his worst.

I turned slowly and looked at my friend. Who would have liked nothing more at that moment than to punch me in the mouth. "Yes. Why are you bringing me in?"

To my surprise, his voice went furious. "Am I stupid? Do I look stupid to you, McCabe?"

Young me or Gee-Gee would have said something rude and gotten smacked. Not me—I bit my lower lip and shook my head. "No, sir."

"Sir is right, you little fuck-joint. I'll tell you what you did wrong. I'll tell you in one word—*Dalemwood.* Does that name sound familiar to your diseased brain? Painting the Dalemwood house?"

My junior year in high school a new family named Dalemwood moved to Crane's View. They had two children, both odd. George was a sophomore and his sister was a senior. Odd kids stick out whether they want to or not. But what really got my attention was hearing these people were Jehovah's Witnesses. That was all I needed. I knew absolutely nothing about the religion other than having heard somewhere that they didn't believe in doctors. They let their children die when they got sick rather than getting them medical treatment. Suddenly I had something new to hate. Decisive action was needed. I took a can of silver spray paint from our garage and wrote JEHOVAH'S WITNESSES FUCKER CHILD KILLERS in three-foot-high letters on the side of the Dalemwoods' freshly painted white house. George saw me, told his parents and I was brought in by the police. My father came to get me but was so fed up with me by then that he worked a deal with the chief of police. They left me in the jail cell overnight to think about my wicked behavior. It had no effect. When I got out the next day I went on my fateful date with Monica Richardson. The only thing that shook me up was seeing her parents naked.

But if that was what was about to happen to me now— seriously bad news. If I was locked in a jail cell for the next twenty-four hours it would be another of my seven days gone.

"Come on, house painter. Time for you to go to the basement."

That's where the cells were in the police station and it was a very bleak part of the building, believe me. Later when I became chief the first thing I did was hire an architect and a builder to make that space a lot more humane. But thirty years ago it was a big dark basement with three holding cells and three sixty-watt bulbs to light them.

Why was I reliving my seventeen-year-old life as a forty-seven-year-old? Or at least a day in that life? The last time I returned from my future to my now, everything had been correct. Why was it now so wrong? Now life inside my house was all right (excepting Gee-Gee) but one step onto the porch and it was thirty years ago. Why had I been returned to the day that Bucci put me in jail? I could have thought a lot about these matters sitting in a cell for twenty-four hours. But there was no time to fuck around. I had five days left—maybe only four. There was only one thing to do and I hated it.

Closing my eyes, I said, "Holes in the rain." The phrase that sent me back to my future.

Or so I thought.

When I opened them again, fully expecting to be back in post-millennium Vienna, I was still in the patrol car sitting next to Pee-Pee. The only difference being he wasn't moving and neither was anything else. It was like the time on the street with Astopel in Vienna when he told me I couldn't talk to George. Who, it later turned out, had transformed from a friend into a centuries-old dog sitting on a hotel bed.

"How do you row a boat on a wooden sea, Mr. McCabe?"

Despite all my confused looking around, I hadn't checked the backseat of the patrol car. Sitting there was the recently dead student Antonya Corando. Today she looked pretty good.

"What's happening here, Antonya?"

"You must answer my question first. It's important."

Resting an elbow on the seat I watched her in the rearview mirror. "I don't know how you'd row that boat. I haven't seen many wooden seas, to tell you the truth."

"Neither have I. It sounds like a Zen koan. I liked those when I was alive. They tickled your brain so much you wanted to scratch it. Like 'I am turning out the light. Where did it go?' "

I reached into Pee-Pee's shirt pocket, took out his cigarettes, and fired one up with the car lighter. "How do you row a boat on a wooden sea? Well, if the water was made of wood then you wouldn't need a boat. You could get out and walk to wherever you were going."

She smiled and had a beautiful mouth of big white teeth. "I

don't know if that's the answer, but it sounds like a good one to me."

"Why are you here, Antonya?"

"Astopel wanted to come but they wouldn't let him because he messed up too many things. He was the one who killed me. And made me start doing those notebooks with the drawings of you. I didn't know what I was doing when I made them—they just came to me and my hand acted like a slave. Astopel also sent the other you, the young one."

"Gee-Gee?"

"Yes."

She started giggling which only confused me more. "Why are you laughing, Antonya?"

"Because of all the 'ee ee's' in your life. There's Gee-Gee and Pee Pee Bucci . . ." She laughed out loud now and it was a great sound, a girlie sound, something that reminded you life could be your friend.

"And you know what? I wouldn't mind making wee-wee right now—too much coffee this morning. So that makes three ee ee's for me-ee."

That set her off more. I sat basking in her loud free laughter like it was Italian sunshine. Nothing moved. I smoked Pee-Pee's Pall Mall cigarette and looked around. Out my window a candy-apple-red Chevy El Camino driven by fat Russell Pratt stood waiting for an unchanging red traffic light to change to green. Which reminded me—

"Antonya, since you already died then you know: What comes after? Is there a God?"

Her new laughter came like a tidal wave. After it washed over everything she had to wipe her eyes. While looking at me in the rearview mirror her laughter came again. What the hell did I say?

"What the hell did I say? I only asked if there's a God."

"But you asked like you wanted to know what *time* it is. Like it's no big deal."

I rubbed the top of my head. "My life couldn't get any stranger than it is right now. The way things have been going, maybe *you're* God dressed up as the dead girl who drew pictures of my future. I don't know. There are no rules in my life anymore."

As if on cue, the door on my side of the car flew open and someone grabbed my shoulder. Hard.

"Get out. Come on, get out of the car!" Gee-Gee. He looked and sounded very scared.

"What's up? What's going on?"

"Just get out of the car and let's go."

"Hi, Gee-Gee!" Antonya called out from the backseat.

He gave her a quick eyeball while pulling on my shirt. "Get-the-fuck-out! Let's go."

Starting to move, I looked in the mirror one last time. Antonya was still smiling. It was bizarre because her facial expression was exactly the same as it had been moments before when she was laughing at me. It seemed like her face would stay like that forever.

"Bye, Frannie!"

"Run, motherfucker. Just run like a *fuck!*" Gee-Gee took off like a cheetah. My middle-aged legs and Marlboro lungs were no match for the kid. He'd blast down the street half a block then stop short to check on me. Gesturing me forward with a big wave of his arm, he'd call out hurry, move it, *come on.* I tried but it was no use. Trying to keep up with him, I knew my days of running hard on this earth were finished. Plus why the hell were we running anyway? Why had I followed him when I might have learned important things from Antonya if I'd stayed? Found out about death or God or who knows what else. But no, I just jumped up and ran after myself. Hey me, wait for me!

When I was on my third verge of collapse I gathered enough strength to call out to him, "Where are we going?"

"Home! We got to get home before they get here."

"Who's *they?*"

"Just move, man. Just move."

Back the way I'd come, past Scrappy's Diner, the high school, houses of old friends and enemies. Another dog I'd known stood sniffing a spot in someone's garden. Stopping to catch my breath I felt like I was running past my life, in reverse. But even that strange way, memories continued to fly through my mind like small objects flying around in a tornado. There was no way I could have stopped them.

But something stopped Gee-Gee. Twenty feet in front of me he was suddenly airborne and then fell in a strange way on his side. When he hit the ground it was so loud that I could hear the bounce of his bones on stone. Running up, I was only concerned for him. The boy—the boy—he fell so hard—is he all right?

"Don't worry about me—just get back to the house!" Holding his hip, he kept looking behind me, then all around, very scared. His face was so scared.

"Gee-Gee, what is it? What's happening?"

"Astopel screwed up everything. He interfered. He interfered with your life and shouldn't have. I only found that out for sure now. Before I thought it was okay he was around. It was okay to bring me here to be with you and send us both to the future, *but it wasn't.* He shouldn't have done any of it. Understand? He shouldn't have killed Antonya. He shouldn't have come and tried to influence you. But he did, and now you got to deal with the fallout. His shit comes down on *your* head if things go wrong, but that's the way it is. So get home, please. If you get to the house I think you'll be safe. If not, you're fucked, and that's a guarantee."

"What about Astopel?"

"He's gone. They got him. You won't see that jerkoff again."

"Who's they?"

He tried to stand up but couldn't. He fell back down and started cursing. I reached to help him but he swatted my hand away. "Take off! Get out, will you just go!" And suddenly he began to cry.

I knew where those tears came from. That very deep and secret address: seventeen-year-old McCabe Street. The place no one had ever been allowed to go or see or even know about. The place locked tight away behind walls of cruelty, bluff, and resentment. Where love too fragile or deformed lived, as well as an overbearing fear that everything you ever dreamed of doing would either stink or embarrass you or fail miserably.

I hesitated only an instant before pulling him up and onto my shoulder in a fireman's heave. He was so light. It almost made me laugh how light he was. He screamed at me to put him down, but that's not what he wanted. Not really. Besides, I was already moving toward the house and there was little he could do in that helpless position.

Walking seemed easier with him over my shoulder. I thought about that later and gargled on the symbolism—whenever you're willing to carry your self . . . that kind of baloney.

"Put me down!"

"Shut up and row."

"What?"

"How do you row a boat on a wooden sea?"

"Have you flipped out?"

"No. That's what Antonya asked me back in the car."

"Really? She asked that?"

Our words were broken up by my chugging along—Really? She-asked-that?

"Yes, right before you came. Was that really Antonya?"

"I don't know. Yeah, probably. Or maybe it was one of them. I'm not sure."

I stopped. I could feel his body heat against my cheek. "Who's them? Just tell me that. Who's *them*?"

"Aliens."

"Uh-oh."

"I second that emotion, brother."

At Home in the Electric chair

"Gee-Gee, would you like some more bacon?"

"Oh yes, ma'am, that would be great. It's delicious."

"Ma'am sounds like a cowboy movie. Call me Magda. We're practically related. Frannie, I cannot get over how alike you two look. He really could be your son. Are you sure you're telling me the truth about who he belongs to?" My wife gave me a shame-on-you smile while spearing three more fat slices of Canadian bacon onto Gee-Gee's plate. She handed it back. He immediately shoved a whole piece in his mouth and like a dog, barely chewed before swallowing it. That made seven pieces of bacon he had eaten in two breakfasts over the course of two hours. Was he a black hole? Where did all of the food go? Did he have several stomachs like a cow? Or cheek pouches like a chipmunk where he stored it for the winter? Had I really eaten that much when I was his age?

Magda and Pauline couldn't take their eyes off him, for different reasons obviously. Magda was totally delighted to have this mysterious husband-lookalike sitting at her breakfast table. In contrast, Pauline appeared sexually stunned, or like she had been hit on the head with a wooden mallet. Same difference. Outside our house, aliens waited to devour us, but inside it was full breakfast ahead. I didn't understand how Gee-Gee could suddenly be so calm about it.

The women were sitting in the living room waiting for us when we came in. I had a million questions to ask him but wasn't about to discuss little green men or dead Antonya with these two innocents around. They had cooked breakfast together, a real

181

rarity in our house and a sign of the specialness of the occasion. The only thing I could do was sit with a piled plate in front of me, trying to make eye contact with Gee-Gee to see if he'd communicate anything. The one time I caught his eye, he smiled and did a small cha-cha with his head. I assumed that meant I was to stay cool and wait for the right moment to talk. But he was the one who'd started the scare thing outside. Now he had my fearometer in the red zone (a new experience for me) while he enthusiastically wolfed down bacon and blueberry pancakes.

"Frannie, how come you never told me about Gee-Gee?" Magda looked beautiful that morning although she is not a beautiful woman. And so did Pauline. They were two great-looking women and I was lucky to be living in the same house with them. The house which at that very moment might have been surrounded by space invaders, according to Bacon Face across the table from me.

I looked at her and tried to think up a believable lie. "Because his parents are jerks and I wanted nothing to do with them. I never even really knew about him till recently. Hey, Gee-Gee, remember those *visitors* you talked about before?"

He didn't even look up from his plate. "Yeah?"

"Are they coming over here or not?"

"Dunno. Could I have some more syrup please?"

Magda prodded. "What visitors? Should we be making some more pancakes?"

Gee-Gee waved his fork around. "Some guys I know from out of town."

"Out of town?" I sputtered.

"Are they friends of yours?" Pauline's voice was jumping out of her throat—more Gee-Gees were coming to our house this morning? Yeah, baby!

"They're more just guys than friends, know what I mean?"

Magda looked at Pauline and simultaneously the two grew exactly the same smile—Boys Ahoy!

I was so frustrated by whatever stall tactic he was up to that I couldn't sit still any longer. For want of anything better to do I stood up and walked to the kitchen sink. Looking out the window there I was glad to see only the old rusty swing set and not ET. No flying saucers had landed in our backyard. Turning on the tap I watched silvery water rush into the sink and down the drain. When it had run a long time Magda asked what I was doing.

"Counting molecules." I didn't look up. I felt like I was going to pop.

"Frannie—"

"Nothing's wrong, Mag. Don't worry about me."

Gee-Gee said, "Look out the window, Uncle Frannie."

"I just did."

"Look harder. Look really carefully at the backyard."

I ignored him and kept looking at the water. I turned it off. Then on. Then off again.

Pauline piped up, "Are your friends here, Gee-Gee? Are they in the backyard?"

"Naah. There's just something out there I want Uncle Fran to see."

A chair scraped the floor. A moment later Pauline stood next to me. Putting a hand on my shoulder, she rested her chin on it. This girl was not a big displayer of affection. I assumed her cuddle was for Gee-Gee's benefit. I didn't care—it was nice having her there. I tipped my head till it leaned on hers. "You smell good."

"I do?"

"Yup. You smell like cloves and burning leaves."

"Wow, that's a cool description, Uncle Frannie. Cloves and burning leaves. I like that a lot."

I turned toward Gee-Gee. Surprisingly he was watching me with real admiration.

"I swear to God—I never heard anyone described like that."

"Well, kid, when you're older I'm sure you'll think up clever things like that to say too."

He grinned while a small continent of yellow and spotted blue pancake dropped off his fork.

Pauline pinched my side. "That was mean. He was only paying you a compliment."

"You're right. Put your head back on my shoulder—it feels good."

After she did I turned back to the window to see if there was anything in the yard that I'd missed.

"The swings are gone."

"What swings?" Pauline said dreamily.

"Keep watchin', Unc."

As I said, our house once belonged to the family of my boyhood friend Samuel Bayer. In the corner of *their* yard a kid's swing set sat dying all through our childhood. The people I bought the house from had had the swings removed. But because the world outside this morning was the 1960s, the backyard view had included the rusted, brown, sad-looking flying machine that had sent any number of kids into almost-orbit for a few happy years. The view *had* included those swings. I knew because when I looked at the yard minutes before, I saw them and instantly remembered. Now they were gone.

"Gee-Gee, what's up?"

"Keep looking. Keep watching."

"Holy shit!"

"What's the matter, Frannie?" Magda asked.

"Could I have some more pancakes, Aunt Magda?"

"Of course, honey. You all right, Frannie?"

"Yeah."

Out in the yard the swings were not the only things that were gone. As I watched, the entire landscape changed. It wasn't fast like a time-lapse film. But if you watched one spot for a few seconds you'd see it and everything around it change to one degree or another. Behind where the swings had stood was a wooden fence. A few months earlier, Johnny Petangles and I spent a Sunday afternoon painting it brick red. In the 1960s when the Bayer family lived in the house the fence was white. And it had been that white a few minutes ago when the swings stood in front of it. Now there were no swings and the fence was green. Then it gradually became navy blue, white again, a different shade of green, then brick red. When I bought the house the fence was white. I had painted it that second shade of green and only recently covered it with the red.

While the colors of the fence changed, so did objects on or near it. The first thing I noticed was a large orange flowerpot hung from the top of the fence on a piece of what looked like black coat hanger. Orange pot on white fence. The pot disappeared and so did the white behind it. A silver BMX bicycle leaning against the fence appeared and disappeared. Just like that. A brown basketball here and gone. A yellow Big Wheels tricycle. Blip blip blip—they all showed for a few seconds and then were gone.

Barely able to tear my eyes from this fast-forward show, I asked Pauline if she could see it too.

"See what?"

"All the things changing out there." I pointed. "Do you see

the silver bicycle? Look! Now it's gone."

Pauline gave me a push. "*What* bicycle? What are you talking about?"

I looked at Gee-Gee. Shaking his head, he mouthed the words, "She can't see."

Frustrated, I went back to the view. "Holy shit!"

"Why do you keep saying that, Frannie?"

Because for maybe five seconds I saw my old pal Sam Bayer, age maybe fifteen, standing completely naked in front of the fence and pissing on the lawn. I think I laughed and gasped but had no time to think about it because it was gone too fast. Up popped one of those cheapo, above-the-ground swimming pools. Two kids frolicked in it until they frolicked right back into invisibility.

"This is stupid," Pauline said and stomped out.

A little later the telephone rang. Magda went to get it. I heard her leave the room. Gee-Gee came up behind me. "They're bringing the world out there back to now. But they got to do it slow, like a diver coming up after he's been too deep in the water. That's why I said before we had to get back here. They needed to fix everything that Astopel fucked up."

"Nothing can happen to us while we're in here?"

He shook his head.

"But if we were out there—"

"We'd probably get zapped. That's what happened to Pauline's tattoo, I guess."

The history of my backyard in a few minutes. The thirty-year history of Crane's View in a few minutes. What was going on all over town while we looked out the window? I would have given anything to be standing in the middle of Main Street at that moment.

"So they're bringing the world out there back up to date? To today?"

"Right."

"They meaning aliens?"

"Right."

"Then how come you're still here?"

"Because I guess you need me, Uncle Frannie."

"Like I need a brain tumor."

A large basset hound walked into sight, collapsed on the ground, started to scratch itself, and disappeared. Voila "The Judge." The dog belonged to the Van Gelder family who owned the house before me. It was infamous around town for repeatedly being hit by both cars and trucks and surviving. It also smelled like a swamp, but I suppose that's the price a dog pays for having nine lives. The Judge died peacefully of old age in its bed a month before the Van Gelders moved out.

As the fence turned red again, my vintage Briggs and Stratton lawnmower reappeared nearby. Magda came back into the room holding the portable phone. "It's George. He says it's important."

I took the phone. Gee-Gee went back to the table and began eating again. "George. What's up?"

"The dog is back, Frannie. It's sitting next to me right now."

"Your dog? Chuck?"

"Chuck and Old Vertue. They're sitting side by side in my living room. And it's alive, Frannie. Old Vertue's alive again. And there's someone here you've got to meet. He's the one who brought them. He says he knows you. His name is Floon?"

"Caz de Floon," Floon called out in the background.

"I'm coming over." I pressed the disconnect button on the phone and let my arm drop to my side.

"Are Gee-Gee's friends here?" my beautiful wife asked.

"Yeah. One's over at George's house. We're going over to get him."

The boy and I stood on the safe side of the front door. I had my hand on the doorknob. He had his on a cinnamon bun Magda warmed for him to eat on the way.

"Do you think it's safe to go outside again?"

He bit into the bun and spoke through the gooey sweet. "We waited long enough to see if anything else would change after your fence turned red again. I'd say we're back to today. Hey, there's really only one way to find out—"

Eyes squinted almost shut I opened the door. I guess I figured if either the end of the world or creatures from outer space were waiting outside, by closing my eyes I could make them go away.

Things looked all right. I slowly let out my breath. What exactly had Crane's View, or at least my street, looked like a day ago? The white Saturn was parked in front of the house across the street and not my dad's Jaguar. Check. The jumbo hammock hung on the porch next door. Check. My motorcycle stood like a mean yellow toad in the driveway. Check. All systems go.

Taking it slow and uneasy, I walked down the porch steps. When I reached the last one, a step away from terror firma, something grabbed my shoulder and jerked me backward.

"Watch out!"

I was so shook up that I forgot to have a heart attack. Gee-Gee was laughing like a fool. I grabbed his hand on my shoulder and made to flip him. He shouted, "No, don't! My knee! My knee's screwed up!"

"Why the hell did you do that? Do you think that's funny?"

"Take it easy. It was a joke. Lighten up, man."

"Lighten up with all this shit going on? Are you stupid?"

"No, Uncle Frannie, I'm you."

"Well then, behave yourself like me. I mean . . . Look, let's just go and stop fucking around, okay?"

Pauline called out from our bedroom window. "Bye, Gee-Gee. See you in a little while!" She was leaning on the sill and it did *not* look like she was wearing a shirt.

"Bye, Pauline! I'll be back soon."

"Let's take the Ducati. It'll be faster."

He shook his head. "Bad idea, boss. Better to walk there."

"Why?"

"Look around. Look at the trees and the street. They're still working on bringing things back to now, can't you see? We're not up to full power here yet."

After a heavy rain the world is different for a while. Rich new smells are everyplace, grass shines, leaves on the trees too as they drip water and change color. Branches fly up, things steam, animals reemerge from their hiding places shaking off water with furious twitches . . . all small things but *all* things. When I did what Gee-Gee said and once again paid close attention to the things around me, I saw he was right—it would not be a good idea to drive to George's house. Because like the world after a rainstorm, everything around me seemed to be changing too. The aliens *had* brought us back up to the correct time, true, but they weren't finished yet and that was now evident.

First I noticed a long black crack on a neighbor's white wall disappearing like a piece of spaghetti being slowly sucked into someone's mouth. Next a pair of large whitewashed rocks reappeared at the beginning of another neighbor's path. A moment ago they weren't there. I knew these details—I saw them every day but they had been so trivial, so much a part of the humdrum ho-hum of life that I'd never given them a second thought. Only now did they matter when they were literally being re-placed in a world I once thought I knew. What's that famous line? "God is in the details." Amen.

If we'd driven to George's on my motorcycle there was a hell of a good chance we might have fallen into a pothole along the way that was there twenty years ago but some forgetful alien forgot to fill.

Despite the urgent need to get over to George's fast, we kept looking around.

"Look at the telephone wires."

"And that tree—the white birch. It was half the size a minute ago."

"Those curtains just changed."

These changes went on and on, almost all of it small stuff, but happening everywhere to what seemed like everything.

"It's kind of cool. These guys really take care of business."

"Gee-Gee, have you seen them yet? I mean actually seen them?"

He hesitated, seemed to be weighing what he could and couldn't say. "Yeah, I have. That's why I got you out of that car and back to your house—they told me to. And they also told me to keep my mouth shut if you asked questions. After seeing what they can do here, I sure as shit ain't gonna disobey them."

Halfway to George's house, Little Me had a new revelation. "I gotta tell you something. I don't think you're gonna like it."

I'd been wondering what would happen if you sprayed an alien in the face (faces?) with Mace. A bird flew across our path and disappeared. Tweet tweet—gone. "Jesus, did you see that bird?"

"Yeah. Listen, I think I got the hots for Pauline."

Silence. Keep moving.

"Did you hear me?"

Silence.

"Come on, man, say something."

I pointed a stiff finger at him. "The more one knows, the more silent he becomes."

He whistled. "That's a neat line. Did you just make it up?"

"No, Gee-Gee, I read it. And at one point in your life you're going to realize books are cool and being a tough guy is stupid. Believe it or not, you'll give up one for the other. It'll save you a lot of time."

"Say another one. Quote something else you read." He was serious. His face was wonder and please-tell-me.

"Here's one that fits this moment—'I go to search a great perhaps.' The dying words of a famous writer."

Hands in his pockets and limping, he matched his pace to mine. "Meaning, like, no one knows what death is but I'm going to find out?"

"Or I'm dying and there's nothing else I *can* do but go find out."

"Yeah, that's what I meant."

"Take a right here."

"I can't believe you're friends with George Dalemwood. That guy was a spaz."

"And you were a sadistic dumb fuck bully. Why haven't you asked me anything, Gee-Gee? I'm the future standing right next to you, but you haven't asked even one question about what my life is like. Why? Aren't you interested? Don't you have any curiosity at all?"

It was his turn to be silent. We walked on. Twice he turned to look at me but said nothing for a long time.

"They told me something. They said I shouldn't tell you because it might affect the way you act. But I want to tell you."

"So tell. What is it?"

"They said after this is over, if it works and things go right, I'll be sent back to my time and never know this happened. I'll live my life I guess the way you already did and then end up . . . like you." He made an unhappy, impatient face.

"And you hate that?"

"Staying in Crane's View? Marrying Magda Ostrova? I was hoping for maybe more."

"Like white shag rugs in an LA bachelor's pad? There *is* more. First you'll go to Vietnam—"

He cringed. "No thanks."

"Be quiet and listen to your life, especially if you're going to forget it later. After Vietnam you'll travel around the world. Then you'll go to a terrific college in Minnesota."

"Minnesota! Are you crazy? It's a thousand degrees below zero out there in the winter."

"Sssh. You'll meet your first wife there. She's a beautiful woman who'll make a lot of money in Hollywood as a producer. A good chunk of that dough will go to you because you'll come up with the idea for a so-so TV show that becomes very successful. You'll get a taste of the LA life but it will mess you up. When you've had enough of it, you'll come back here and be really happy for the first time in your life. Not a bad résumé. So don't worry, there's lots of things for you to look forward to, believe me."

"Isn't that your dog up there?"

Seeing Old Vertue alive again, hobbling down the street toward us wasn't a shock. Stranger things had been happening. The shock came from the fact the dog was much larger than the last time I'd seen it. Larger than *any* time I'd seen it. And something else—it was moving too fast. How could it walk so quickly on only three and a half legs?

"That ugly mutt don't look friendly and it *don't* look happy to see you, Uncle Fran. I think it's time we stepped up our fucking pace."

Vertue came straight at us, tail wagging too quickly, head down. It was moving too damned fast. A lot faster than a moment ago. Without checking for oncoming traffic, Gee-Gee stepped out into the street and limped/sprinted for the other side. I hesitated because part of me wanted to get close up to that dog. The last time I'd seen it, Floon said Old Vertue was George. What was it now? Why was it so much bigger? It began to growl. It was very loud.

"Get out of there. It's gonna bite you." Gee-Gee had wisely climbed onto the roof of a shiny black Audi TT. I wanted to laugh—whoever owned that nice little car was going to be *tres* pissed off. But I didn't laugh because when I looked again at the dog, it had halved the distance between us and was coming on fast.

When in Rome do as the Romans do. I was near an old Volkswagen bus. Very high off the ground, the vehicle was virtually Vertue-proof if I could only get my ass onto its roof. But it is very goddamned hard to climb onto the roof of an old Volkswagen bus. There is no place to put your feet, no handholds to grab onto, or—

Clock clock. That's the sound the dog's jaws made as they snapped their way through the air toward me. Hadn't I saved this dumb animal's life before it died? And given it an agreeable burial two times, even though it refused to stay buried? What kind of gratitude was that? Back from the dead (again), this beast was trying to attack me. And could it jump! As I scrambled up onto the roof of the VW, the three-legged monster was leaping like a pro basketball player at my ass.

Gee-Gee stood on the roof of one car while I stood on

another. I was higher, his car was classier. I preferred the altitude. Meanwhile the dog looked up at me like I was the anchovy pizza he'd ordered from Domino's.

Frustrated, I threw up my hands. "Now what are we supposed to do?"

Vertue growled and *clock-clocked* some more.

"Let's call the police," Wiseguy said from atop his Audi and honked a big fat fake laugh.

That inspired Old Vertue and it started jumping again. Ominously it got higher and higher.

"He gonna bite you, boss. Them teeth of his go *clack-clack*. You'd better think of something fast!"

"Like what?"

"Why don't you kill it? You got your gun?"

"You can't kill this dog. It's already died twice since we met."

He wouldn't stop grinning. "Maybe the third time you'll be lucky."

"Gee-Gee, help me out here, willya? Don't be a dick all day long. Helping me is helping you, don't forget."

"What's its name?"

"Old Vertue."

"What kind of dog's name is that? Vertue! Come here, boy."

It didn't move. Now it was drooling. Drooling and *clock-clocking*. Its gums were showing. They were shiny bubble-gum pink.

"We gotta get out of here. We gotta get over to George's and see what's going on with him."

"Well, we ain't got no stilts or a hot air balloon." He put a hand in a shading position over his eyes and pretended to look toward the horizon. "No ladder in sight. It'd be nice if there was a tightrope, but there isn't."

"Thank you for sharing that with me."

"You're welcome. You know what that dog is? It's a FUDD."

"Meaning what?"

"Meaning most dogs are just *dogs*, you know? Not one thing special about them. Dog-dogs. But that one—that is a fucked-up-dog-dog. A FUDD."

Clock-clock. I looked down into Vertue's bubble-gum mouth and noticed for the first time that its teeth were tobacco-brown. Pink and brown and shiny. *Clock-clock.*

"Hey, Uncle Fran?"

"What?"

"I got an idea."

Straightening up, I looked over at him. "Yes?"

"We fly."

"That's brilliant. In what?"

"We just fly, man. Everything else around here is crazy, right? So why can't we fly? Why can't we just jump off these roofs and fly? Who says it won't happen if we try?"

"Gravity."

"Look, *Zio*, since I got here, this whole experience has been like sitting in the electric chair getting five thousand volts through your head all day long. It's fried everything, but 'specially our brains. So I say we just try it and see what happens. We've seen again and again anything's possible. So now we start using that. This whole world around us is nuts: Me and you are here together at the same time. Isn't that crazy? We've been time traveling, that dead dog rose up out of its grave, birds disappear in plain sight . . . so why not flying? We want to fly, we try. If it don't work, then it don't work. Why not?"

It was me talking, but a me I hadn't known for years. The me who believed in why not? Rather than no way/no can do/ no exit or no, period. Middle-aged, this-idea-is-ridiculous me started to get up and leave the movie theater. But the rest of me shouted at him to sit down again and watch the rest of the show. Why not fly? *Why not?*

"Let's go."

Gee-Gee grinned like a carved pumpkin and clapped twice. "Excellent." Without a moment's hesitation he extended his arms as if he was preparing to dive into water. Then he jumped off the roof of the Audi. And hit the ground a second later, hollering in pain. Old Vertue looked at him and back up at me just as I sailed off the roof of the VW bus—and flew.

Could I describe to you what it was like to fly? Certainly. Will I? Never in a million years. I will tell you this: Remember the best kiss you ever had? How suddenly all sound, all life, all matter, disappeared? How for that holy while all of your life was only on your lips? That's some of what it was like in that first moment when I realized it was happening, that it was real.

I flew like an astronaut on the moon. The leap off the car roof drifted me forward at ten feet off the ground. Slowly I began to descend. Touching down, I pushed off with one foot and at once rose up again up up and back to the height I'd been. Floating gently forward, flying . . . sort of.

"You bastard, you bastard, you're up there! It's working! I told you. I knew it would work. Get the hell away from me, dog!"

Gee-Gee ran along below me, waving his hands excitedly. For a few moments my shadow actually passed over him and the earth, as if I were a plane casting its dark image down. He shouted when Old Vertue ran into his leg and made him stumble. As I was coming down for my first landing, fifty feet from where I'd started, I saw the kid kick the dog full-bang in the head. Orange cowboy boot on dog skull. Result? A draw. Vertue stopped and gave his head a couple of shakes. Which made enough time for me to push off again and for Gee-Gee to start running.

"You got it now, Uncle. You are definitely airborne!"

I turned halfway around in midair to check on Vertue. It was keeping its distance now but wasn't about to give up the pursuit. As I was turning again, I felt my body beginning to descend. But now I had the hang of it and when I touched ground it was only that—a touch. A push off and I was gone again.

"This is the coolest thing! You-are-*flying*."

"It's your doing, Gee-Gee. If you hadn't said try, it wouldn't have happened."

"Yeah, yeah, I know. Who cares how it happened? It's just so damned cool."

This was true, but what was I going to do when I got to George's house, besides land? Floon was there, George was there, Vertue was here trying to bite me while I tried to get there—

As if he'd read my mind, down below Gee-Gee asked, "What are we going to do when we get to Dalemwood's house?"

Before I could answer, I saw a jogger coming down the sidewalk toward us. I started to smile. How would he react to: a man floating overhead like a kite, a boy in thirty-year-old clothes and a bad Elvis haircut following below, and a dog with three legs, one eye, and a jaw going *clock-clock*? This was going to be rich.

He wore one of those ridiculous-looking jogging suits that no real jogger ever wears. It was a traffic jam of clashing colors, all of them made more ugly because they were on top of each other. What kind of person would actually buy clothes like that? I'd seen something like it recently, but didn't register or remember that until later. When I had a chance to think about the details.

I was so tickled that another person was seeing the three of us now like this. I was so eager to see how they'd react to the absurdity of our picture. I didn't pay attention to anything but the fact a man in a jogging suit was coming toward us and what would he think?

He shot the boy first. The man shot Gee-Gee.

Ten feet from us he casually reached into his pink-on-yellow pocket and pulled out a pistol. I saw it, realized it, took the image into my slow brain. Ten feet above the ground I was powerless to do anything. I shouted out, "A gun! Look out, he has a gun."

Blank-faced, Caz de Floon pointed it at Gee-Gee and shot him in the throat, the chest, the stomach. The boy collapsed, dead before he hit the sidewalk. Floon then turned to Old Vertue and shot it in the head.

Bang Bang Bang.

The Rat's Potato

I'm sure I fell from the sky the moment Gee-Gee's heart stopped beating. Because when he died, so did the "why not?" and renewed sense of wonder in me he had brought back. I don't remember dropping or even hitting the ground because I was so horrified by what had happened.

Arms at his sides, Caz de Floon, looking exactly the same as I'd seen him in Vienna, stared indifferently at the two bodies. I got off the ground but stayed where I was. I had no idea what he'd do next. Maybe I was going to die too.

"*Why?* Why did you do it, Floon?"

"I don't like the future I was living in, Frannie. I want a different one. Had to make a few changes. You had an unfair advantage with those two. I know who the boy was." He pointed at the dead dog. "Now it will be different."

"How did you get back here?"

"I don't know. Divine intervention—*manus e nubibus*—a hand from the clouds; I suppose someone powerful wants me here. In the same way they brought the boy back to help you."

I remembered Gee-Gee saying Astopel had made a mistake by manipulating my life. Because the result of that was anything could happen now. Floon here with a gun in his hand was immediate proof of it.

"But you killed them. What for? Do you know who they were?"

"Yes, George explained. I just told you why, McCabe. You'd better be careful too. From now on I'm going to be as close to you as the vein in your neck. Or the eye in your socket."

199

"Or the shit passing through my bowel. Put the gun down and we can get *real* close to each other, Caz. I'll French kiss you while I cut out your brain." A bad thought blinked on in my head. "Where is George?"

Floon furrowed his brow and sounded surprised. "At his house. Where else would he be?"

"You didn't hurt him?"

"No, I need him. I need George and you but I don't know in what way yet. When I do, we'll see. But don't follow me now because I'll shoot you in an instant. You know that?"

"Yes, Floon, I know that."

"But don't be sad when I'm gone because I'll always be nearby. I'll check in with you now and then." His voice was cheerful, all good will.

"What are you going to do?"

"Make some changes here now. So that life will be even nicer than it was."

"For you. Not for anyone else."

"Of course for me, Frannie. At least I'm honest about it."

Disgusted, I turned away and looked toward Gee-Gee to show myself again that it had really happened. But his body was gone and so was the dog's.

Floon must have seen my expression change; aiming the gun at me, he looked over and grew a smile. "Ah, that's considerate; they saved you the trouble of having to explain two bodies to your colleagues on the police force."

"Who's doing all this, Floon? Do you know? Did you meet Astopel?"

"No. But my guess is God. And if it is, I like this deity. Maybe He decided to get involved again. Wouldn't that be interesting? I'll see you." He waved with his gun hand and walked away.

When he was gone I stood-stock still without a single idea of what to do next. The obvious move was to go to George's and see if he was okay. Instead I stared at the spot on the sidewalk where the boy and the dog had lain when I last saw them.

I'd always thought of him as the boy, the pain in the ass, or Gee-Gee. Now that he was gone I remembered, if that was the right word, he was me. And he was dead. That me was gone and I was sure there were more things he still had to show me but never would now.

I was back in my own time with too many bits and pieces of information to swallow but no time to digest them. I assumed that there were only a few days left to complete whatever it was I was supposed to accomplish. I couldn't return to the future for another look because my magical phrase "holes in the rain" hadn't worked when I tried it. I couldn't ask Astopel or Gee-Gee any questions. And the cherry on top of this shit was Floon had gotten loose in the here and now and would surely snarl things up more. All I could hope was that he would stay out of my way while I tried to figure out what had to be done.

"Hey, Frannie, how come that guy was pointing a gun at you?"

Johnny Petangles is a tall fat man. He exists on Burger King Whoppers and candy. Physically he has looked the same for fifteen years. There are people in our town who think he's some kind of idiot savant. I don't know about that. The only unusual thing Johnny ever did that shows he's more than mildly retarded is memorize decades of television commercials—not a talent that's going to get you a job at the White House or Microsoft. Since his mother died a few years ago I've kept an eye on him. That isn't hard because so do most of the people in Crane's View. We feed him when he'll accept it, give him odd jobs that pay for his hamburgers and Arnold Schwarzenegger video rentals, and feel very protective toward him. He may not be a rocket scientist, but he's our Johnny and that's enough. I have always tried to be as straight with him as I can.

"Where are you coming from?"

"Mrs. Darnell made me French toast for breakfast. That was nice, wasn't it?"

"Yes, it is. He's a bad man, Johnny. His name is Floon. If you see him around town steer clear of the guy."

"Shouldn't you arrest him? He held you at gunpoint." Johnny loved movie phrases like that—"held you at gunpoint." Sometimes when he was watching a video he would hear one and laboriously write it down in block letters on a pad he kept near the television.

"Maybe later. Not right now."

"Okay. But would you like me to follow him? I could give you a secret report on where he goes."

My first instinct was to say forget it, but I stopped. What could it hurt? Even if Floon noticed him, he only had to speak with Johnny for two minutes to realize his mental Swiss Army knife didn't have all its blades. Who would feel threatened by a fat retarded guy reciting Isuzu commercials? What Floon didn't know was that once John got his mind set on something he was as tenacious as a mongoose battling a cobra. Why not let him follow Floon?

"You'd have to be very careful, Johnny. If he saw you he might make big trouble."

Johnny never smiles but he did then. "I know how to hide. I used to hide from my mother and she could never find me anywhere. I'll just hide from him too. You watch—I bet you ten thousand billion dollars that guy will never see me."

"Then go ahead, John, but be careful. Don't do anything stupid."

"I am a little stupid, Frannie, but not about hiding." He was still smiling when he left.

So much had already happened in the last few hours that it was a wonder I arrived at George's house on two feet rather than crawling on all fours. My brain felt like it had been fucked by demons on acid and then tossed away. On reaching his street I began walking faster and faster without realizing it. I wanted to see my friend George Dalemwood, someone real and solid and an important part of the life only a few days before I had taken so blithely for granted.

I climbed the porch steps and pressed his doorbell. No one answered but that was no big deal. Even when he was home George frequently ignored a ringing telephone or doorbell. "They want me," he was apt to say, "but I probably don't want them, no matter who it is." And he would go on doing what he was doing, oblivious to whatever bell scolded him in the background.

Before trying again, I walked back down a few steps and looked toward the roof. That's where he'd been sitting the other day when my world was a simpler place, a world where "only" dead dogs reappeared and not versions of myself past present and future. Who then subsequently got shot by Dutch industrialists from the twenty-first century.

My friend wasn't sitting on the roof today, but while looking up there I heard something that calmed my heart. George is an exceptionally good guitarist. He's such an original that that shouldn't be surprising but it is. And knowing his strange and conservative tastes, you'd expect him to play only classical music but not so. He ranges from Mozart to the Beatles to damned good imitations of Michael Hedges or Manitas de Plata. He spends at least two hours a day practicing on the most beautiful guitar I have ever seen. I would love that instrument just for its name alone—a very rare model called a "Church Door." When I asked

George how much it cost, he swallowed hard and got colloquial on me, saying only "five figures." It's worth it. He handles that wooden box like he's making love to it and maybe he is.

While standing with one foot on a porch step, I heard him playing Scott Joplin's darkly beautiful waltz "Bethena," a great favorite of his. Relieved, I blew air out through my lips in a quiet raspberry. Hearing it told me he was all right. George played certain pieces depending on his moods. I knew "Bethena" was performed when he was stuck in his work and trying to figure his way out. Normally that tune meant stay away if you happened into his neighborhood; George was definitely not fun to be around when he was thinking something through. But today he would have to put that Church Door down and listen to me.

The music flowed out from behind the house. I made my way around to the back. George sat on the ground in the middle of his yard with the guitar propped between his knees. An unopened Mars chocolate bar lay on the ground nearby. Music filled the air. Chuck the dachshund sat nearby staring at his master like the dog staring at the old victrola on the RCA label.

"George?"

He looked at me and smiled. The dog ran over to say hello. I bent down and lifted him up. He attacked my face with hot fast licks. "Glad to see you back, Chucky."

George heard that and his smile widened. "Did you see Caz de Floon? Did he find you?"

"Yes, Caz found me." I walked over with the dog in my arms. He was a bundle of warm squirm and kisses all the way. George played two chords—a resolve—and stopped.

"When did Chuck reappear?"

"Caz brought him. He said he was a gift for me. So many things have happened, Frannie."

"I know."

It was a while before he spoke again. "And you talked to Floon?"

"Yes indeedy."

"What did you think of him?" The question was unbelievable. George never, ever asked what you thought of people because he didn't care. Neither about people nor what you thought of them. As a rule of thumb, George Dalemwood's interest in humanity was akin to the average man's interest in feldspar.

I sat down nearby and put Chuck on the ground. He walked over to George, curled confidently against his side, and closed his eyes. "What did I think of Floon? I already met him."

George opened the candy bar. "Me too."

That straightened me up fast. "You knew Floon before?"

"According to him I did." He bit into the candy. A thin thread of tan caramel looped down and around his thumb. He licked it off. "He said we'd met back when he was in his thirties."

"Why?"

"Supposedly he hired me to write the instructions for something he had invented."

A warm gust of wind picked up the brown and red candy wrapper and flipped it into the air. I snatched it. "Do you remember him?"

"You have the fastest hands I've ever seen, Frannie. You really should play an instrument."

"Is that true about his hiring you, George?"

"No, I never saw him before. And even though my memory is perfect, I checked my records to be sure. I never worked for anyone by the name of Floon."

"So he's lying?"

"He doesn't think so. Plus he knew exactly who I was and specific aspects of my life. He cited both old and obscure examples of my work."

"He could have found that out anywhere."

"True, but the breadth of his knowledge was impressive. He must have done a lot of homework to find out what he knew. Would you like some of my Mars bar?"

"No. So Floon appears at your door with Chuck in,.tow as a little gift to gain your confidence. Tells you who he is and says you once worked for him. Did you know he was carrying a gun?"

"Everyone has guns today, Frannie. You said that yourself. That's why you gave me one." He offered a piece of chocolate to the dog, who sniffed it but turned away. George shrugged and popped the chunk into his own mouth.

"I've gotta tell you what's been happening to me. It'll make you see things differently."

"Maybe, but Floon's already told me a lot."

That pissed me off and my voice reflected it. "Floon's not me, George. He wasn't where I was. What did he say?"

For the next half hour I told him my news and he told me his. To my great surprise and dismay, everything Floon told George was true, down to the last particulars. No exaggeration, no shading of the actual details of the story so that he would come out looking better. He answered all of George's questions and then—get this—they tried to figure out what was happening to me and why.

"That's rich! You two compared notes about me?"

"Yes."

"George, Floon's fucking Citizen Kane with a gun. He just shot Gee-Gee and before he shot the dog I think he did something bad to it so it became like a killer dog. You're gonna take this man's opinion as valid?"

"I didn't say that, Frannie. I said we discussed you."

Fuming, I began pulling up handfuls of innocent grass and throwing them at innocent Chuck. They were too light to reach the dog, but he woke up and kept an eye on me just in case. "Yeah, well, tell me, what did you two *prognosticators* decide?"

Inside his house the phone rang. Suspiciously, George got right up to answer it. That wasn't like him. I had the feeling he did it only to stall for time. He came hurrying back out with a portable telephone extended in front of him stiff-armed. "Frannie, it's Pauline. Magda just collapsed. She's unconscious."

In the minutes it took for George to drive me home, the ambulance I'd called from his place was already coming down the other end of our street, siren howling. As both vehicles pulled up to the house, the word "oxymoron" came to mind. Because that is exactly what this situation was—an oxymoron. Knowing what was wrong with my wife before a doctor even felt her pulse was of inestimable advantage. The irony being that I also knew her situation was hopeless. Take your time, Doctor. Because no matter what you do it's useless—she'll be dead of a big fat juicy brain tumor within a year. I hadn't told George about it. I'd only said that as an old man in Vienna I was married to Susan Ginnety. In typical Dalemwood fashion he'd paused, taken another bite of his chocolate bar and said flatly, "That's interesting."

The four of us raced into the house. When we slammed the door, Pauline called out to us from the kitchen. Magda lay on the floor in there next to the table. Pauline had put a pillow from the couch under her head and lined up her arms and legs so that she looked at peace lying there but also too much like a corpse. I immediately looked to see if she had "posturing"— where limbs twist inward as if the muscles have drawn too tight on the bones—which is one of the worst possible signs of brain tumor.

The paramedics dropped to their knees and began their grim work. I had been a medic in Vietnam and knew what they were doing. That didn't make it any easier to watch. I kept wanting to say things like "Check the Babinski" and "Is she decerebrated?" but I didn't because they didn't need anyone interfering in their very strict by-the-book procedures. Nevertheless I watched what they did very carefully.

One hand across her mouth, Pauline gestured me over urgently with the other. George saw this and moved over behind the paramedics, as far away from us as possible.

"What happened, Pauline?"

"We were talking and her eyes, like, suddenly rolled up in her head? Then she slid out of the chair. Like she was playing some kind of creepy joke? Mom's been having bad headaches for the last couple of weeks. She didn't tell you because she didn't want you to worry."

I'm sure she was surprised by my reaction. Probably expecting me to go ballistic because I hadn't been told about these headaches, I only looked long at my shoes and nodded.

"I haven't noticed it, but has she acted strange recently? Like has she been grouchy or irrational suddenly out of the blue?"

A paramedic pushed up one of Magda's eyelids and shone a small yellow flashlight into her eye. He said, "She doesn't have any posturing but there's some kind of unequal pupil response here."

I couldn't hold back any longer. There was no point to it. "Look for signs of a brain tumor." Both men looked up at me. "She had blurred vision and bad headaches recently."

"She never said anything about blurred vision to me, Frannie."

I squeezed Pauline's arm to be still.

"Do you know the signs, Chief McCabe?"

"I was a medic in the service. Do a pinprick test. See her response to pain."

One of the guys looked at his partner. "Christ, I never had a brain tumor case before."

Pauline stepped in close. I could smell her breath when she spoke. "Frannie, do you really think Mom has a brain tumor?"

Lie to the girl? Tell her the truth? "I don't know, sweetheart. But I want them to check that possibility. Let's wait to hear what these guys say. It's always better to be safe in things like this. Let them check everything." I moved Pauline so that she stood in front of me. I wrapped my arms around her and held on for dear life. She stood stiff and trembling. I felt so helpless and goddamned sorry for her. I didn't want to know what I knew about her mother's condition.

She moaned. "Mom. Oh, Mom."

For the first time in my life, my heart began beating erratically. It was the damnedest feeling. Suddenly it appeared to climb higher in my chest until it felt like it was at the bottom of my throat. Then it began pounding hard and unevenly. My cheeks got hot. I touched one of them and my fingers felt very cold on it. My heart pounded throughout the whole top of my chest. It went fast fast fast, then seemed to stop, go fast a couple more times, stop . . . The normal rhythm was gone, it was on its own, lurching around inside me like a car being parallel parked at high speed.

While still holding Pauline, I slid my hand down from my cheek to the left side of my chest. I thought I could feel my heart banging away under there. It was strange, fascinating and terrible.

"Frannie, are you okay?" George was watching me.

"Yeah, I'm just having some arrhythmia. It makes sense though with the stress."

"What is that, Frannie? What's wrong with you?" Pauline's voice was afraid. Was I going to collapse next?

"It means my heart's beating fast. No big deal. Don't worry."

"You want me to check you out?" One of the men asked with the blood pressure cuff in his hand. I shook my head.

They moved Magda onto a stretcher and hooked up an IV. Pauline kept asking what they were doing at each step and she deserved to know. I carefully described the procedures, keeping my voice cool and confident throughout. That tone appeared to work because her shoulders unhunched and after a while she stopped nervously licking her lips every few seconds.

"We're all done here. You want to ride with us to the hospital?"

"Pauline, you want to go with your Mom? George can drive me over in his car." I thought I needed about ten minutes alone with George to talk about things. Just enough time to ride from our house to the Crane's View hospital.

Her body immediately clenched again. "No! I'm not riding in any ambulance. I don't want to, Frannie. Please let me go with George. Please!"

Her quick, unexpected hysteria threw us all off. Bypassing the diplomatic, I took her firmly by the shoulders and gave her a shake. "Stop! It's okay, honey, everything is okay. You don't have to go in the ambulance. Go with George and I'll ride with Mom to the hospital. Just take it easy, huh? Everything will be okay."

While I spoke she looked at the floor, nodding the whole time like her head was mounted on a spring. "Good. Okay. I'll come right behind you. But, Frannie? Should I ask the doctors about my tattoo when I get there? Do you think I should ask them why my tattoo disappeared?"

What the hell was she talking about? When it eventually dawned on me I had to squint to focus my mind on what had happened to her earlier that morning. "Uh, no. We'll do that another time. Right now let's take care of Magda."

"Okay. But Frannie, will Gee-Gee be at the hospital?"

"I—I don't know, honey. I don't really know where Gee-Gee is right now."

Magda regained consciousness riding in the ambulance. I had been talking to one of the paramedics who, it turned out, went to the high school the other day to pick up Antonya Corando's body. I hadn't recognized him.

"Frannie?" My wife's voice sounded very soft and sexy. It sounded perversely like she was inviting me to bed. She might even have said my name more than once but her voice was so faint that it would have been easy to miss.

"Magda, how are you? How do you feel? Are you a little foggy?" I touched her temple and stroked it. Her face felt cold in some places, hot in others.

She blinked a few times, never taking her glassy eyes off me. Once she opened her mouth a long few moments but said nothing. Her tongue looked gray and shriveled. Moving her head slowly from side to side, she looked blankly around, apparently trying to figure out where she was.

"You fainted, Mag. We're in an ambulance going to the hospital because I want them to check you out. I've called Dr. Zakrides and he'll be waiting for us there."

She gently touched the back of my hand with one of her fingers. Slowly she stroked it once and then her finger fell away. She said something I couldn't hear. I leaned in closer. From whatever well of small energy she had left, she was able to say it again: "Knock-knock." I gasped back a short harsh breath. It was our password and secret smile. Whenever one of us felt sexy and wanted to make love, we went to the other and said that,

"Knock-knock." Not so much knocking on their "door" as meaning the silly line kids have used forever to begin a million bad jokes. I don't know where it came from or remember which of us had been the first to use it in that context. But the *only* time we said the phrase to each other was for that reason alone.

Hearing those wonderful words now in this place and circumstance was hideous. But how amazing that that's what she wanted to say to me now, when fear would own most people. Every couple has an intimate, secret vocabulary only they speak or understand. Until this moment, "knock-knock" had been our great lewd line that meant only one thing to us and was therefore irresistible. My heart galloped up a hill in my chest. My wife was going away.

One side of Magda's mouth twitched. Seeing it, I was afraid she was about to have a seizure, a common side effect of brain tumor. But almost worse, that twitch turned into a smile. How did she do it? Everything was gone in her but here she was smiling. When she tried to speak again she had no energy. All she could do was mouth the words but that was enough. She said slowly, "I like you." Another major phrase from our shared history; the result of an old wound that had healed into a joke, then a joy and a memory neither of us would forget.

A decade before we married, Magda and I had a very serious affair. But it blew up and rained pieces of pain down on both of us for a long time. It was all my fault. By some miracle years later Magda was able to forgive my great shittiness and give me another chance. Nonetheless both of us had scars up and down our souls from what had happened. So when we started dating again, we moved around each other like two dogs that have never met before—slow approach, backs stiff, tails up, circling. Even when we knew we were onto something big here, neither of us dared say any of the magic words or phrases that seal the deal.

This went on for more than a while. Eventually after one particularly nice time together, I screwed up my courage. Looking her square in the eye I said, "I like you." Of course I wanted to say the big stuff but was worried she might bolt if she heard "I love you" or "I want you" or "you're the one for me." Instead, she smiled like someone who's come home and said, "I wish we were in a bedroom now."

I smiled back. "Why?"

"Because I could be naked for you there. No, nude. No, naked. Well, *both* and then you could choose."

Naturally both "I like you" and "naked and nude" became honorary members of our relationship. Both were frequently used as assurances, reminders, and surefire alternatives to "I love you."

"Don't talk anymore now, Mag. Save your strength."

What strength? Nothing in her expression or the broken lie of her body indicated there was more than a firefly's light of strength left in her. Whatever owned Magda now had taken full charge and it was definitely not her friend. She closed her eyes and I took her hand. She gave a weak squeeze and stopped.

I closed my eyes and summoned the image I always did in situations like this: A close-up of a finger going into the white number holes of an old black 1940s style telephone. Finger in a hole—turn the wheel—do it again, dial the number digit by slow digit. It rings on the other end. Two, three times, sometimes four but eventually it is picked up. A nondescript male voice asks calmly, "Yes?" I've got him—it's God. He always picks up and always listens. It does not mean He'll do what I ask. He only listens and that's our deal.

This time I silently said, please leave Magda out of this. If it's her fate to go like this, then okay. But if it's because of something I did, break *my* skull. Break me—but please leave her alone. That's all. I thanked him and the hand in my mental image put down the phone. No pleading or elaboration because He knows what I'm talking about. And He's got a lot of phones to answer.

"All right."

My eyes were closed but I jumped hearing the voice. Magda's limp hand lay in mine. God had just said all right. I opened my eyes and was looking directly at the paramedic. He smiled and said it again in that unmistakable voice, "All right, Mr. McCabe. We can save your wife."

Magda's eyes were still closed. Her face looked very peaceful. I knew no matter where she "was" she wouldn't be able to hear us now.

"We can do what you ask, sir. But you'll have to do something for us."

"Are you God?" I asked timidly.

His smile grew warmer. "No, but we are more powerful than human beings. We can facilitate making certain things happen that you can't." He had a big face—big eyes, wide nose, his teeth were the color of a yellowed meerschaum pipe. Altogether there was nothing special about his face. You wouldn't notice or remember it. Maybe that was the point.

"A small group of us, including Astopel, came to Earth—"

"So you *are* aliens? Gee-Gee was right?"

"Yes." He wouldn't' stop smiling. Now he looked encouraging, like a teacher pleased with a student's answer to a hard question.

"There are aliens on Earth that look like people? This is a goddamned 1950s movie! Why aren't we in black and white? We've already got the Pod People here!"

I was too loud. He put a finger to his lips to shush me. "If you saw what we really looked like you would be alarmed. We didn't come here to cause a disturbance. That was Astopel's doing and why all these odd things have been happening to you."

He reached into his breast pocket and pulled out a blue and white pack of gum. The writing on it was Cyrillic. The black plastic identity tag on that pocket said his name was Barry— Barry the alien.

"How long have you been here, uh, Barry?"

"A little over a month. Some of us longer, like the Schiavos. As you know the two of them have been here for years. Would you like a piece of Russian gum? It's very good."

I was dumbstruck. "The Schiavos are—Geraldine Schiavo is an *alien*? Oh-my-God! That's why they disappeared like that and their house . . . Holy Christ! Why are you here?"

Leaning forward he spoke to the driver. "Nate, stop the car. We need some time before we get to the hospital."

"What about my wife?"

"She'll be all right until we get there. Don't worry. This is all within our control, Mr. McCabe. Or rather this *part* is. Please trust me."

What else could I do? More importantly what parts *weren't* under their control?

The ambulance slowed and made a hard right turn. Looking out the window, I saw that we were in the parking lot of the Grand Union market. Ironic because it was where Old Vertue had been found that first day.

"Are we stopping here on purpose? Is this place some sort of symbolic gesture?"

Barry Smiles lost the smile and looking bewildered said no; we simply needed a place to talk and this was convenient. I didn't believe him. Sliding the door open, he gestured for me to climb out. After checking Magda again, I did. The parking lot was mostly empty, but the heat of the day was already beginning to rise from the pocked, cracked pavement. A lone white seagull drifted above us. Seeing something on the ground, it dropped for a landing. The flattened body of a mouse turned out to be the object of the bird's affection. It pecked away at what was left of the squashed blob.

Barry watched this and said, "There are no animals where we come from. They're extraordinary things. You're very lucky to have them. That's what I like most on Earth—the animals."

"What's your favorite?"

The gull rose into the air carrying the flattened carcass in its beak. Landing on top of a streetlamp, it looked around like it didn't know how it got there.

Barry chuckled, his head bent way back to watch the bird. "That's an interesting question. Off the top of my head I would have to say either the dodo bird or the stegosaurus, although you couldn't really call that an animal, could you?"

"No, most people would call it a dinosaur. And the dodo is extinct." I waited for a response but he just kept looking up.

The seagull lifted lazily off its high perch and flew away with the ugly prize still in its beak.

"Yes, both creatures are extinct."

"But you've *seen* them alive since you've been here, right Barry? Or am I wrong?"

My Favorite Martian shook his head. "No, you're not wrong. The first thing we did when we got here was review mankind's history. We visited every era of the earth's past to familiarize ourselves with where humanity came from."

I said, "Hmm." Standing in the Grand Union parking lot listening to a man from outer space say he'd paid a quick visit to the Jurassic period to see dinosaurs while on a field trip for his class in Mankind 101. What else could I say but *Hmm?*

"It must be hard to believe. Would you like some proof, Mr. McCabe?"

"Barry, once again you read my mind."

"Fair enough. What can I show you? What would you like to see? A stegosaurus?"

"No, it would crack the pavement and then I'd have to arrest both of you for disturbing the peace. But are you serious? Can you call up whatever I want to see?"

"Yes, so long as it exists now or once existed. Nothing beyond that. As I said, we do have limitations here."

"I know exactly what I want to see."

"Really, a stegosaurus would be no problem—"

"Skip it, Barry. You want to prove who you are? I'll tell you what I want to see."

After I did, his shoulders sagged like they were silently complaining "that's *all*?" But he straightened them again and said okay, follow him. He started across the parking lot toward the market.

"And Magda will be all right?"

"Trust me."

"You keep saying that. Why should I?"

"In five minutes you'll know why. For five minutes trust that nothing will happen to your wife." His big open face was one you immediately felt you could trust. It was perfect for the job he'd been sent to do. You saw this guy and right off you thought, I'm in good hands. Maybe I'm in trouble, but here's a man who looks like he can help me. I'll trust him.

Too bad he happened to be an alien.

He stopped walking, turned, and looked straight at me.

Paranoia hit like a glass of ice water thrown in my face. "What? What's the matter?"

"Something . . ." Touching his chin with three fingers he slid them back and forth as if feeling for stubble. "Something just happened here in town that matters. I don't know what, but something important. I just felt it. It's very strong. It'll affect things."

"What?"

He raised a hand palm up. "I don't know *what,* but something . . . something very definitely just happened in your town that will affect things."

"That doesn't help, Barry. If you traveled from your planet to here and can change time, conjure dinosaurs, bring back the dead, how come you can't . . . Where *are* you from anyway?"

"It would be best to express it mathematically but since that's not your bent, I'll say it phonetically: Hratz-Potayo."

"Rat's Potato?" My gut jumped in before my head had time to think. A laugh burst out of me that sounded like a bizarre jungle bird: Yee-Yee-Yee—Caw—caw—caw. "You come from *Rat's Potato?*" I couldn't stop laughing. The name sounded so stupid—like a name from a TV show for little kids. Plus I'd reached some kind of breaking point—after all that had gone on it finally felt as if my brain was melting like hot candle wax.

While I laughed, Barry lifted his thumb and began carefully writing with it in the air. As his finger moved, two words in thick white script appeared between us and hung there unmoving: HRATZ-POTAYO.

"Where is that?"

"Seen from the earth, it is behind the Crab Nebula."

"Oh. So you rats are behind the crab. That's fitting." I pointed to the lunatic words hanging in the air, as vivid as if they were on fire. "If it were any other time, seeing this would impress the hell out of me, Barry. But you know what I feel now? Tired. That's all—just fucking tired. Let's go see if you're telling the truth." Now I was the one who started walking toward the market, although I didn't know if that was where we were supposed to end up.

He hesitated. Reaching toward the white words he plucked them out of the air and put them into his pocket. "It wouldn't be good for others to see them there like that. Who knows what they would think."

"Whatever. Are we going to the market?"

"Yes. That's what I want to show you."

Long before we got there I knew it was all true. I knew Barry was the real thing. I knew that what I was about to see was impossible but I was about to see it anyway. I could already hear it. And what I heard half the Western world would have killed to hear.

I stopped and looked at the spaceman, but he continued walking. Without looking at me he said, "Come on, you'll hear better inside."

At the market door he pushed it in. The moment the door swung open the music swelled louder and I almost swooned. I could not believe it. You know instantly when music is live compared to when it's on the radio or piped-in shit. The hyped-up rawness of it, the blare and bang of too much guitar, feedback wrecking your ears, or drums that push everything else out. This was live and it was them because now I could see them. And Jesus Christ, it was *them*.

I had been in the market a thousand times before but it had never looked like this. Where aisles of food should have been, a stage had been erected in the middle of the store. But nothing professional—you must understand that. Nothing glitzy, expensive or in any way appropriate to who was standing on that stage playing live for only Barry and me.

They saw us moving toward them but none reacted with any

more than a shrug or a hi-how-you-doin' head tip. Their indifference said we weren't interrupting them because they were used to an audience.

John Lennon sat on the edge of the small stage with a cigarette stuck in the corner of his mouth and a Rickenbacker guitar held in his hands. He looked twenty-five years old, maybe thirty—they all did. Paul stood on the other side of the stage next to George. The two of them were weaving back and forth, goofing around. Paul sang a lousy version of "I Feel Fine." At the back of the stage Ringo played the drums with eyes closed. "I Feel Fine" performed badly by the Beatles. Bad or not, it was *the boys* and their sound was un-fucking-mistakable.

That's what I'd asked Barry to show me and that's what this was a quarter of a century after the group broke up, twenty years after Lennon was murdered. For a million reasons I wanted to reach out and touch Lennon's arm—only that—but I resisted the impulse. He must have sensed my excitement and awe though because he abruptly looked up and wiggled his eyebrows at me. It was the same expression he'd used in a famous TV interview he'd done after the group broke up. I had the interview on tape at home. I owned way too much Beatles memorabilia because no one, not no one, was ever better than they were.

The Beatles, dead and alive, together again in the Crane's View supermarket. Brought to you courtesy of the Rat's Potato, that friendly little planet just behind the Crab Nebula.

On finishing their own song, the Fab Four started playing the Zombies' "She's Not There," another of my all-time favorites. It was a song in the McCabe Music Hall of Fame. But why were the Beatles doing a cover version of *this* one? None of them said anything—just moved from one tune right into the other. I sighed like a boy who's fallen in love. I didn't even have to die to know that this was heaven.

As they reached my favorite part of that eerie song, Barry leaned over and asked, "Would you like to talk about it now or wait till the music is over?"

"Now. If I stay any longer I'm never going to leave here."

"Okay, let's go back outside. As long as we remain here they'll continue to play."

The Beatles were playing only for us? I moaned, "Is that true?"

"Yes. They're what you wanted, Mr. McCabe, so as long as you stick around here they'll just keep playing your favorite songs."

"Help!" My head flooded with songs I loved—"For No One," "Concrete and Clay," "Walk Away Renee" . . . They would have played those too, I suppose. Just like I said—Heaven. "Come on, let's get out of here." On the way out I didn't risk looking back over my shoulder. But for the first time in my life I understood why Lot's wife wasn't so stupid after all.

Out in the sunglare and heat of the parking lot things were quiet again. All the music was gone and I knew that meant *they* were gone too. If we'd walked back into the store it would only be a market again—cans of Campbell's soup and frozen legs of lamb back where they belonged, having replaced my dream come true for a little while.

Two crummy green lawn chairs had appeared in the middle of the parking lot. On the seats were large Styrofoam cups. Somewhere nearby a person was cutting wood with a chainsaw. The sound and smell were on the air. A dog barked wildly— row-row-row—like it was going out of its mind. A car pulled into the lot. Someone whistled high and long. A woman's voice said hello. The day was wide-awake and coming downstairs for breakfast.

Coffee was in the Styrofoam cups, perfectly sugared and boiling hot—exactly the way I liked it. None of this surprised me. Barry was turning out to be a dandy host. Sitting on the edge of the cheap metal chair, I stared across the lot at the parked ambulance. For a few moments my heart started doing its weird jumpy dance again. Blowing on the steaming drink, I took it in quick careful sips. "All right, story time. Tell me what's going on."

"You're not very religious are you, Mr. McCabe?"

"No, but I believe He's there. I believe that wholeheartedly."

"Oh, He is, but not in the way you think. Would you like me to describe this situation in detail or would you prefer an abridged version?" He was grinning when he said it but I knew he was serious.

"Abridged, Barry. I've got Attention Deficit Disorder. I have a hard time sitting still very long."

"All right. Then the best way for me to begin is to quote something to you from the Bible:

> Thus the heavens and the earth were finished, and all the host of them. And on the seventh day God ended His work which He had made; and He rested on the seventh day from all His work which He had made.

"That is a passage from Genesis, a word that literally means 'a coming into existence.' That first chapter of your Bible is where the creation of the universe is accounted for."

"The universe? I thought Genesis only described the creation of life on earth."

"Noooo, it is the origin of everything—every planet, every being, every cell. But mankind is predictably vain and sees things only in relation to itself. The most important thing in all this is that symbolic seventh day when God had finished His work and rested. That day is now coming to an end, Mr. McCabe. We're getting very close to the time when He will wake again, so to speak, and reassert his authority."

"Armageddon?" I asked the question in the same tone I once asked an emergency room doctor, "Am I dying?" after having been shot and feeling myself dropping steep into a coma.

This pleased Barry. Having just heard *the* most frightening word in the human vocabulary, he chuckled and took a long swallow of coffee. "No, it's much more interesting than that. For a moment think of God as a bear."

I looked up at two slivers of silvery airplanes moving in different directions across the cobalt blue sky drawing separate vapor trails behind them. "Did you say a bear?"

"Yes I did. Imagine God as a bear that, having created the heavens and the earth, went into hibernation for billions and billions of years. Time out of mind."

The idea was so mind-boggling that for the moment all I could do was feebly repeat him. "Billions of years."

"Right, but before He went to sleep He arranged to be awakened at a certain point."

I blew up. "Get the hell out of here! You're saying God-the-bear made all this and then went to sleep? But not before arranging a *wake-up call*? Who did He call, the front desk?"

Barry put his cup between his thighs and brushed off his hands. His till-that-moment-friendly voice turned red-hot sarcastic. "You can be snide and waste time or you can listen, Mr. McCabe. I would advise listening because it may end up saving your wife's life."

"Go on."

"The brilliance of God's plan was in its simplicity." He stretched out both arms and opened them as if showing the size of a big fish he'd caught. "He created it all—the universe, you, me . . . everything, and then rested. But before He did, He arranged to be awakened by all of us, in concert. He gave us the knowledge and the resources as well as sufficient time to develop individually so that *together* we could build a device that would awaken God when it was time."

"The whole universe works together to make a machine that will wake God up?"

"Overly simplified, yes. And He's been remarkably benevolent about it, considering the differences between species. Every civilization has developed at its own speed. Some are eons further along than others are, but that makes no difference. When it comes to this, no matter where a culture may be on the evolutionary scale without every one of them working together, this world machine cannot be created. And that is the essential thing. It is the only thing."

"It sounds like the Tower of Babel."

Picking up the cup he began breaking off small pieces of the plastic around the rim and dropping them inside what was left. "That's true, but on an empyrean scale."

"Empyrean. What does that mean? Forget it, doesn't matter. Barry, let's get to the point: I know it's egotistical but what does it all have to do with me? How come my life has turned into a Salvador Dali painting?"

"Every civilization in the cosmos has a specific task to perform in this undertaking. Think of us all as workers in a factory creating one single product. Many have already accomplished what they were supposed to do. Some of it took place billions of years ago, some five minutes ago. It is happening all the time—piece by piece the world machine is being assembled."

"Why don't you call it the God Machine?"

"Because worlds are assembling it, Mr. McCabe, not God. That is the whole point of the endeavor."

"Why me? What does a cop in Crane's View, New York, have to do with the World Machine?"

He abruptly looked away. "We don't know."

The next thing I knew, coffee was all over my hand and my fingers were stuck through my white plastic cup. "You don't *know?*"

He sighed like an old man who's just taken off too-tight shoes. It was a while before he spoke again. "We don't know what needs to be done on Earth. We have only been able to figure out approximately who must do it."

"Me?"

"No. For a while we thought so and that's why we permitted Astopel to manipulate your life. That's why the old dog appeared, Antonya's notebooks, why we allowed you to experience your future . . . all that. We thought experiencing all those things would help stimulate you to do whatever was necessary. But we were wrong. You're not the one, Mr. McCabe. We know that now. But time is growing very short and we must find the correct person quickly."

"Because of the Millennium?"

He dismissed the question with a flick of the wrist. "The Millennium was Earth's party, no one else's. Work on the World Machine has been going on far longer than two thousand years. But every piece must be finished and incorporated within a spe- cific time. Mankind has been given millions of years to complete theirs. Unfortunately they haven't yet and now there are increas- ing concerns about a delay.

That cannot happen. All of this work functions within a rigid schedule, although in Earth-time it wouldn't sound rigid at all."

"What is your job on Rat's Potato?"

"Hratz-Potayo. We're administrators and troubleshooters. Our task is to make sure that every component comes in completed and on time. We walk around the factory with clipboards checking things off as they arrive and are attached to the overall structure. When something goes wrong or there are mistakes it is our responsibility to rectify them."

"Has this sort of thing happened before?"

"More times than there are molecules in a peppermint."

"All this makes me feel pretty small, Barry. What could I possibly do to help build the World Machine?"

"Die."

Lions for Breakfast

We were silent driving out of the parking lot and back onto the street. Barry had told the truth—nothing changed between the time we left the ambulance and when we were back moving again-toward the hospital. Although she appeared unconscious Magda looked more peaceful than before, as if a weight had been lifted from her. I suppose it had. I only wanted to sit there and watch her. Thinking about how much she meant to me, I knew she would be all right now. In a way that same weight had been lifted from me too and to my great surprise I felt relatively calm. I knew I had done the right thing although it meant the end of everything I loved and hoped for.

Sometimes happiness is like the sound of a plane overhead. You look up to see it but the plane's not there. No matter where you look you can't find it on the sky, although the sound is still there and growing louder. You get a little frantic searching. At the same time you're thinking, this is stupid. But you keep looking and if you do finally see it, you feel absolved. Most of my life I'd been looking for happiness in the wrong parts of the sky. I told this analogy to Magda after we married and she said it sounded like a country-western song. I said fuck you and she said please do.

"Where's George and Pauline?"

"Behind us, just like before."

"What will happen now when the doctors examine Magda?"

"Find that she has dangerously low blood pressure and recommend she take a variety of medications."

"When will this . . . thing start to affect me?"

"In a few days you'll begin having headaches. The situation will deteriorate quickly. It won't take long."

"If you're able to give me her brain tumor, why can't you find the person who's got to make the piece for the machine?"

"We tried, believe me. But in essence we can only manipulate what already is or was, Mr. McCabe. For example Antonya Corando was a very good artist who had already begun taking heroin. She would have died within six months. We showed you your future as it would happen if you continued living the way you do. But to be frank, we haven't been able to comprehend a great many things on Earth. There are huge gaps in our understanding. By interfering in your life, Astopel showed us our limitations."

"So that means you might be wrong with this too—maybe giving me her tumor *won't* work and she'll still die of it."

"Possible but unlikely. I can guarantee that if you were both given CAT scans now, Magda would not have a tumor and you would."

"But you're still not one hundred percent sure of the final outcome?"

"No, and I would be lying to you if I said so. We're still trying to understand how systems work on this planet, but the overriding problem is we simply don't have enough time now to figure them out."

"How did old Floon get back here?"

Barry shrugged. "Astopel fucked up. He sent him and shouldn't have. He thought having him here might spur you on to working faster."

"Floon knew about me and Gee-Gee. Did Astopel tell him that?"

"Yes, and almost as much as you know now."

"Couldn't he cause big trouble, knowing that?"

"Yes, he could."

"Why don't you kill him?"

"We're considering it."

"Should I?"

"I'll let you know what we decide. In the meantime don't worry about it."

"You're sure who you're looking for is in Crane's View?"

"Absolutely. We're sure they're someone you *know*."

Barry told me something else: There was not just one person responsible for mankind's contribution to the World Machine—there were four. Three had already done their parts. When I asked what they'd made or if I could see it, he reached into his pocket and pulled out *the* feather.

"Son of a bitch! That's why the damned thing kept following me around. But people don't make feathers—birds do. Find that bird and your problems are solved."

"This feather was man-made. And there's something else." Reaching into the same pocket, he took out the silvery piece of bone I'd found while burying Old Vertue the first time. I looked expectantly at Barry, assuming he had a good punch line to this show and tell.

None came. Instead he held the objects in an open palm and looked at them. Without thinking, without pausing, connecting or considering or any other goddamned thing I asked, "How do you row a boat across a wooden sea?"

He snapped the fingers of his other hand. The noise was very loud in that small space. It sounded like a tree branch cracking. "Very good, Mr. McCabe, you remembered Antonya's question. *That's* the third part. Now all we have to do is find the fourth."

"How did I know that, Barry? How did I know that question was the third part?"

"Because you've tuned into our frequency. You found our

channel." Smiling, he reached over and began taking Magda's blood pressure again. "Now you'll be able to receive our broadcasts."

"Don't be cutesy. What does it mean?"

"It means you're beginning to understand."

"But what do a feather a bone and that question have in common?"

"Don't know. We're hoping the fourth piece will tell us."

At the hospital both Michael and Isabelle Zakrides were waiting for us. They immediately took over from the paramedics, shooing away even the nurses who came to help. The Zakrideses are old friends and both of them are very good doctors. After I was shot years ago Mike saved my life. Watching him and his wife push Magda's stretcher down the hall, I realized he would take care of me again soon when lights started going out *chez moi*. Before that delightful idea could land and make me miserable I saw something down the hall that caught my attention. After checking to make sure Magda was all right for the moment, I went down there.

Bill Pegg stood at the other end, listening intently as a short woman doctor with a monk's haircut lectured him. Her pedantic tone of voice set my teeth on edge ten feet away. When I arrived, he put up a hand to stop her.

"Hold it, Doctor. This is Chief of Police McCabe. He'll want to hear all of this."

"What's up, Bill?"

"Chief, this is Doctor Schellberger. Brunhilde Schellberger."

He lifted one eyebrow one millimeter but that said it all.

"Hello, Doctor, what's going on?"

"A Caucasian male named John Petangles was brought in half an hour ago with gunshot wounds to the stomach and thigh."

I looked at Bill but heard myself tell Johnny it was all right to follow Caz de Floon only minutes after that shithead shot Gee-Gee and Old Vertue.

"Put out an all points on a white male, around sixty years old wearing a multicolored jogging suit. He's about five-nine, got a big head of white hair, weight . . . a hundred and fifty. A little less."

Bill took a notebook out of his pocket and wrote it down but his eyes kept coming up off the page and looking me over. "How do you know this, Chief?"

"Just do it, Bill. How's Johnny?"

"Not good. They're operating on him now."

"Doctor?"

She turned her hand back and forth and again. "We'll know more after the operation."

"Who is this guy, Frannie? How do you know who to look for?"

"I'll tell you later. Right now I've got to find a paramedic here named Barry."

Dr. Schellberger said, "Barry? There's no paramedic at this hospital by that name."

I turned to go. "That doesn't surprise me."

George and Pauline were sitting in the waiting room holding hands. That picture struck my heart like lightning splitting a tree down the middle. Two people who mattered so much to me. I would have them for only a few more days and then they would be gone. George gone, Pauline, Magda, Crane's View . . . my life. How do you ride the wave of *that* thought into the beach without falling off? Your life will be over in days.

"Is she gonna be all right, Frannie? Is Mom going to be okay?"

"Yes, I think so. I hope so. They said things looked good. But we have to wait till they've finished the tests. Pauline, can you wait here a minute while I talk to George? It'll only take like five minutes."

She grabbed my arm. "Are you not telling me something? Is there something I should know about Mom?"

"No, no, it's nothing like that. Believe me. It's just something I have to tell George—"

"Don't lie to me, Frannie. Please don't. I know that you think I'm a baby—"

"That isn't true, Pauline. Magda's your mother. If I knew something was really wrong with her I wouldn't hide it from you. Why would you think I'd do that?"

"Because you think I'm a child and—"

There was so little time left now that I felt it imperative to get through to Pauline on at least this one thing. Taking hold of both her arms, I pulled her close to me so that we were almost nose to nose. "I don't think that at all. I'm proud as hell of you and I think you're going to be a contender, like you said you wanted in the garage the other night." That's all I could think of to say but knew I had to say more because it was all breaking up inside me, breaking up and crashing together at the same time. An impossible thing, but there nevertheless.

Life is only contradictions and learning how to adjust to them. I wanted to tell this smart, naive girl to be quiet and listen—I'll tell you some of what I've learned and maybe you can use it. At the same time I wanted to tell her nothing and let her live in her silvery soap bubble of innocence until the very last moment when of course it would pop and she would fall to a much harder earth than she had ever imagined.

"Listen to me—" But then it was her turn to hold me because I completely lost it, couldn't say anything more and started to cry.

"Are you lying to me, Frannie? Is that why you're crying? Are you lying to me about Mom?" Her voice was soft and kind as cashmere. It asked its question but reassured at the same time. It held no grudge. Okay, even if you lied to me about this it's okay. I forgive you and will hold you till you're feeling better. All these new sides of this girl I had never seen before this morning. All of them appearing at once. Sexy Pauline, Flirty Pauline, Forgiving, Understanding . . . Why hadn't I seen them before? Why hadn't I known her?

"Am I good to you, Pauline? Have I been a good stepfather?"

"Well, yeah. Yes, definitely. Why are you asking? What's the matter?"

"I just want to know. I need to know. Your Mom is okay. I swear they didn't say anything I haven't told you. But this is different: I just want to know if I've been a good guy to you."

She smiled small but warm. "A *very* good guy. The other night when we were sitting in the garage talking I loved you so much. You made me feel like what I was saying wasn't stupid or crazy. You made me feel normal."

We hugged. We hugged and I felt tears on my face and the heat of her thin body in my arms. "Don't be normal, Pauline. Don't ever try to be normal because it's the first symptom of a terminal disease. As soon as you feel the need to be normal coming on, get the antidote."

"And what *is* the antidote?"

I wanted so badly to come up with a brilliant ripping riposte that she would remember the rest of her life. All I could think of was, "Just make sure that you're living your life, Pauline; don't let normal pretend to be you."

Isabelle Zakrides came over with papers to sign and asked if she could speak with one of us about Magda's condition. With a glance I asked Isabelle if anything was new. Her eyes back said no, this was just a formality. I told her to talk to Pauline and the girl's face showed happy gratitude.

"Will you tell me what's going on with my mom?"

"Sure, Pauline. Let's sit over there and I'll give you the whole scoop."

Standing outside the hospital, I told George what had happened to Johnny Petangles and that I was sure Floon shot him. I also described what had gone on between Barry and me. When I was finished, the blown-fuse look on George's face said it all. "Digesting all this is like eating a whole turkey in a couple of bites, Frannie. It's staggering. What are you going to do now?"

"I was going to look for Barry and ask some questions but he's disappeared. I have a feeling he'll be back when it's necessary. In the meantime I don't want that cocksucker Floon roaming around with a gun. He's already shot two people and a dog and it's not even noon."

"But if you find him what are you going to do then? You only have a few days, Frannie."

"First let me find Floon. The guy's dangerous. Then I'll look for this fourth thing they're so hot to have, whatever the hell *it* is. What else can I do, George? I don't exactly have a lot of options open to me."

A look of deep sadness swept onto his normally impassive face and stayed. He was frightened for me and to my surprise a lot of love was in his look as well. Very quietly he asked, "How can I help?"

"Go back inside and keep an eye on Pauline for me. I can't be worrying about her now. Carry your cell phone so I can reach you when I need to. And answer it for Christ's sake, George. Don't just let it ring till the battery runs out."

"All right. Where are you going now?"

"Home to get a gun and get changed. Then out to find Floon the Flying Dutchman."

We stared at each other and more than a lot passed between us in those silent seconds.

Finally a small guilty grin flickered at the corners of his mouth. He couldn't resist asking, "Frannie, you really saw the Beatles? What was it like?"

"They were all shorter than I imagined. Even Lennon. I always thought of him as ten feet tall."

The phone was ringing when I got to my house. In the rush to leave for the hospital, we'd forgotten to lock the front door. I walked in and caught the phone on its last ring. But by the time I said hello whoever was gone. Had Floon done something else in the meantime? God forbid. I thought about that familiar phrase as I walked into our bedroom and started getting dressed. How could "God forbid" if He'd been asleep all this time? Or "God damn" or "God save us"? And was He actually unconscious the way we are when we sleep, or did Barry mean it as some kind of cosmic metaphor?

With a pair of trousers in my hands and one leg up ready to insert, I realized I was staring at our bed. Did God sleep on a mattress? Or use a pillow? How big was His bed? Why was I suddenly smiling? I was going to be dead soon because my poor brain was going to explode. In the meantime I had to catch mad Caz de Floon before he shot someone else, *then* find the fourth whatever so as to save the universe. Why was I smiling?

After slipping on the pants, I straightened up and struck a pure Bruce Lee pose—arms up in inverted "L's" ready to deliver lethal blows. I swatted one out while growling, "Heeee-ya!" in my best Hong Kong karate movie voice. McCabe, dying Master of the Universe. Because George was right—it was too much to even imagine, much less absorb. It just seemed logical to do whatever I could and then leave the rest to Barry, his gang and whoever else was out there in the stars.

I didn't have a solution but I had to admire the enormity of the problem.

Where to find Floon? In his situation where would I go? Hmmm? Where *could* I go with no money or identification? I was assuming he arrived here with only the clothes on his back. Plus he had no clue of the specifics of what was going on today. If I were suddenly shot back thirty years with no preparation and no resources to work from, I don't know what I'd do. He'd said he wanted to "change some things" which I took to mean take greedy advantage of what he knew about the future to affect his fortunes then, i.e., buy a zillion shares of Microsoft stock the first day it goes public. But how could he do that? Rob a bank to get some startup capital? He had his gun and certainly the balls to do something like that.

Standing in front of the dresser slipping things into my pockets, I looked at myself in the dresser mirror trying to figure this out—where would Floon go? What's the first thing he would be likely to do?

Magda is an orderly woman. Everything in its place, our house is always spick-and-span, her desk is empty of any extraneous papers, and monthly bills are paid punctually. It's one of her qualities I deeply appreciate because I am not usually tidy in either mind or checkbook. Every morning when the mail arrived she put whatever letters were for me in a neat pile on top of my dresser. When I came home from work and changed clothes, I'd fan through them and read any that looked inviting. The others I left on the dresser for when I could summon the small interest to open them. Magda and Pauline kidded me about how many contests I'd lost or orphans I let starve because I didn't open most of those letters for days.

Today on top of that pile was a quarterly report from my stockbroker. When my pockets were filled with what I thought I would need—money, notebook, pistol . . . I mentally ran through the list to make sure I hadn't forgotten anything. While doing this, my eyes remained on the broker's letter, specifically the company's mailing and email addresses. Something dawned on me.

"Elementary, my dear Watson!" And then I was galloping out of the house like a horse on fire.

Our town library was the pet project of Lionel Tyndall, the only obscenely wealthy resident of Crane's View. A lonely old eccentric who made a fortune in oil prospecting, Tyndall gave the library so much money before he died that the place is a joy to visit. Not only do they have a wide array of constantly changing books, but their equipment is always the most tiptop, cutting-edge, and up to date. The head librarian, Maeve Powell, patiently taught me how to use a computer and, when I had it down, how to surf and make the most of the Internet.

That morning when I entered, Maeve was sitting behind the front desk looking at a large coffee table book on wristwatches. The library's computer room is behind that desk and off to the right. There was no way I could see into it from where I was standing. It made me nervous knowing Floon might be a few feet away but I had no way of knowing it.

Librarian Powell is as serious as a postage stamp, so when she smiles you should consider it a special gift. She looked up from her book and smiled. "Good morning, Francis."

"Hi. Have you been here since the library opened today?"

"Yes. I was just reading about the Breguet Tourbillon—"

"That's nice. But did a guy come in here in an ugly-colored jogging suit, around sixty years old and with a lot of white hair? He speaks with an accent."

"Yes. He was quite nice. Asked for the CDs of the Encarta encyclopedia and dictionary we keep on reserve. Then he went into the computer room with them."

"I knew it! I knew he'd look for a computer and that god-damned Internet! Is there anyone else in the library?" I looked around. A fat woman in a yellow dress sat at a table reading an *Utne Reader* magazine. "Anyone besides her?"

Maeve got my message. Her voice turned grave and quick-ened. "Yes, there are a couple of children in the computer room too."

"Shit." I took a deep breath and let it out slowly. "All right, we'll just have to deal with it."

"Who is this man, Frannie?"

For a moment I was tempted to tell her but something held me back. "It doesn't matter. I just have to talk to him and it might be dicey. Who else is in the library besides her and those kids?"

"No one."

"Then why don't you go outside for a while and take that woman with you."

"Should I call the police station?"

"No, let's see if I can take care of it without a fuss. You two go ahead outside."

She stood immediately but then hesitated. It was clear she

wanted to say something. Instead she walked around the desk and over to the woman. Both of them stared at me while Maeve spoke. Fatso clearly did not want to leave. But she heard something that changed her mind. She jumped out of that seat like she'd been ejected from it. She motored by me toward the door at a speed that said it all.

When Maeve was passing me she stopped. "Frannie."

"Yes?" I looked from her toward the door to the computer room, wishing she would leave so I could get on with this.

"My daughter Nell is in there. Nell and her friend Layla."

"I'll take care of it. Don't worry."

"If anything were to happen—"

I spoke lightly—as if this were no big deal. "Nothing's going to happen, Mrs. Powell. I'm going in there and come right out again with this guy. Zip zip and we're gone. Please, trust me."

"I do trust you, Frannie. But it's *Nell* in there. Don't let anything happen to my child."

"Never." I touched her cheek with my hand. Her eyes were brimming with tears and her eyelids trembled.

When she had left the building I walked slowly around the desk. Pressed flat against the wall, I took out my Beretta and checked to see if the safety was off. Holding it at my side, I slid slowly toward the computer room. On reaching that door, I got ready to sneak a look through the glass. Without warning a nova of unimaginable pain burst in my head. Because my back was to the wall I sort of crumpled against it and slid to the floor. If I hadn't been leaning I would have fallen on my face. I had no control over my body.

I thought I'd been shot. Then my mind blanked because there was no room for anything else in that space but pain. The breath froze in my throat. I could not see. No agony was worse than this, nothing. The most terrible part was I remained conscious throughout—no blackout, no physical escape. I must have looked like a drunken man, sitting on the floor dazed and gone. It was like an underground nuclear test. You know—when the bomb goes off the only visible sign is the earth collapsing inward toward the fifty megaton fire in its belly half a mile below.

I don't know how long it lasted—five seconds, a minute. I don't know how I survived. When it stopped I was stupefied. Is that the word? Stupefied, paralyzed, nothing in my brain would ever work right again. Nothing ever could after that.

Sitting on the floor outside the computer room I stared unseeing at a large black-and-white photograph of Ernest Hemingway on the opposite wall. Next to him was one of Fitzgerald, then Faulkner, Emerson, and Thoreau. I knew the faces but it took an eternity to dig their names out of the rubble of my mind. To make sure it was Hemingway, I said his name. It sounded correct although it came out of my mouth slowly, as if the word were made of chewy caramel.

I felt the cold of the floor under my palms, the hardness of the wall against my back. Nothing in me was safe or to be trusted anymore. One of the first realizations I made when my mind started focusing again was the brain tumor had just taken over my being. Despite what Barry said about me having a few days' grace period before it killed me, what just happened proved he was wrong—I might not have any days left.

I tried breathing normally but it was impossible. My lungs took only short fast panting breaths like those of a small animal that's been cornered. I tried willing myself to breathe slow and deep but it didn't work. My eyes moved down the opposite wall, across the floor and onto my hand. It still held the gun, but for the longest time I literally couldn't recognize what that object was.

From inside the computer room came children's laughter.

That more than anything sharpened my thoughts. Why I was there came back to me: Floon—get him, Maeve's daughter—save her. Get up.

"Get up, mullerfucker." I smiled at my mistake. One of my favorite words in the English language I couldn't even pronounce now. So I tried again, carefully. "Mother-fucker." Good, and now it was time to stand up. I tried. I tried pushing myself up off the floor but I was heavy, so incredibly heavy. Gravity had doubled, tripled. How was I ever going to rise?

For one grisly instant my head went on fire again—the pain blasting across it like a miles-long dance of heat lightning on an August night sky. But that was all—that flash, my breath freezing again, but then it was gone. It was gone.

And then I spoke again but it was not in my own voice. "Get the fuck up, motherfucker." I said, someone said, the word perfectly enunciated this time.

"I can't. I have no strength." I said without self-pity, with perfect calm.

"No you can't, but I can. So do it." Gee-Gee's voice came out of me.

I said, "Where are you?" and waited.

He said, "Everywhere you need me. Just get up."

I decided it was a good idea to leave the gun on the floor while trying to stand. I put it down gently, not wanting to make noise. It was black against the yellow linoleum. I don't like yellow things.

"Forget the yellow! Pay attention. You have to pay attention to what you're doing."

"Okay." I licked my lips and pulled some energy together to stand. It was slow going at first. As I was propping myself up, I suddenly felt a massive jolt of both strength and energy in my arms. But only my arms, no place else. They felt like they belonged to someone strong and agile. To someone maybe seventeen years old . . .

"It isn't me doing this, is it, Gee-Gee?"

"Yeah, it's you. Don't start getting philosophical on me. Just get a fucking grip and do it." He sounded exasperated, like my helplessness was a pain in his neck.

Standing again, I looked down and saw my pistol on the floor. It looked like it was five miles away at the bottom of the Grand Canyon. I needed it for what I was about to do but didn't know if I'd be able to get down there again without doing a nosedive.

"I don't think I can do this."

"Get the goddamned gun."

Like an old man, like *the* old man I'd been in Vienna, I carefully bent my knees and went down in a slo-mo squat for the gun. It worked and I felt like I'd really accomplished something. Because despite the strong arms, the rest of my body felt useless.

"Now what do I do?" I asked the emptiness around me. No answer came. Just when I needed Gee-Gee most he disappeared.

I stood there with ashes and smoke coming out my ears from the Mount Vesuvius that had just erupted in my brain. There was no guarantee I wouldn't keel over again any instant. Yet I was supposed to step into a room and disarm a lunatic billionaire murderer with two children nearby?

Three children. When I was able to rummage up the strength to get me to that door again, I looked in and saw three little backs standing around one big one. Two little girls, a boy, and Floon were all staring at a computer monitor. He was seated while they stood but none of them was higher than his shoulders. The kids were close enough to be touching—they didn't want to miss any of the fun flying across the screen. It showed so much information so fast that it was impossible for my eyes to absorb

any of what was there. Since all of their backs were to me I
continued watching.

Now and then Floon put his hands on the keyboard and
proceeded to type faster than anyone I have ever seen. That's
what set the kids off laughing so much. Every time he put his
fingers down and attacked, they squealed their delight and kept
trying to push in even closer to the monitor. I've heard the fastest
typist can do a hundred and sixty words a minute. Forget it—
Floon was eons beyond that. From the look of things, he was
going faster than the damned machine could take. I swear to God
there appeared to be a kind of infinitesimal lag between what he
put in and what showed up on the screen. Typing, he looked
like a cartoon character on fast forward.

Eventually he sat back in his chair and waited while the computer caught up and did what he had asked. Seconds later there
would appear a burst of words and graphics or a flying myriad
of mathematical something. He'd watch it a while and then assault
that old keyboard again. Every time the kids cracked up at his
frenzy. The interesting thing was, from all appearances, Floon
didn't seem to mind them being there. Or else he wasn't even
aware they were there at all.

But I was—even more so when, turning to Nell Powell, the
boy gave her a hard push into the other girl. Nell shoved him
back just as hard. Off balance he staggered back from the girls,
trying to catch his balance. He couldn't and fell on his ass. At
which point I saw his face and he was me, age nine or ten or
thereabouts. Ten-year-old Frannie McCabe was in that room with
Floon and the girls. Forty-seven-year-old Frannie McCabe stood
outside alone and watched.

When I asked Gee-Gee where are you he had said, *"Wherever
you need me."* So this was what he meant? That me was no longer
only me, and then Gee-Gee, but now other McCabes from all

my eras. Including little boy Fran in there with Caz de Floon. A living greatest hits album played all at the same time.

Still on his butt the kid looked at the door. His small face was a mixture of sneaky rat and choirboy. Without the slightest sign of surprise on his face he smirked like we were in on an in-joke together and flipped me a big thumbs-up.

I turned from the door. Back to the wall again, I closed my eyes tight. Okay, go with it. This is how it's going to be till you die: Chaos everywhere, no answers to your questions, a head ticking like a time bomb, and a different McCabe every time you turn around. So go with it, use it; embrace it if you can. Because you ain't got time to do anything else, bud.

Once more at the window, I watched as the boy stood up and looked my way again. He made a face that clearly asked, what do you want me to do? Seeing this, Nell turned around to see what he was mugging at. I pulled back quickly, not wanting her to know I was there.

What were my options? What could a little boy do with Floon that I couldn't, although at the moment the kid probably had more strength and clearheadedness than I did. The blowout in my head had left me drained and very shaky, too aware that I could collapse at any time.

As a boy I had the patience of a housefly. I should have remembered that when I was watching little Gee-Gee in the computer room. After we stared at each other some more he gestured again, all impatient exaggeration. His whole jiggling twitching body asked, what should I do?

As best I could I used hands and charades to outline a computer monitor. He got what I was saying and nodded. Next I showed him what to do. He lit up like a thousand-watt lightbulb. Boy, did he love these instructions.

Without a second's hesitation he stepped over to where

Floon was typing away. With both hands the boy shoved the monitor off its base, and that big fucker *flew* out into space and crashed on the floor. Time passed. All four of them froze where they were. But then that bastard Floon didn't do what I expected. I thought he would go nuts, berserk, rip himself in half Rumpelstiltskin-style at the loss of his data or the time he'd already put in on the computer doing whatever the hell he was doing. None of the above. With a coolness that was disconcerting he rose from his seat, moved over to the next computer, and started wailing away on that one, not missing a beat.

My one idea flushed, I shoved the door open, walked over to Floon, and smashed him good on the back of the head with my pistol. That did the trick. Rocking forward, his face hit the screen and cracked it. He had a lot of white hair. I grabbed a handful and banged his head down on the keyboard.

"Kids, get out. Nell, your mom is waiting outside."

The girls took off like water bugs but not McCabe Junior. "That was super cool!"

"Go outside."

"No way! I'm stayin'. You think I'd miss this? Hit him again."

"Go or I'll tell your mother you stole fifteen dollars from her purse so you could go to the car show in White Plains."

His jaw dropped. "How'd you know that?"

Trying not to smile I managed, "Because I'm psychic. Go outside and wait for me."

"Jeez, what a hot turd." On that note he started to leave. "But I'll be waiting for you. Just remember that."

As soon as the door closed, I banged down Floon's floppy head once more only because I felt like it. Thoroughly unprofessional but I was no longer a professional. I searched for his gun. It was in one of his pockets. I took it out and put it in mine.

"McCabe——" he mumbled.

"Shut up, Caz, or else I'll dribble your head some more. Don't think I'm not tempted."

"McCabe, listen—" He sounded half-in-the-bag drunk.

A blast of pain blew across my brain. Not now! Not now, please not. Raising my shoulders and pulling my head down into my neck, I waited for the worst but none came.

"McCabe, at least look at the screen."

What was displayed there looked like a densely detailed train schedule.

"So what?"

"Tan—" He took a deep breath and started coughing halfway through it. Blood dripped from his mouth onto the table. "Tancresis. It hasn't been invented yet! Or if it has, there is no public mention of it. Is that amazing? There's not even the word for it in the dictionary. Nobody knows about it yet."

"I don't know what you're talking about, Caz. And I don't much care."

"*Don't care?* Tancretic spredge? Nuclear transmutation? *Cold fusion,* you idiot! How to do it hasn't been discovered yet!"

I banged his head down onto the keyboard again. This was getting to be fun. My anger at him brought a good adrenaline load of energy back into my veins and heart. "Don't fuck with me, Floon—your dick's not big enough." And to the tune of the Sam Cooke song "Wonderful World" I sang:

> *"Don't know much about cold fus-ion,*
> *Don't know much about Caz de Floon.*
> *But I do know that I'll kick your ass*
> *And you do know it'll happen fast—*

"I don't care what you're looking for or what you've found, Floon. Right now you and I are going to leave here. If you do anything along the way that pisses me off I will kill you without the slightest hesitation. I give you my word."

"You can't kill me—you're a policeman."

"Past tense, Caz. Past tense. It's a brave new world. Get up."

"Please, McCabe, listen to me for two minutes. What I tell you will change your life."

I snorted. "What little there is left of it. I don't need my life changed any more than it already is. What do you want? You've got one minute to say it. So talk."

"All right." He touched his forehead and winced. He looked at his fingers and didn't appear to know what to do with the big smear of blood there. That made me feel just fine.

I looked at my bare wrist and put an imaginary watch against my ear to check to see if it was functioning. "My watch tells me you've got about thirty seconds left on your minute, Caz."

"Stop! You should be grateful to me for what you are about to see. If nothing else I will show you how to become very rich right now. In five minutes. Just give me five minutes—"

"Two. I already have enough money."

"Two. All right. I'll show you." Once again he slid over—to computer number three. At the rate we were going there would be no more machines left in the library by the time we left. His fingers started machine-gunning away and whatever info he was calling up flew onto the screen.

"I know that site! Yahoo! Finance."

"Correct. Now watch," he said while typing something in. A moment later a full screen of market research appeared on a company called SeeReal. The stock ticker abbreviation for it was SEER. Individual shares in the company were selling for four dollars and fifteen-sixteenths. SeeReal had been in business three years but hadn't made one penny's profit yet.

"SEER. Very symbolic name, Caz. Selling for four dollars a share? Wow, right up there with Intel, huh? Time to go."

His voice went up up up. "No, no, you must listen! SeeReal has discovered a substance called naterskine. That line of research will lead them to creating something called tancretic spredge. Once that happens this company will become ten times more important and powerful than General Electric. Believe me, McCabe. That is why I was so shocked to realize it hasn't happened yet. None of this information is in either the latest dictionary or encyclopedia. It's as if someone named Bill Gates asked if you would be interested in investing in a new company he was founding called Microsoft. And if you give me a little bit more time to work here I will find a great many more of these things for you. Invest in them now and within five years you will be as rich as Croesus."

"Floon, you're shit on the bottom of my shoe. The sooner I scrape you off, the better. For some unimaginable reason you were given the great privilege of being allowed to travel back in time thirty years. Time travel, for Christ's sake. An absolute all-out four-star miracle. But what's the first thing *you* do? Get online so you can surf the Web for ways to make money. You disgust me."

"That wasn't what I was doing."

"I don't care what you were doing. Get up."

"Don't be an ass, McCabe. Neither of us knows why we were sent back here. Nor do we know if we'll ever be returned to our proper time. So why not make the most of this while we're here?"

He believed I was here for the same reasons he was. "You think I was sent back here from *your* time?"

He blinked exaggeratedly and slowly several times. When he spoke again his voice was pure sarcasm. "Well, *hello,* are you not standing here with me now when the last time we saw each other was in Vienna?"

"Floon, you're sixty years old. Do I look sixty years old?"

"That doesn't matter—"

"Yes, it matters a great deal. Your being sent back here was a mistake. My being sent back here was a correction. This is my time; it ain't no mistake for me."

Clearly unimpressed, he crossed his arms. "How do you know?"

I was about to answer but then thought why bother? "Because the aliens told me. Let's go."

"What aliens?" Now he looked like he believed me.

"You haven't met them yet? The Martians from Rat's Potato? Nice fellows. They live behind the Crab Nebula. When they come to Earth they disguise themselves either as paramedics or well-dressed black men wearing expensive watches. Move."

"Where are we going?"

Where *were* we going? Until that moment I hadn't really thought about it, what with all the swirl going on. But Floon had a point. I couldn't take him to jail because that would involve too much time explaining to the people down at the station house and I had no time to explain.

"Don't you want to know what I was doing on the computer, McCabe?"

"No and be quiet." Where the hell was I going to take him?

The door flew open and little me appeared. "The cops are here."

"Where? Didn't I tell you to go outside?"

"I did, Mr. Stupid. But now the cops are out there. That's all I came in to tell you. I thought you'd want to know. They brought two cars and now they're talking to that librarian across the street."

Thinking out loud I said, "Maeve must have called them."

With a taunt on his face and in his voice Floon asked, "Are you going to have me arrested, McCabe?"

"I'd rather have you stuffed. Now shut up. I have to figure this out."

The two regarded me as if I knew what I was doing. Floon was impassive, the boy very happy and excited. I hadn't ordered him out again which meant that for the time being he could stick around for whatever was coming next.

As fast as my limping head could think, I tried sorting through my options. If we stayed in the library, Bill Pegg would eventually assume some kind of hostage situation was going on and take the appropriate steps. That did not bode well. I liked Bill very much but knew he had dreams of glory, most of them unfulfilled. Here was a chance for him to take charge big-time but that was not necessarily a good thing.

A simpler way would be for us to just walk out of the library. But both choices led to the same thing—hours wasted explaining and sorting this bizarre situation out afterward. I could not afford to waste that time.

"What about the basement?" Junior asked but his question didn't register in me until some beats had passed.

"Huh?"

"The basement. What if we snuck out of here through the door in the basement?"

"Why sneak?"

"Because the cops are outside, dumbbell! Jeez, you want them to catch you or something?"

"Who is this child, McCabe?"

"He's my son."

"I am not!"

"Well, close enough. How do you know about the basement?"

"Because I know a lot about this place. I have pretty well explored everything around here. Me and this guy, we found a way to sneak out downstairs through a fire door—"

Scorched brain notwithstanding, I remembered what the boy was talking about, remembered jimmying the lock on a door downstairs when I was his age. Al Salvato and me. I spoke that name before I had a chance to think, "Al Salvato."

Little Fran nodded because it was obvious that's who he was talking about.

And he was right—we could easily sneak out that door and after a few strategic lefts and rights, be gone from this neighborhood in five minutes.

"You're a smart kid. And since you came up with the idea, why don't you lead the way?"

"Okay."

I took Floon's arm and pushed him in front of me. He didn't resist, which was clever, because if he had I would have hit him on the head again. We left the computer room and, turning right down the hall, walked till we got to a wide staircase. The kid took it two quick steps at a time. Us old men were slower but we made it to the bottom too.

The kid waved for us to follow him. "That door's over here."

"How 'bout this quick-witted boy, Floon? He's actually going to get us out of here. No wonder I'm so smart—I started young."

"What the hell are you talking about, McCabe?"

"Never mind. Just follow that little genius."

As I was reaching out to push the door open, at the last moment I noticed a sign on the wall saying it was an emergency fire exit. When it was opened an audible signal would be heard.

I assumed that meant some kind of horrendous screeching racket to scare off any rascals trying to weasel out of the library with stolen books. Any horrendous screeching racket would not help my plan to tiptoe out of here and make a stealthy escape.

"May I make a suggestion?" Floon didn't wait for permission. "When you open that door it will set off an electronic alarm. Just in case you didn't read the *schild* there."

"It's called a plaque, Floon, or a sign. Not a *schild*. I already know there's an alarm."

"Yes, well, I would guess that if you looked a bit you'd find a wire to it that you could disconnect."

That made me suspicious—especially because he spoke in such an even tone. "Why do you care if we get out of here now?"

"Because I don't want to be arrested. There are other things I would rather be doing than sitting in a jail cell."

"You won't be doing anything until I'm finished with you. And then I'll put you in jail myself."

The boy scowled at us, hands on hips. "Are you two guys going to talk all day or are we getting out of here? Come on, let's go!"

It took five minutes to locate the wire and with a snick of the boy's fat brown Buck pocketknife, seconds to cut it. Then we were outta there and the door was banging shut behind us. We walked up a small hill, down past a thin creek, looked back, and the library was gone. And so was my uncertainty about where to go.

"Take a right here."

"May I ask where we're going?" Every time Floon spoke it came out sounding both pedantic and amused. It was a voice you wanted to hit with a baseball bat.

"To George's house."

"Why? We were just there!" For the first time his voice
cracked into something annoyed and vaguely human.

'The boy poked me in the side. "Who's George?"

"Junior, I really am grateful to you for helping in the library.
But if you're going to come along now, I don't want any questions—nothing, not one. There's too much happening and my
head's jam-packed. Questions from you won't help. *Capice?*"

"Yeah. I *capice.*"

"Good. But I'll answer you this one time: We're going to a
friend of mine's house. His name is George and he's very smart.
I want him to help me figure something out. Okay? That's the
whole plan."

We walked across the familiar backyards and back streets of
Crane's View. A little boy leading two middle-aged men. Some-
times he skipped along smiling to himself, alone in his own world.
Watching him, I tried to remember pieces of that world where
I'd once lived: Good & Plenty licorice candies, bunkbeds in my
bedroom, Early Wynn pitching for the Cleveland Indians, *Famous
Monsters of Filmland* magazine, the Beatles singing "I Wanna Hold
Your Hand," the Three Stooges on TV. I walked on, remembering the delicious trivia that had filled those days. Some of it came
back but so much was gone. That part made me very sad. I
wished there would have been time to sit down with the boy
and ask him to tell me about his life, my life. Then I could have
known it again in detail and carried that knowledge with me for
as much time as I had left.

Sometimes the boy looked confused because the town he'd
known forty years ago was not the same as today's. Houses he
knew were not where they were supposed to be. Houses were
not supposed to be where they were. The layout looked different.
Who were all these strangers? No one knows a small town like

the kids living there. They live on the streets, memorize the residents, the cars, and what's in the store windows. In the summer when school is out they have little else to do. Stay home bored or be out and around in the town. So they stand by their bikes and watch as cars get put up on the rack for a lube job at the gas station, or people moving in and out of the houses. Kids can tell you about a new member of the community before anyone else can. How many children do they have, what kind of dog, the color of their furniture, and if the husband yells at the wife.

Crane's View was Little Fran's town while at the same time *this* town wasn't. But the changes he must have seen everywhere didn't appear to bother him much. When puzzled he would only stop, look back at me, and wait for instructions. Keeping Floon a few steps in front, I mainly watched the boy and found myself continually smiling. I liked his willingness to accept changes of scenery; anything different from his own world seemed okay. The expression on his face said he was open to it all.

"McCabe?" Floon turned to look at me.

I gave him a shove. "Keep moving, asshole."

"I *am* moving. Why do you think we've been sent back here?"

"I know why I've been sent back, Caz. You're here by mistake. You're a fucking blemish."

"How do you know?"

"The aliens told me."

"That's very helpful."

"Glad to be of service."

We walked on, the boy still a ways in front of us.

"Hey, Caz, how do you row a boat across a wooden sea?"

"I couldn't care less. Cute little arcane questions don't interest me."

"With a spoon."

Both of us looked at the boy. "A spoon?"

"Yes, because there's no such thing as a wooden sea. So if there was then it'd be a crazy thing, which means you'd have to use something crazy to row across it, like a spoon. Or maybe it's not a wooden sea, but a wooden C, like in the letter? *See?*" He grew a wicked grin. "Which one of 'em do you mean?"

"Christ, I didn't even think of that."

Floon looked from one version of me to the other and back again. "Didn't consider what?"

"That it might be a C and not a sea."

Floon frowned. "I take it back, McCabe—maybe he is your son. There's a real family resemblance in the recondite way you two think."

"Recondite. You sure know your vocabulary, Caz. Wasn't that word on our last spelling bee?"

The boy fell into step next to me. He skipped a few steps and then to my real surprise, took my hand in his. I didn't know what to say. It felt strange but sweet too. Holding hands with yourself, forty years apart.

"What do you want to be when you grow up?" I knew the answer but wanted to hear him say it anyway. Wanted to hear him living inside that dream again as I had for many of my boyhood years.

He actually puffed out his chest a bit before answering. "I wanna be an actor. I wanna act in monster movies. Maybe be the guy inside the monster suit."

"Oh yeah? Do you know *The Seventh Voyage of Sinbad*? That's my favorite movie."

He dropped my hand and jumped aside. "Mine too, mine too! That's the greatest movie in the world. The Cyclops in it is my favorite. I made one just like it out of clay in my art class." He put both hands up and curling them into three-clawed paws, roared Cyclops-style. "That part where Sinbad sticks the torch in his eye and burns it out so he's blind and he stumbles back and falls off the cliff? Do you remember that?"

I nodded in complete understanding. "How could I forget? It's the best." How many times had I watched that scene both when I was his age and sitting with my buddies in the fourth row of the Embassy Theater, and then after my thoughtful wife gave me a copy of the video for Christmas a few years ago? Whenever she was angry with me, Magda would call me "Sekourah," who was the villain in the film.

The short rest of the way to George's house we talked about the movies we loved and our favorite scenes in them. It was nice to be able to agree on absolutely everything. Floon got fed up and disgustedly asked if we would *please* change the subject? In happy unison we said "No!" and kept talking.

"What kind of car is that?"

Parked in front of George's house was a very futuristic looking four-wheel-drive vehicle. I'd seen it advertised on TV—an Isuzu, some kind of Isuzu. Everything about it was more round and aerodynamic than those weekend-warrior standbys. It looked like the kind of too-cool car you see in music videos on MTV.

Floon spoke before I had a chance to answer the boy's question. "It's an Isuzu Vehicross. A marvelous car. Two hundred fifteen horsepower, torque-on-demand four-wheel-drive. I owned one exactly like it when I was a young man. The first new car I ever bought." He sounded so smitten with the car that I half expected to see little hearts come rising off his head like lovebirds in a Disney film.

"It's really ugly if you ask me. Looks like a big silver frog. Can you drive it in the water? It looks like one of those cars in a James Bond movie that you can drive off the road into the water."

Floon looked positively miffed at what I thought was the kid's fair assessment. "No you can't drive it into the water, for God's sake. But you can go off road with it, although sometimes that's dangerous because there is an awful blind spot in the back. That's what caused my accident."

"What's a blind spot?"

Floon ignored the kid, all the while grinning at the Isuzu as if it were his child.

"My goodness, Caz, you're actually smiling now. I didn't think you knew how."

Sliding a stubby hand across the roof of the car, he patted it affectionately. The sound was louder than usual because everything else around us was very quiet. "Seeing this brings back nice memories. I was twenty-nine and working for Pfizer. They gave me a raise and at the time all I wanted in the world was one of these. I thought if you owned a car like this you could rule the world: You would be so cool you could eat lions for breakfast. Remember when a car could fill your life, McCabe? I distinctly remember the day I realized I could afford to buy one—in exactly this color. But I purposely waited two weeks before going to the showroom. It was like standing outside a candy store with a pocket full of money. You put off going in as long as you can bear it just to prolong the pleasure of anticipation. I had been mooning over the catalog for months. I'd memorize all the details and the specifications I wanted on my car. I still remember most of them to this day." He stopped talking. Staring at the car, he let the good memories wash over him.

Unimpressed, Junior crossed his arms and frowned. "I still think it looks like a frog."

Floon started to walk around the car. I tensed, not knowing what he was about to do.

"I'd only had the car two months when I backed into someone at a parking lot because of that ridiculous blind spot. It was a really stupid flaw in the car's design. I put a big dent right—" Bending down, his head disappeared behind the other side of the car. Things got even quieter and stayed that way. Finally the boy and I looked at each other and simultaneously walked around the car to see what was going on.

Floon had squatted down and was busily running his hand back and forth across a large dent on the lower left side panel. Although he said nothing, his busy hand would go slow then speed up, then slow . . . so that it looked like he was trying to sand the section with the flat of his palm.

"Whacha doin' there, Caz?" I said it as gently as I could, not at all sure where the hell his mind was at that moment.

When he looked up his eyes didn't tell a happy tale. "This is exactly the same dent." He tried to stand, winced, stopped. Putting a hand on his lower back, he rose much more slowly. Without a word he shuffled toward the front of the car and opened the driver's door. Surprised by his calm chutzpah, I was about to play cop and say hey, you can't do that but this looked too interesting. I decided to wait and see what he'd do next.

Floon climbed into the car. Instead of sitting down, he stayed on his knees on the driver's seat and appeared to be searching for something on the floor. Then he started talking to himself. Not just a word or two but whole long sentences. When I got close enough to hear what he was saying I couldn't understand anything because he spoke in a guttural foreign language. It sounded like German but later turned out to be Dutch. Every word sounded like he was trying to clear his throat. Everything he said came out sounding like a loud distressed mumble; the kind of annoyed/worried conversation you have with yourself when you can't find your keys and you're in a big hurry.

"Telemann! Hah!" His back to me, he held up a CD jewel case and shook it as if it were a crucial piece of evidence he had discovered. Caz dropped it and kept reaching around on the floor and under the car seats.

"Floon—"

"Wait!"

Because I was such a nice fellow I'd give him a few more seconds to find whatever he was looking for. Besides it was interesting seeing him melt down into a molten nutcase.

In English he said, "Hah, there it is! I was right."

"What's he doing?" Junior came over and went up on his toes for a better view.

Deepening my voice, I tried to sound like Orson Welles, "I'm afraid the man's coming unhinged."

"Huh? Waddya mean?"

"Just hold on. We're waiting to see what he'll do next." I put my hand on the boy's shoulder. He quickly shook it off and stepped away from me.

"Frannie? Is that you?"

Looking up, I saw George standing on his porch next to a stranger. At first I didn't know the other guy. A young man, he looked vaguely familiar. Then recognition came like a cannon going off in front of me. And I knew who he was—big-time. I almost laughed out loud. "Oh boy! Uh, Caz?"

He kept rummaging and mumbling but would not turn around.

"Floon!"

That got his attention. He glared at me over his shoulder. There was something in his hand but his body blocked my view of it. Anyway I was in a hurry to tell him and watch his reaction.

"What do you want, McCabe?" The words came out too loudly; his voice was full of hatred and hurry.

Pointing a finger at him like a gun, I spat back just as meanly, "Don't talk to me like that, you piece of shit. Look at the porch. Just look over there." I threw my arm wildly in that direction. Anything to get his goddamned eyes to look that way.

"What did you say?"

"*Look on the porch*, Floon!"

"I cannot. I have to—"

"Okay, that's it. Get out of that car. Come here—" I reached for him but he was faster. The next thing I knew, Caz de Floon had a new pistol in his hand and was pointing it at me. Where did he get that? It almost didn't matter because what he was about to see was a lot more powerful than a gun.

"Get away from me, McCabe."

I stepped back, hands up. "Please look at the porch?"

Twisting back and forth, he awkwardly worked himself out of the car. The gun remained pointed at my heart the whole time. Only when he was standing again did he look where I'd said. The stranger next to George watched all of this with a kind of vaguely curious passivity. What was happening was sort of interesting but not enough to make him excited.

These two men looked at each other. Watching I got a chill up my back because to my great surprise, the expressions on their faces didn't change a bit. The younger man seemed engaged but aloof. The old man was just plain pissed off.

"Don't you know who that is? For Christ's sake *even I* know who it is! How can you not recognize him, Floon? It's you! It's you when you were young!"

"I know. I knew he was here as soon as I saw the dent in the car. That's why I was looking around inside it. I knew this was my car. I always kept this gun under the passenger's seat. I taped it there the day I brought it home from the dealer."

I remembered Floon in Vienna telling me George and I had given him the feather when he was young and that it had changed everything. I remembered George saying old Floon knew him from when he was young.

George followed by the thirtysomething Caz de Floon clumped down the porch steps and toward us. Neither Floon seemed particularly interested in the presence of the other. Their coolness at this meeting astonished me. Then I realized it was one-sided because Floon Junior could not possibly know who this white-haired man with a gun was. Because if you look in a mirror and try to imagine what you'll look like in thirty years, I don't think your guesstimate will be right. Mine certainly wasn't when I saw myself in a mirror in Vienna for the first time.

But there was a piece to the Floon puzzle I didn't know about that was going to reveal itself and change everything.

The younger man had the same big head of hair (only his was chestnut-brown), army officer posture, and thick stubby hands. But what fixed the resemblance between the two was the tone of voice when he spoke—it was identical. "Father? Why are you here?"

Floon said to Floon. Young to old. The floor was all theirs now—the rest of us were just house lights dimming for the beginning of their show.

Old Floon said nothing but watched his younger self intently, as if trying to figure out what the other was getting at. He kept the gun tight against his side, still pointed at me. I saw it was a Walther PPK. Nasty gun. Nasty man.

"I'm not your father."

Ignoring what the other had just said, Young Floon stepped

forward and spat out, "You promised to leave me alone for two years. Two years later, Father. That was our deal and you agreed to it. But it's not even been six months. Why have you come here?" His voice was blistering now. If he'd thrown it on someone it would have burned their skin off. It was in complete contrast to the look on his face which was empty, indifferent and said nothing.

"I am not your father! How can you not see the difference?"

"I see an agreement we made which you are now breaking, in typical fashion. You are a contemptible man. Do you know that, Father? Both you and Mother are contemptible people. Please get away from my car." He looked the old man up and down like a guy does to a girl he's sizing up. His eyes stopped when he saw the pistol. "Where did you get that gun?"

Old Floon looked first at his hand and then back at the other man. "Where did I get it? Under the car seat. You know that."

"I thought so. You went into my car and took it without asking. My car, my gun—it's so typical of you. That's what I'm talking about. Because it's not your gun to take, Father. I bought it. I bought it with my money, not yours. Nothing I own anymore came from you, nothing on this earth. Nothing ever will again."

"I know that! I remember doing it. One of the great days of my life!" Old Floon said.

Then it became so quiet you could have heard a body drop, which I more than expected to happen at any moment although I didn't know whose body it would be. The whole situation had turned so fucking weird that it chewed up logic and fact like they were Juicy Fruit gum. Anything could have happened at that moment. I wouldn't have been surprised if anything had. Floon shoots me. Floon shoots Floon. Floon surrenders to Floon. Floon . . . You get the point.

"Look at my hands, for God's sake! Look how fat they are.

Don't you remember his hands?" Pistol dangling from an index finger, Old Floon put up both hands like he was surrendering to us. "Those long fingers? The ones he used to stab into my ear whenever I did something wrong. You don't remember?"

The younger man appeared unimpressed. Arms crossed over his chest and eyes closed, he shook his head. "You have the same hands I do, Father. Why are you lying about it? What is your problem?"

Old Floon exploded. "My problem? My problem is I am not your father! He had thin hands! And when I did anything wrong he used them on me! Oh yes, oh yes. Stabbing those terrible fingers of his into my ear. Saying '*My* son will not *do* things like this. *Not-my-son.*' 'We are living in Amer-i-ca now! So you will talk like an Amer-i-can.' Once a week, more, sometimes five times a week he would find a new reason for torturing me with those goddamned hands, those fingers like pencils." Voice crazed, Old Floon's eyes stayed in his head but at the same time they were somewhere else very far away. "Look at my hands, you fool. They are like catcher's mitts. Do these really look like his?"

When there was still no response, the old man got even angrier. Grabbing little Frannie by the arm he jerked him over. The kid grunted and tried to twist away but it was impossible. Old Floon stuffed the pistol halfway down the front of his pants to free up his other hand.

The next time he spoke his voice sounded completely different—it had a thick guttural accent and his words slowed so they had more weight and flavor when you heard them. He sounded like Henry Kissinger talking. "A hero eats lions for breakfast." He stuck his index finger so hard into the kid's ear that the poor boy's face collapsed in on itself while he let out a screeching catlike yelp.

"Do you want to be a hero, or do you want to deliver mail?

Or iron another man's shirts? That would be a good job for my son—iron another man's shirts." Another finger stab into the ear, another startled scream.

George, Floon Junior, and I watched the lunatic vent his festered fifty-year-old gripe on a little boy. It was so bizarre and crackbrained that for too many moments we did nothing because all three of us were simply hypnotized by the force and ugliness of it. What's more interesting than a car wreck when you first see it? Why do you think traffic always backs up for miles? All those eyes want to see what's left. A car wreck or another's bad news, a person losing control in public . . . Because they are all different kinds of death in action, folks. Step right up and see life bite—someone else.

"Lemme go!" The boy struggled wildly, twisting every which way but he could not escape. No way.

Leaning against the house a few feet away was a long and quite heavy metal pole. On the porch was a black plastic dishlike thing with several color-coded wires hanging off it. This contraption was meant to be bolted onto the pole. If done correctly and with proper adjustments, the completed outfit became an outdoor TV antenna. A few days before George had been sitting up on his roof, imagining himself as this very antenna so that he could write a good description of how to properly assemble it.

I had seen the pole earlier but what with all the action taking place it didn't much register on me. Old Floon watched with interest as the boy flipped and jumped frantically around in his hand. While his attention was distracted, Young Floon stepped over to the house, took up the pole, and without a second's hesitation swung it full force at the old man's head.

The sound of metal on skull came out a mix of *clong* and *thunk*. It was a deep, dull noise, not loud but oh-so-vivid. You remembered a sound like that even if you didn't know what caused it. After the hit, the pole shook so violently in his hands that it looked alive. My eyes followed that jittering pole up all the way to Young Floon's eyes. They were still blank/empty of anything but just being alive. That's all—that's the only thing they showed. As far as he knew, this man had just crushed his father's skull with a five-foot-long metal pike but the only emotion that showed on his face was nothing.

Old Floon fell to the left, Little Frannie to the right. He had been pulling so terrifically hard to get away that when the old man let go of him, the boy just dropped toward gravity. They separated like a wishbone snapping. As soon as the kid hit the ground he crawled lickety-split away on all fours, not sure of what had happened except for the physical fact he was abruptly freed and was not about to be recaptured. As he moved he screamed, "Asshole, asshole!" in a high, hurt little boy's voice. It was a strange sight—him crabbing away, shouting that word over and over at an old man who lay on his back with nothing left but some escaping body heat.

I looked at the others and then eventually bent down to feel for a pulse. Nothing. Anyway Floon's head told the tale before I even touched his throat—one look and anyone would have known. Because what had once been the man's temple was now fresh bread dough and red oatmeal.

I glanced at his killer. "Home run, bud. You knocked this guy out of the park."

Raising his eyebrows only a little, Young Floon dropped the metal pole on the ground. It landed with a clang and rolled away from him. I think all of us spent a moment watching it roll till it stopped. Lying there, it suddenly had a whole new personality: It had gone from being an antenna pole to a murder weapon in a minute and a half.

Dreampilot

Just about everything that took place after that was strange, but strangest of all was what happened immediately after Floon killed Floon. Without a word the three of us adults moved into action with the kid looking on.

I went to the car and gestured for Floon Junior to open the back gate. He unlocked it and as soon as it swung open, we went back for the body. I looked at George and said only, "Get those big Baggies." He went into his house and came back a few moments later (followed by Chuck the dachshund) with a box of giant, industrial-size garbage bags he used when he cut branches off his apple tree. Walking to the back of the car, he pulled out several and rapidly lined the floor of the trunk with them. Not once did I look to see if anyone in the neighborhood had witnessed our goings-on in the last ten minutes or even if anyone was watching us now.

We picked up the body, awkwardly maneuvered it into another of the shiny black bags, and hefted it into the trunk. Its plastic landed on the other plastic with a clunk and the sound of a lot of crinkling while we pushed and shoved it flush into a corner. Then I slid the murder weapon in next to the bag. Obviously it would have to disappear too.

That done, I put out my hand for the car keys. There would be no debate about this—I was driving. Floon gave them right over. All four of us (and the dog) got into his brand-new Isuzu and drove off.

We rode through town in silence. Once in a while I looked around remembering how different the place looked earlier that morning when it was Crane's View of thirty years ago. From what little I could see, the Rat's Potato crew had put everything back in its proper place. But then again I wasn't about to stop to check the details, what with the serious cargo we were carrying.

George and Floon sat in the backseat, the boy up front next to me. Our silence continued until I realized, hey, I don't having a fucking clue where to go now. I looked in the rearview mirror and checked the passengers to see if they looked any less confused than I. Both were staring out the windows with their hands in their laps.

"Hey."

Blinking, I shifted my eyes over to the kid. "What do *you* want?"

He just happened to be holding the famous feather, twirling it back and forth in his little fingers the way anyone plays with a feather in their hand.

"Where'd you get that?"

Saying nothing, he jerked his head toward his shoulder.

"What? What does that mean?"

"I got it from him. The guy. The guy in the *bag*."

"How?"

"I just got it." Suddenly he had changed from a chatterbox into Mr. Laconic.

"Give it here."

He didn't. Looking full at him, I snapped my fingers under his nose. *"Give it to me."*

With a dramatic sigh he handed it over. "That big stupid jerk hurt my ear inside. It still hurts."

"I bet it does." Glancing in the rearview, I saw that Floon was watching me. I reached backward and gestured for him to take the feather. "You're going to need this."

He took it, gave it a look, didn't say a word.

"You've also got blood on your cheek, so you'd better wipe it off. Now listen, Floon, there's something incredibly important about that feather but don't ask me what 'cause I don't know. The thing's not what you think it is, it's not even from a bird. It's just something completely *different*. You'll understand that when you examine it in your lab or wherever. That feather is going to play a really important part in whatever you do with the rest of your life, so take good care of it."

"Frannie, how do you know these things?"

"I just do, George, so let me talk now and don't interrupt. Next, if you have any money, buy stock in a company called SeeReal—"

"Cereal?"

"No, see—real. Like see with your eyes, and real like genuine. The two words go together as one: SeeReal. The ticker abbreviation for it is S-E-E-R. Buy stock in that company as soon as you can and buy a lot." I tried hard to remember what else Old Floon had told me earlier in the library but I couldn't think of anything. Only later did I recall "tancretic spredge" and cold fusion but by then the men were long gone in the direction of their next thirty years.

"What are we going to do, Frannie?" George held Chuck on his lap. Even that goofy dog must have sensed something serious was going on because it wasn't hopping around as usual, trying to kiss everyone.

"We're going to my house to get a shovel. Then we'll go to the woods out behind the Tyndall place and bury the body. Unless you have a better plan."

"Someone could find it. Those woods aren't *that* large."

"True, George, but the alternative is to drive around until we run out of gas trying to decide what else to do with our body. Then we can tank up at CITGO, hope no one sees what we're carrying in the back, and then drive around some more. Does that sound like a better plan, or do you have another in mind?"

Silence.

"All right. I say we go with my plan, hope our luck holds and no one sees us."

"Why are you even doing this, Frannie? If we're caught they'll put us in prison. We'll all be in terrible trouble. You're the chief of police!"

"He *is?*" Floon gulped, his voice climbing way up.

"I'm doing it because I have no time left, George. That's the only thing I know for sure now. We have to get him out of here without anyone knowing what just happened. Please don't ask me to explain it—that's just the way it is. I have no time left to worry about what else to do with this body. We gotta dump it, and Floon's gotta get out of here. I may be wrong but I gotta go with that instinct. There are other things way more important."

"More important than *this,* Frannie?"

"Much more, believe me."

The backseaters looked at each other.

"Floon, why were you at George's house just now?"

"Because I have invented something and I need the best person in the business to write the instructions."

I slapped the steering wheel for emphasis while keeping eye contact with George in the mirror. "You mean he came to you out of the blue *today,* this morning, to ask if you'd work with him?"

"Not exactly. He called yesterday to say he was in New York and asked if we could meet."

"That's still too much of a coincidence. This whole thing ain't no fluke."

"What isn't?"

"It can't be a coincidence that Mr. Floon here was visiting you *today* at the same time as I came to the house with *him*. I hitchhiked a thumb over my shoulder, assuming everyone knew who I was talking about.

A flame of pain seared across the inside of my forehead forcing me to squint my eyes almost closed. It shot to the back of my head where, for an excruciating few seconds, it flickered on and off like a blazing neon sign. It stopped. But I realized I had better not drive anymore because if another big one hit there was a good chance I would drive this snazzy new car right into someone's living room and solve all our problems.

When I pulled up in front of our house, loud music was coming from an open window upstairs. Pauline's room. I wondered if George had brought her home from the hospital before meeting with Floon. Despite everything I had to smile. A yellow and green summery day. Loud techno music pouring out of a teenager's bedroom. What could be more normal and reassuring than that scene? Her mother was in the hospital but she would be all right now. There was nothing to worry about. Magda would be home soon.

I stood on the sidewalk looking at our house, loving what I saw. I knew I must get moving but give me one more minute to look and remember, just one more. How happy I'd been here. How much I would have given to spend the rest of my life knowing these women day to day, getting older, watching Pauline grow up and into a valid and interesting life of her own. Maybe if I'd had more time I would have been able to figure out a little of what made my own life tick. Maybe not, but it wouldn't have even mattered so long as I could live it here, around these people, in this town I loved. No matter what was about to happen to me, I had no reason to complain.

I was tempted to run upstairs and check on Pauline to see how she was doing, reassure her that everything was going to be fine now. But there was no time. Nor did I want her to see Floon's car and ask questions about what was going on.

Instead I went to the garage to look for the shovel. My car was parked in there, which reminded me of finding the resurrected Old Vertue in its trunk the other night. Which reminded me of having that nice chat with Pauline in the car about what she wanted to do with her life. On and on, everything in that dusty place reminding me of something else, and my nostalgia for my flickering life grew even keener.

I searched the crowded garage for the tool I had already used to bury both my father and a four-hundred-year-old dog (twice). I discovered it leaning next to a rake against a far wall. Next to it was a window that gave a view of the street. Reaching for the shovel I glanced out the window and saw a police car coming up the street. It stopped almost directly across from Floon's car.

Of course the cops would eventually show up here when they discovered I wasn't being held captive at the town library (by a man who had just been killed by himself and whose corpse was lying in that car directly across the street from them). The situation was so surreal that it should have been funny but it was way too late for that.

Adele Kastberg and Brett Rudin got out of the police car. That was good to see because both of them were dimwits. I would have been much more concerned if Bill Pegg had showed up now at my door. These two cops walked up our path, but at a certain point I lost sight of them because of my limited view. The doorbell chimed its familiar ding-dong. Unconsciously I found myself mimicking those sounds quietly—*ding-dong*—just so I could hear them another time and memorize a little more of what would be gone soon. All three of us waited for someone to answer the door. When no one came they rang it again. Pauline had her music cranked way up. I could hear it through the walls of the garage. Could she hear the ring behind that wall of sound in her room? I closed my eyes and willed her to come answer the door. In the middle of that willing, I heard a car engine start. Opening my eyes, I caught sight of the tail end of Floon's car slowly driving away down the street.

"Where the hell are they going? You gotta to be shitting me!" I bit my hand. It hurt, but I had to do something to vent my frustration.

Two stupid cops stood on my doorstep, effectively trapping me in my own damned garage. And even if I was able to escape, what was I supposed to do now that the car with the evidence had just taken off? Where *were* they going? What did they think they were doing? In truth I knew exactly what they were doing and it made total sense—they wanted to get out of there because they carried a body in their car. But what the hell was I supposed to do in the meantime—wait there with the shovel until either they decided to come back or my head popped?

Luckily a little police muscle went into action. Knowing Officer Adele and her diplomatic manner, she was probably the one who started banging on the front door so loudly that they could have heard the sound down the block. That was Adele's way of doing police work, but for the first time in all the years we had worked together I was happy for it.

The Isuzu disappeared completely from view just as the music in the house stopped. Some more time passed but then there was Pauline's voice, joined by the others. I was so relieved that I stuck out my tongue and crossed my eyes. The three of them spoke a while, but I couldn't make out what they were saying. Then came the sound of the front door closing. I assumed they had all gone into the house. Which meant I had very little time to escape before they came out again. I looked around the garage for anything beside the too-loud and obvious car that could get me away from there fast and silently.

At the beginning of the summer Magda was inspired by some rah-rah article on fitness she read and bought a mountain bike. Pauline and I were struck dumb by the gesture. As expected, my wife used it maybe three times before deciding she wasn't the big calves/wet armpits kind of girl. The minute she showed me the bike I christened it Tinkerbell because of its ridiculous color—gold-metal-flake pink.

I hate bicycles and bicycling. They poke you in the ass and make you pant for no good reason. Bikes are also dangerous as hell and serious traffic hazards. Furthermore, people who use them are invariably self-righteous about various unappealing subjects—ecology, fitness, or their resting pulse rate. The hell with them—when I want my heart to beat fast I'll have sex.

So dig this—the ultimate indignity: there goes Chief of Police McCabe pedaling furiously down his street like a fucking wacko on a cute little pink bike. And is that a dirty shovel lying across the handlebars of the bike? Indeed it is. But can't the man see that the tires on it are so low on air that they might as well be flat?

The bike was small, and because I didn't adjust the seat before launching myself, my knees came up almost to my chest as I pedaled, making the whole experience ten times more uncomfortable and ridiculous-looking.

Follow that Isuzu! But how could I when it had a five-minute head start on me and two hundred more horsepower than I did? Down one street, down another. Looking everywhere for their car. The shovel slipping around on the handlebars and almost dropping a half dozen times.

Passing too many people I knew, I tried as hard as I could not. to be seen. Failed miserably.

"Whoa there, Chief. Nice bike!" Smirk.

"Hey, Fran, you suddenly going athletic?" Big laugh.

Or just plain smiles and more chuckles as these people—my friends and neighbors—watched a fool roll by with his high-pumping knees and semiflat tires.

I thought I saw their car going left at the intersection of Broadway and April Street but most likely that was wishful think-ing. I kept trying to figure out where they might go. All at once I dropped the shovel and, braking hard, listened to it clatter and dance down the street. I picked it up and started again. George must have been driving the car now because he knew Crane's View. But where would my friend go? If he were writing the instructions for how to get out of this fix, what would he say?

Pedal pedal pedal—pedaling through town I kept imagining the music from *The Wizard of Oz* when Miss Gulch rides away on her bicycle with Toto the dog her captive. Pedal pedal pedal—this was definitely not how I had imagined my last days on earth.

I was miserably out of shape; my cigarette lungs were screaming help; every moment I felt like my whole body might just cave in and stop. The number of possible places they might have gone was just too big. I had to make a choice now and go with it before my body disintegrated.

"All right, the woods. Let's go to the woods." And that's what I did. At Mobile Lane I hung a left and took a shortcut toward the Tyndall house that I had been using for forty years. Now that I knew where I was heading I felt better in my head but my body was shot. When she was enthusing about the benefits of her new exercise regime, Magda had told me that riding a bicycle was second only to swimming in total aerobic training. I said uh-huh and continued reading the newspaper. Now sadly I knew what she meant. I was sweating, panting, and cursing at the same time. Simultaneous breakdown on all fronts. Was that aerobic too? And those woods behind Lionel Tyndall's house suddenly seemed a *lot* farther away than I remembered. Then again it had been many years since I had gone to that part of Crane's View on foot, or any kind of pedal other than a gas pedal. Exercise fiends always crow that you see more when you're walking or biking. But the only thing I saw more of at the moment was my fury and frustration at trying to move Tinkerbell forward at more than a crawl.

When it felt like things couldn't get any worse I heard the sound of a siren coming up fast behind me. For a molten moment I felt like I had when I was a kid and forever in trouble with the law: All I could think was *run*—get out of there. Don't let them catch you! I even considered jumping off the bike and sprinting for cover. But if I was the cop in the car and saw that, I'd wonder gee, how come that fellow on the pink bike is running away? So instead of fleeing, I put my head down as low as it would go and bravely pedaled on, hoping the gods or maybe even the gang from Rat's Potato would help me out here.

And I guess someone did because the patrol car screamed by me way too fast and straight on down the road. I'm sure whoever was driving was having such a good time playing with the siren and high speed that he didn't think a second about the sunken-headed man puffing along on a bicycle. Which gave me something new to think/worry about as I took the last few lefts and rights: Where *was* that car going in such a dangerous hurry? It was departmental policy not to speed in town unless there was real trouble somewhere. What new complication or calamity had just happened?

Luckily there was Tyndall's big house, and immediately behind it the aqueduct that was another part of the shortcut to the
woods if you were on foot or a bike. For the only time since I'd
set off from my house I was happy to be riding these wheels.
Another five minutes and I would come to the road that led off
into the woods. If there was no sign of George I hadn't a clue
of what to do next.

There was no sign of George. I took the road anyway and
drove into the forest. If you'd said there was a steep hill ahead
that I had to climb, I would have gotten off the bike, turned
around, and pushed it home, to hell with the consequences.

I rode slowly on, seeing nothing, growing more confused
and disappointed by the foot. Still, when I got to the end of the
woods I turned around and came back, looking just as hard as I
had before. An old policeman's instincts die hard. Looking back
and forth from one side of the shadowed road to the other and
then in among the trees for a sign—any sign that they had come
here to bury the body. But how could they do that if they didn't
have a shovel?

"Damn you, George, why didn't you do what I said? It would
have been the easiest way out of this mess." Which I knew wasn't
really true but it felt good to say it to no one but the trees and
Tinkerbell.

Cars flew past. I wobbled/pedaled as close to the side of the
road as possible. I didn't want to be seen but how do you avoid
that when you're in the middle of nowhere riding a pink bicycle?
Never once did it cross my rattled mind that the Isuzu boys were
in a four-wheel-drive vehicle which—ergo!—meant they could
go off the road.

Shortly before I gave up and was beginning to think about
my next move, I looked to one side of the road and saw Little
Frannie emerging from a dark clump of pine trees. He saw me

but didn't appear one bit surprised. Hands stuffed deep in his khaki pockets, he didn't look happy. Rolling slowly over to him, I put my feet down to stop.

"Hey."

"Hey." He wouldn't look at me. "That's a pretty cool-looking bike. Except it's pink."

For one ridiculous second I felt embarrassed and an urgent need to explain. "Well, it's not mine. It belongs to my wife. Where are the other guys?"

"Back there in the trees." His voice was sad and quiet. He sighed deeply when he finished the sentence.

"How come you're out here?"

Looking at the ground he mumbled, "They told me to go home."

"Can you show me where they are?" I tried not to sound impatient. If I pissed him off now I was in big trouble.

He brightened right up—this was an adult's invitation to go back into the action. "Yeah, I'll show you! Are you going to take the bike? How come it's got such big tires?"

Back when I was his age, things like mountain bikes didn't exist, so I understood his skepticism.

"It drives better that way; especially in the woods, over rocks and stuff. Hop on—we'll ride it in and you can show me where they are. Then you can take it for a ride yourself if you like."

He jumped on, shouting gleefully, "You steer and I'll be the Dreampilot! I'll tell you where to go."

"Okay, Mr. Dreampilot. Hold the shovel."

I hadn't seen them because they had driven a good ways into the woods and down into a small ravine that couldn't be seen from the road. When we reached Floon's car no one was around, but the body still lay in the trunk—not a good sign.

"Where are they?" Leaning the bike against a tree, I turned in a complete circle but saw nothing.

The boy looked too. "They were looking for a place to bury him before; somewhere under the trees. But they wouldn't let me come. That Floon guy called me a little pisser."

Instinctively I touched his head and almost said when I was your age I was a lot more than just a little pisser. But I held back and tried to sound reassuring instead. "Hey, that's a compliment! I'm a big pisser and proud of it, but that's only because I'm grown up. Give me the shovel. You want to take the bike now and go for a ride?"

He shook his head. "No, I want to go with you."

"Okay, come on. We'll leave the bike here and go find them."

We walked around for minutes but found nothing and heard nothing. The woods were fragrant and full of leaves and flickering shadows. Soon autumn would arrive and the smells in here would change—they'd become thicker, funkier—things would die, fall, cover the forest floor, and rot. Old wood, old leaves, later on it would snow and all those dark final colors of winter would be covered by the white.

I would never see any of it again. The thought was unbearable. I tried with all my strength to clear it from my mind. We walked on, stopping once in a while to listen for the others.

"Who are you?" the boy asked.

I hesitated, smiled. "I'm you, grown up."

He studied the ground and thought that one over. "But how can we both be here at the same time?"

"I don't know. It just happened. I can't explain it. I guess it's magic."

"Okay." He rocked back on his heels, saw something on the

ground, bent to pick up an interesting-looking stick that was lying against a rock. His voice was calm and reasonable when he spoke. As if what I'd said was no big deal. "I knew we were kind of related or something but I didn't know how. You're really me when I grow up?"

"Yes. I'm you when you're forty-seven years old."

"That's pretty old. But you look okay. Do you still have a penis?"

That stopped me. "A penis? Well yeah. Why wouldn't I?"

"Marvin Bruce told me your penis grows back inside your body when you get to be forty."

Just the name and memory of that skinny, yellow-toothed, brown-nosing sewer rat shot the hair up on the back of my neck. I said a little too adamantly, "Marvin Bruce picks his nose and *eats* it. Are you gonna trust a guy who does that?"

"You know Marvin?"

"Sure. He's a jerk. He probably grew up and became Kenneth Starr."

"Who's that?"

"Never mind. Let's go."

We found them as far into the woods as you could go. Both men were sitting on the ground staring blankly into the distance. Chuck lay asleep on Floon's left foot. Only George looked up slowly when we approached. The expression on his face said he was trying to wrestle his mind back from a place very far away but having a hard time doing it. Maybe that was why he didn't appear surprised to see me.

"Frannie. Here you are. Are you all right? You look very pale."

"I'm okay. What are you doing? Why are you just sitting? There's a body in the back of that car. You can't just leave it there like that."

"We were about to go back for it. We stopped to rest and then Caz started giving me details about his project. It's absolutely astounding. You can't imagine the ramifications of what he's attempting to do."

"I'll take your word for it. Get up, George. We have to dig a hole now and stop wasting time. Did you find a place yet?"

The boy wandered away, poking his stick into the ground.

"Anywhere around here should be all right, Frannie. It's as far from the road as we can be. We'll have to go down deep, though, to prevent the animals from digging it up when we're gone."

I stabbed the shovel into the earth. It clanged loudly against a tree root. It was like the day I had tried to bury Old Vertue out here—thick roots crisscrossed the forest floor just below the surface. I had learned the hard way that cutting through them was impossible.

I walked back and forth pushing the shovel into the ground every few feet but it was all the same—roots galore. The only sounds were the birds, me poking with the shovel and the boy swishing his stick, hitting trees, swatting at their branches.

"I don't think we can do it here. There are just too many goddamned roots."

"Should we go get the body or not?"

I dropped the shovel on the ground and crossed my arms. In my mind all I could picture was a giant traffic light stuck on red. Something had to be done, a decision had to be made fast, but what?

A wind kicked up. The air was suddenly filled with the lush scent of pine and the sexy hiss of a warm breeze through summer's trees. Without thinking I lifted my head and sniffed the air. "My God, what a beautiful smell."

As if it couldn't decide on whether to go or stay, sunlight

flickered across different parts of the boy's body. His head was bowed. From the look of it, he'd recently gotten his hair cut by Vernon the town barber, dead twenty years now.

Seeing something on the ground, Little Fran dropped his stick and slowly began to bend down. His eyes were glued to one spot. "Hey, look at this!" He was twenty feet away. I was annoyed that he was distracting me, plus I couldn't see what had him so excited. A kid thing probably. No time for that now. George and Floon stood waiting for me to decide. Ironic—these two megabrains waiting for instructions from F. McCabe, once deemed "a candidate for the gas chamber" by an enraged high school principal before expelling him. But I had no idea what to tell them to do—the traffic light in my mind was still red.

"Look!" The boy snatched at something on the ground.

Rising again, he held something between his thumb and index fingers. The rest of his fingers were splayed out like he didn't want them to touch whatever it was he held. Until it moved, I thought it was only another stick.

It was a lizard or a chameleon, I don't know which—I ain't no herpetologist. I should have asked George the expert on everything but I was too excited to care. The poor little fucker had been minding its own lizard business, taking a little sun on the forest floor. Until without warning it was yanked up in the air by its long tail. For a moment. For a moment it stayed that way, swinging and twisting in circles desperately trying to get away. Then its tail snapped off and Mr. Lizard hit the ground running. The boy squealed his delight and dismay. More important, when the lizard ran away it skittered up, along and then over my shovel. The picture of those two things together, one on top of the other—lizard on shovel—touched something in me like flame to dry paper.

Without a second's hesitation I remembered George and me

looking at Antonya Corando's school notebooks. And I heard him say there were only two images that kept recurring in all of her strange, prophetic drawings—that shovel and a lizard.

My eyes glued to the spot on the ground where the kid had picked up the lizard, I stepped over and said, "Dig here."

"*There?* It's right under that tree. There will be roots everywhere."

"Pick up the fucking shovel and dig *here*, Floon. Or I'll stick it up your ass, blade first."

"But, Frannie, he's right. The roots—"

"George, remember Antonya Corando's notebooks? Remember the two images you said kept coming up over and over?"

Sucking in his lower lip, he raised a hand to make a point. Like he was raising it in class to be recognized by the teacher. But his hand slowed going up as the understanding of what I'd said hit home. His hand abruptly snatched at the air and turned into a tight fist. "The lizard and the shovel!"

"Exactly. Start digging. Right here."

"Yes!" He whipped around to Floon who was now looking at both of us as if we were the enemy. "It's here, Caz. Frannie's right—this is where we have to dig."

"I'll start! Let me." The kid cried out happily, picking up the shovel but dropping it again in his excitement. He picked it right up again and began digging like a little machine.

"No, we'll do it. It'll go faster. You just stand back." I gestured for him to hand over the shovel.

He wouldn't. He tried putting it behind his back. "No! That's not fair! I found that lizard. I did. And I found these guys too when you couldn't. So I should get to dig first."

I tried to sound reasonable, like a good guy who was only on his side. "My man, we just gotta do this ourselves and as fast as possible. We gotta dig this hole and then get out of here."

His face tried turning to stone but you know how little kids are—they haven't learned how to be cool yet. They know passion cold and hot, but not cool. His next voice came out a sob. "That's not fair! I helped you twice today and you know it! I helped you get out of the library too. I—"

"Give me the goddamned shovel. *Now!*" I stepped toward him. Whatever was on my face scared him. He held the tool behind his back, but when he saw me coming, he dropped it. Stumbling backward over it, he fell down. His eyes stayed scared on me. There was no more time to waste. I picked up the shovel and turned away from him.

"You're the pisser! You're the big fat pisser and you *don't* have a penis!" His outrage turned to singsongy taunt. "You don't have a penis, you don't have a pe-nis!"

Ignoring the boy, I gave Floon the shovel and pointed out the spot on the ground. I was dizzy and needed to sit down.

"Frannie, watch out—" George's voice, then something hard hit the back of my knee. It buckled, but I didn't fall. Turning, I saw the kid running away into the woods.

"He kicked you."

"Doesn't matter. Let's go."

But it did matter. When we decided it would be better for George and Floon to first go back for the body, I stood alone thinking about the little boy. Where would he go? Would he be coming back?

I felt weak but clearer in my mind than I had all day. Some sort of plan had taken shape: Dig the hole, bury the body, return to town—The snap and click of twigs under their feet announced they were returning. The body in its bag on their shoulders looked smaller.

As if it was still alive and they were concerned for its comfort, they lowered it very gently to the ground. Floon picked up the shovel and began digging. He worked with precise gestures and no wasted effort. The hole grew quickly not least because there was nothing in the way—no roots, boulders, nothing unseen or unexpected. I was sure there wouldn't be. The lizard had been the X to mark this spot and I knew that the minute I saw it.

When George took over digging he asked if I had ever heard of Kilioa. When I said no he explained it was a mythological creature—one of two lizard women who keep the soul of the deceased imprisoned. By then I didn't give a damn whether the lizard we'd seen was Kilioa or a normal forest reptile catching a few rays on a sunny day.

"Yes, but lizards have always been very important in world mythology, Frannie. They can symbolize all sorts of profound things."

"Fascinating. Just keep digging."

"You don't care do you?"

"Not at all."

The excavation went on. We talked some but not much. I didn't feel up to joining in the work yet so I let them do it. Periodically I checked to see if the dead Floon was still with us.

They'd gotten pretty far down when I heard two sirens go by out on the road, one right after the other. It made me crazy not knowing what the reason was. Normally you didn't have to use the siren in a Crane's View police car. Assuming the worst, I decided the best thing was to get these two guys out of here now, finish the job myself and go home.

When I told them neither seemed unhappy about stopping. We stood above the hole looking down into it.

"George, I want you to leave town for a while. Just go and don't come back for maybe a week or two. Have you got money on you?"

"Yes, but where should I go?"

"I don't know. I want you and Floon here to just disappear for a while. Call me in a few days. I'll tell you when the coast is clear to come back. I want to clean up every trace of anything we might have left back at your house. I'll lock it up when I'm done. Who knows if anyone saw what went on back there."

"Okay."

Floon said, "We can go to my apartment in New York."

"No, that's a bad idea. Go away for a while. Take a road trip, go somewhere neither of you is known. Go to the ocean and talk about Floon's plans."

I remembered that hotel room in Vienna and seeing the dog on the bed. Astopel had said it was George Dalemwood. I remembered Susan Ginnety telling me George had simply disappeared from Crane's View thirty years ago and was never seen again.

"Floon, you go ahead. I need to tell George a few more things."

When the other was far enough away not to hear, I put both hands on my friend's shoulders and moved toward him till we were almost nose to nose.

"Frannie, you don't look good. You look very ill. Let's finish this and then let me take you home."

"No, I'm okay. George, listen to me: I know some things about the future. I know that you and Floon are going to work together on something very big. It may take years. Maybe it's even this project he was telling you about. Do it but be very careful. Watch your ass at all times. Don't trust him much, no matter how brilliant you think he is.

"Get out of town now and stay gone for a while. I don't know how things are going to go down around here in the next few days. But I don't want you anywhere in the vicinity if shit hits the fan. And, George?"

"Yes?" His face was all questions and worry. It broke my heart but there was nothing more I could do about it.

I was about to tell my friend that I loved him but something else came to mind. "Tancretic spredge. Can you remember that name?" I spelled it for him. "Do you know about cold fusion? *You do?* Great! Then this has something to do with it. And if you can't find it yet, keep looking because that's what cold fusion is all about. It's going to change the world. Tancretic spredge, okay?"

"Okay. When should I call you?"

"In a few days. Wait till things calm down." I knew he would never be back but I didn't want to say that and scare him. "Take care of yourself. Take care of Chuck." I kissed him on the cheek. "You're a good pal. The best."

"I'm frightened, Frannie."

"So am I."

"You? You're never frightened of anything."

"I'm frightened that one day I'm going to lose all this and I won't have loved it enough. Remember that—love this all the time. Love it for me too when you remember."

I gave him a slight push and he started away. Chuck danced around his feet, running this way and that; happy to be on the move again with the person he loved most. George turned once. I said only "tancretic spredge." He repeated it, but by the time he got to the end, he was too far away for me to hear.

I waited for the Isuzu engine to start but heard nothing. A long wait, too long. But then there it was—faint, so faint, as if the sound came from half a mile away. I imagined them slowly driving out through the trees, avoiding ruts, stumps, stones.

George at the wheel or Floon? George—he knew the town, knew to turn right when they reached the road and go that five winding miles till he hit the parkway.

I maneuvered my way awkwardly down into the hole and started digging. The earth was soft and damp—it gave up a lot to each shovelful. Digging, I busied my mind by imagining their car driving down the road toward the parkway. I tried to remember all of the landmarks along the way—the large copper beech tree that had been struck by lightning. The small white cross by the side of the road marking the spot where a fatal accident had happened years ago. The still pond nearby that was always covered by green scum and water lillies. We'd caught so many frogs there when we were kids. I once pushed Marvin Bruce into it and made sure his head went all the way under.

For no reason my heart began racing. Closing my eyes, I willed then begged it to calm down. After some more crazy uneven beats it eventually quieted. I waited to see if it would stay that way. My chin rested on my chest. Quiet down, heart— everything is going to be all right. I couldn't trust my body anymore. How much time did I have left? Maybe I should have let them finish digging the grave and drive me back to town. Maybe that would have been a whole lot smarter than what I was attempting to do now.

Opening my eyes I saw the ground at the bottom of the hole. Slowly I lifted another shovelful. It uncovered something. My heart stayed calm but I could feel it beating throughout my body.

Something white down there. Something white covered by moist black dirt. Pushing the shovel up out of the hole, I went down on my knees for a closer look. Tentatively I brushed some dirt aside. More white appeared. It was cloth, cotton, some kind of clothing. A T-shirt? With cupped hands I dug way more dirt until yes, I saw it was a white T-shirt and oh Christ, it's a body.

The lizard and the shovel said Dig here. There's a body here. Find it. All the time I'd been moving toward this without knowing it. Dig here.

Dig here.

I carefully brushed away more dirt until the face showed. A child. I knew who it was. It was impossible. I knew who it was. No! Run away, get out of here. His small mouth, nose, the peacefully closed eyes.

It was the boy. The boy I had just sent away, Dreampilot, me. He was dead now and covered with dirt at the bottom of this hole. This hole we had just dug, this hole he had wanted to help dig. He lay dead in it now and I had unearthed him. His face was still warm when I touched it. His lips separated under the pressure of my hand. They were still wet. The bottom one shone.

"No!"

I found a way through it. I found a way through it by going crazy a little but that helped. He was dirty. He was lying under the dirt and needed to be brought out, cleaned. I set to work rescuing him. That wasn't the correct word but it's the one that stayed in my mind. Rescue him—get him back to us—back from where he shouldn't have been in the first place.

I talked to him while I got him out. I talked to him when I lifted him up, had him in my arms, was brushing dirt off him, off his soft child's skin, his clothes, any dirt I could see. I talked while I lifted his body gently up to the rim of the grave and lay him down next to the shovel.

I climbed out. I felt weak, sick, but strangely exhilarated at the same time. I had this job to do, this rescue mission: Bring the Dreampilot back. All of my own problems must wait till that is accomplished.

I had to stop and rest. I sat down next to his body. I had to

hold him to make sure nothing else happened to him. We were
too close to the hole. I didn't like that. It was too close to us.
We had to move farther away. The hole was dangerous and deep.
No matter how careful you were you could still fall in.

I stood, picked him up, and walked away from there. I think
I probably would have kept walking out of the forest if my body
hadn't said stop. It said stop now or I won't give you anything
more. So I did what it demanded—stopped where I was, waited,
hoped that it would let me go on. I wasn't talking to the boy
anymore, wasn't apologizing for not letting him help us dig. I
only wanted everything to be silent then.

His body was light. Was that because he was a little boy or
because death had taken his weight? Standing in the woods with
my back to Floon's grave, I waited for something to happen, not
caring if anything did. I knew I should put the child down, go
back to the hole and finish that job. I knew I should do that but
I didn't.

I guess I just stood with the child's body in my arms, dream-
ing. Is that possible? I stood there without even thinking now
what? Yes, I just stood there.

Until I heard maybe the third or fourth *whump*. There are
sounds you know but don't recognize till you see them happening. With my back to the hole I heard it one-two-three times—
whump whump whump. Slowly, not fast in any way. I knew the
sound but could not place it. It came from behind me in the
forest where no one was. But I didn't turn to see. Not yet.
Whump whump.

Not until more of those heavy dull, familiar sounds came did
I want to look. Pulling the child tighter to my chest, I turned.

There were five of them. They were all shoveling dirt back
into the hole. *Whump-whump.* Although none spoke they all looked

really happy, smiling, delighted to be doing this chore together. Their ages varied widely. The youngest looked around fourteen, the oldest forty-five. I am only guessing. Every one of them wore what the dead boy in my arms wore—khakis, a white T-shirt, black high-top canvas sneakers,

And all of them were me. They were finishing filling Floon's grave. His body bag was gone. They must have lowered the black bag into the hole and now were filling the dirt back in. Together they had done the job for me.

I watched until they were finished. With five of them working it didn't take long. The shovels were light in their hands. Giant loads of dirt flew back into the hole. All the time they worked they kept looking at each other and smiling. They were having a ball. It was as if this were a family outing—all the brothers together again and goofing around. Digging a hole, having fun. But they weren't brothers, they were me.

When they were finished they stood back from the hole and, leaning on their shovels, surveyed the work. From where I stood there was no sign of anything on the ground. No one could have known that a deep wide hole had been dug and filled there. The forest floor looked as untouched as it had been when we first came to it.

The diggers looked at each other and the oldest nodded his approval. Another slapped the youngest on the shoulder and, winking, handed him his shovel. Was it the one I had used? All of them were identical. The boy took it, an adoring look on his face. They all loved each other—being together like this was the greatest thing in life.

And then as one they came toward me. When they were near, the one who had given over his shovel reached out his arms and gently took the dead child from me. I didn't resist.

He said, "It's okay. We'll take care of him now." Holding the body more carefully than I had, he looked at it with wonderful warmth. Of course he would know what to do with it.

"Come on," another of them said but I didn't know which. They started to walk out of the woods, and it felt like the most natural thing to follow. They walked on either side of me. I kept looking from one to the other. I knew them all, each one a different version of myself when I was younger.

My body felt calm and okay as we walked. I felt peaceful and at the same time deeply, deeply sad. Because seeing them all together like this, seeing them work together with such pleasure and concentration, seeing how much they liked each other, seeing the dead child lying in one's arms, I finally understood.

How do you cross a wooden sea? I still did not know the answer to that question but seeing all that was around me, I now knew how to find the answer. Was this what Astopel and his kind wanted us to know? That nothing is more important than keeping every one of our individual selves alive. We must listen and be guided by them.

Not know thyself, know *thy selves*. All the yous, all the years, the days of Magda and Pauline, and orange cowboy boots, and when you believed penises grew back inside a man at forty years old.

We look at who we were, once upon a time, and see that person as stupid or amusing, but never essential. Like flipping through old snapshots of ourselves wearing funny hats or big lapels. How silly I was back then, how naive.

And how wrong to think that! Because now when *you* are incapable of doing it, those yous still know how to fly, find the way into a forest or out of a library. Only they can see the lizards and fill holes that need to be filled.

Gee-Gee, Dreampilot, the diggers . . . Now I knew how

much I needed all of them to really understand my life. How do you cross a wooden sea? Ask them and listen carefully to their different answers.

"I don't think I can go any farther." My head was throbbing and there was a strange prickly tingle in the tips of my fingers.

"We'll help you." One of them said and came up under my right arm to support me. Another took me up on the left. Held that way by them I felt almost okay again.

"The road isn't far. We're almost there."

Mayor Susan Ginnety found the body of Frannie McCabe. Driving back from a trip to New York, she was musing about how nice it would have been to be returning to a home, a husband and a life rather than just her job now. She was as lost as she had ever been and terrified she would live the rest of her days alone.

She drove past the pond and the sad white cross by the side of the road. Then through the small forest that marked the beginning of the Crane's View town limits. The road began to wind there and she slowed down. She was a careful driver. She was only going thirty when she saw the body lying by the side of the road. At first it looked like some bum had just decided to lay down there of all places and take a nap. Sunlight through the trees played a dancing havoc across the unmoving frame, lying on its back. Clearly it was a man. Susan didn't want to stop because she was frightened, but she was also the mayor and felt it her duty. Anyway, by the time she pulled to the side of the road a few feet up from the corpse she could see the man's face and instantly her mouth was open as far as it would go.

She was barely able to push the shift lever up to park before bursting into tears. The secret that no one ever knew was Mayor Ginnety sat in her car and wept so long and so loudly that her cries frightened birds from the trees directly above her. Minutes passed before she was even able to get out of her car and go to the body.

But what the old stories say really is true—somewhere deep in their hearts, those who love us most *always* know how we are. The moment she recognized Frannie McCabe lying by the side of the road, Susan Ginnety knew he was dead. The memories of her joyful times with him when she was a girl had haunted Susan her whole life and would continue to do so.

Only months later when she felt very sad and alone did a revelation come to her one winter night that made her smile. Only after all that time since his death had passed did she realize how lucky she was to have been the one to find McCabe. It had allowed her to be the first one to tell him goodbye. But in the next instant, life for her suddenly seemed hopelessly long and obscure. Because even when it gave you a gift, what could you do with a first goodbye?

Epilogue

Much against Magda's wishes, the funeral turned out to be a huge event. None of Frannie's friends could ever agree whether he would have loved or hated knowing five hundred people attended. Five hundred people who were genuinely stricken by the fact this still-young man was dead. He was so smart and competent, so funny too. Without doubt the best chief of police they had ever had. The story of how he had saved Maeve Powell's daughter from some mysterious madman on the day he died only polished his star.

Granted, there were also many stories about what a rotten kid he had been. How he had once set fire to a principal's car. Been expelled from school, been arrested, caused his father pain. But his death made those stories into anecdotes, apocryphal, chuckles mostly. Old Frannie, he was some guy, wasn't he? And weren't most good men naughty in their time? And don't forget how he also helped solve only the second murder case in the history of Crane's View.

So what if he'd been a wicked kid—McCabe grew up to be one hell of a man. He was a good friend, one hundred percent dependable; he loved his wife and did his job well. Those things are what count and people were grateful to have known him.

Thank God the boy was there. Gary Graham was his real name but he preferred being called Gee-Gee. A handsome kid. People who knew said he looked just like Frannie when he was that age.

On the day Gee-Gee came to stay with the McCabe's, his aunt was rushed to the hospital and his uncle died! Not much of a welcome but that didn't matter: He stepped right up and won people's admiration by the way he behaved.

He and Pauline arranged the funeral together, brought Magda home from the hospital, and led her to the gravesite when it was time. Then those two good kids stood by while she looked down at her husband's simple coffin.

Someone nearby heard her say only one thing: "I like you." Then she threw a pink rose onto his coffin and returned to her seat. Besides the large turnout the only other things that surprised people were the fact that Frannie's best friend, George Dalemwood didn't attend, Johnny Petangles *did,* in a wheelchair, and the minister no one knew who said the last words.

No one had ever seen the man before. An elegantly dressed black gentleman, he seemed to have the confidence of a politician and the voice of a radio announcer. At the service someone sitting near Gee-Gee asked in a whisper who the fellow was. The boy said in a peculiar voice, "I know who he is. Uncle Frannie and I knew the guy."

People were hesitant to ask Magda what this man's connection to her family was but she appeared to like what he said, particularly the quotation from the Koran: "Consider the last of everything and then thou wilt depart from the dream of it." Which was the only thing in the whole ceremony that made her cry, but again no one had the nerve to ask why.

When it was over and people were walking away, the boy approached the minister and asked in a tense hiss if they could talk a minute. The man tossed him a shrewd smile and said certainly, as soon as he was free they'd talk. Free meant after shaking as many hands as the man could find. He really did behave like he was running for office. But the boy waited, after telling Pauline he would meet them back at the house. The girl gave him a goony, loving look and said okay, but hurry.

Watching him patiently wait with his hands held in front of him, people thought Gee-Gee only wanted to thank the minister.

But when they were finally alone, the boy looked both ways to make sure no one was listening and then he let fly. "You fuck! You bastard! *What are you doing here?*"

"Gee-Gee, you should thank me for letting you come back. I didn't have to, you know."

"No, I don't know. I don't know anything. Why don't you tell me? Huh? You think you could do that?"

The man looked at an exquisite silver-and-black wristwatch on his left arm. When the boy saw it his eyes popped. "That's his watch. You stole his watch!"

"Borrowed. It's a beautiful thing, isn't it? Really a handsome piece. I'll give it to you when we're done here. Then you can pretend to have found it and get points with Magda. Yes, that's the best way to do it." He seemed very pleased with this idea.

In contrast, the boy was seething. His mouth was pinched down into a thin straight line that turned his lips almost white. Any moment it looked like he might jump on the minister and attack him although the other man was much larger.

Now that the service was finished, cemetery workers that had been waiting at a discreet distance quickly appeared all around them. Two started snapping closed the green folding chairs. Another took down floral arrangements. A bulldozer nearby started up but for some unknown reason shut right down again with a few motory burps and coughs. More men came along to fold the chairs. The minister and teenager were clearly in the way so they moved a few feet off.

"Why are you here again? Why am I? I thought I was dead."

"You were. I brought you back."

"And I'm supposed to be grateful for it? Am I supposed to say thank you?"

"That would be nice."

Instead, the boy jumped in front of the minister and shot both right and left fuck-you fingers at him. One cemetery worker saw and whooped. He pointed at them and kept laughing. Giving a minister the finger! That was a good one. Astopel looked at the worker and nodded his approval—he thought it was funny too.

"Why did you do it? And if I was coming back, why not send me to my right time?"

"This *is* your time from now on, Gee-Gee. Get used to it." Astopel reached into his jacket pocket and rummaged around for something in there. He looked at the brilliant blue sky while searching. Sunlight glinted off the crystal face of his watch. Once it shot into the boy's eye and he had to look away.

"Here we go. Look at this and pay close attention." From his pocket Astopel brought out a handful of eight marbles. The colors were not unusual—cat's-eyes, a blue, a red, some were doubles—two yellows. Kids' marbles.

"This is the life of Frannie McCabe." Cupping the marbles between both hands, Astopel shook them vigorously. Their glassy click was loud and annoying. He stopped, opened his hands and showed the marbles again. Gee-Gee half expected something else to be there—it was some kind of trick. But no, there were the marbles on the salmon-colored palm. He looked at the man's face and saw only a clear smile. Suddenly with no warning, Astopel flung the marbles into the air. The kid ducked because he thought they'd hit him. Instead, they froze in the air in a perfectly straight vertical line. Eight marbles—two yellows on top, then a blue . . . They did not move. Sunlight bounced off them into the world. A line of marbles hung perfectly arranged and unmoving in the air between these two men. After a few moments, the still-smiling Astopel plucked each one individually from its place and dropped them back into his other hand.

Shaking them again, click click, he tossed them back into the air. The same thing happened, only this time they spread out like buckshot and froze in no discernible pattern. One here, one there, one higher, two lower . . .

"And this too is the life of Frannie McCabe, Gee-Gee. I could throw them all afternoon and each time they would freeze in a different pattern. The marbles are the events and people in your life. You have one life, but we've had to intervene a little in it now. If you think of these marbles as the raw material we have to work with, what we're doing is throwing them out in different combinations to hopefully obtain a certain result."

"You're using me. You and the rest of you fucking aliens are using my life to get what you want."

"Using? No. We're only moving you around inside your own life." Picking the marbles out of the air, he shook them. They clicked. "At the end of his life just now Frannie came very close to a breakthrough. We were all very excited and impressed. Because he was so close, we decided to bring you back here now and let you try again."

"Why not bring *him* back? Why'd you let him die?"

"It was his decision. We cannot control that."

"But Old Floon killed me."

"Floon couldn't kill you—he met Frannie when he was twenty-nine years old. He never knew *you*."

"Then who shot me?"

"Unfortunately Frannie *let* it happen. That's a very different matter. It's what he learned at the end. So now you must take his discovery and use it.

"Think of it this way, son: In some combination there is a

perfect order for these marbles. Maybe it's a vertical line, maybe a circle, who knows? But you must find it. Francis McCabe. So far that hasn't happened. Now it must because we need that perfect order for something important. Only McCabe in one variation or another of his life can find that flawless combination. So now it's your turn to try. Frannie was married to Magda. Pauline was his stepdaughter. For you, Magda will be your aunt and Pauline your cousin." Astopel smiled. "Or maybe more than your cousin."

Belligerently the boy demanded, "And what if this new arrangement with Aunt Magda doesn't work? What if I can't find the right way to arrange your stupid marbles either?" His hand shot out to grab them from Astopel but the other's snapped closed like an alligator's jaws.

"You don't want to throw these away, Gee-Gee. They're who you are."

"But if I don't figure this out, you'll bring another Frannie back from another age and put him in here in a different arrangement. You'll do it again."

"Again and again until one McCabe finds it and we can add that piece to the World Machine."

Neither had anything more to say. Gee-Gee fumed. His blood felt like it been replaced by pure adrenaline. Astopel felt pretty good. It was a fine day. He was finished working for the time being and maybe he'd go see a movie.

"If you want, we can give you something to help."

"Like what? A laxative?"

"No, a helper. Something that might help you find the solution."

"All right, why not? I mean, why not have help?"

"Good. You'll just have to find a way of explaining it to

Magda." Astopel brought two fingers to his mouth and whistled. A weak tweet, the sound cracked and broke as soon as it came out.

"That's no whistle!" Gee-Gee smirked triumphantly. No one could whistle like him. Putting the same two fingers together, he let one fly that was fabulously earsplitting. Even staunch Astopel winced. When Gee-Gee saw that reaction, naturally he did it again.

Nothing happened. Gee-Gee didn't know what to expect but not nothing. He looked at Astopel who didn't appear concerned.

"Should I whistle again?"

"Not necessary. He'll be coming along."

"He" turned out be a solidly built moving object way far down the cemetery green. It was coming toward them. It was young and had two normal eyes and four normal legs this time which allowed it to trot comically. It approached with its tongue hanging out and its mouth set so that it looked like it was smiling. Maybe it was. A plump smiling dog that looked like a marble cake.

"That dog? He's my *helper?*"

"You'll be surprised how much Old Vertue knows, Gee-Gee."

"Gee-Gee. Do I gotta live with that name forever?"

"It's possible. But remember, for now Gee-Gee gets to live with Magda and Pauline."

"And this fucked-up dog."

"Still sounds like a fair trade. Well, I'm off." The minister dropped the marbles into his pocket and without another word strode away.

Old Vertue walked over and sat down on Gee-Gee's foot as if they were old friends. The young man was about to tell the fat bastard to get off but didn't. Instead he looked at the high mound of fresh dirt covered only partially by a tarpaulin. For some reason no cemetery workers were around now. Only some of their brand-new shovels lay on the ground and the silent bulldozer he assumed would later be used to fill in the hole. Going over, he picked up a shovel and hefted it tentatively. Then the dog watched while Gee-Gee began shoveling dirt into Frannie McCabe's grave.

CPSIA information can be obtained at www.ICGtesting.com
Printed in the USA

239991LV00002B/52/P

9 780765 3